TRESPASSERS

A FERRYMAN NOVEL

CLAIRE MCFALL

KELPIESEDGE

To Cate and John. Finally.

PROLOGUE

He just... he just vanished.

Susanna sat on the damp grass on the side of the hill and contemplated the tunnel mouth where the ferryman who called himself Tristan had disappeared. She'd no right to be there, she knew, lingering, holding off her next soul – but she'd seen him going the wrong way.

Towards the world of the living – him and his soul. And vanishing.

There was only one possible explanation, but that was the thing: it was impossible. She'd sat here for a long time – though time was all relative in the wasteland – and hadn't been able to come up with any other answer except the one that sent equal bolts of fear and excitement coursing through her veins.

Somehow, Tristan had found a door to the world of the living.

Somehow, he'd gone through it.

He was a ferryman just like her, and he'd left his post. The pull of Susanna's next soul, her next job, scraped painfully against her every nerve ending, but she couldn't make herself move from the spot. She couldn't stop seeing Tristan's broad shoulders, his mop of sandy hair, being swallowed up by the darkness as he walked right out of the wasteland.

ONE

Dylan floated in a warm haze. Eyes closed, she lay flat on her back, thick cushioning underneath her and soft covers tucked up almost to her chin. She was comfortable, she was cosy and she wanted to stay that way.

Unfortunately, there were several voices nearby intruding on her peace and one of them, at least, wasn't going to be ignored for long.

"Who, exactly, are you, young man?" Joan's words were frosted with ice. Dylan knew that tone, knew it intimately. She'd been on the receiving end of it more times than she could count. What she'd never noticed before, though, was the undertone of anxiety and fear that sharpened its edge.

"I'm with Dylan."

At the second voice, Dylan's eyes snapped open. She couldn't help it. She'd crossed the wasteland for that rich timbre, faced beings more deadly and terrifying than anything she could have imagined in the world of the living. There was nothing she wouldn't do…

Although there was one thing she *couldn't* do. With her neck trapped by an unyielding plastic collar, she wasn't able to twist and see Tristan, check with her own eyes that he was really there. She tried, though, letting the hard material dig into her collarbone and rolling her eyes so far upwards that her temples throbbed. But he remained frustratingly just out of sight.

"Are you indeed?" A pause heavy with suspicion that made Dylan wince. "Funny how I've never heard of you. Doctor, why have you allowed this young man access to my daughter?" Rising volume, rising anger. "She's lying unconscious. He could have done *anything*!"

Dylan had heard enough. Mortified, she tried to yell, but all that came out was a croaky, "Mum!"

Unable to see anything except an ugly white strip light above her head and the circular curtain rail that typically surrounded a hospital bed, she had to wait a couple of seconds for Joan's face to rush into her field of vision.

"Dylan! Are you all right?"

Joan looked like she'd aged a hundred years. Her eyes were bloodshot and the bags beneath them were streaked with mascara. The tight bun she always kept her hair in was bedraggled, wisps hanging limply round her face. She was wearing her nurse's uniform under a baggy cardigan, and it struck Dylan suddenly that she'd been wearing that when they'd said goodbye – no, when they'd fought instead of saying goodbye – just that morning.

And yet it had been days ago for Dylan. Days of struggling through the wasteland. Without warning, Dylan's eyes filled with tears that spilled hot and fast across her cheeks, disappearing into her hair.

"Mum!" she repeated. Her face scrunched up against the stinging in her eyes, her nose and her throat.

"It's all right, sweetheart. I'm here." Fingers curled around her left hand and even though Joan's grip was icy, Dylan felt comforted.

Dylan sniffed and tried to lift her right hand to wipe her cheeks dry, but a tug followed by a sharp pain brought her up short. She flinched, drew in a startled breath and tried to raise her head, but along with the neck brace someone had run a strap across her shoulders. She couldn't lift herself more than an inch – and even that *hurt*.

"Just hold still, baby," Joan crooned. "You're in the hospital. You've had a bad accident and you need to stay very still." She squeezed Dylan's right hand very gently. "You've got a drip in your other hand. It's best if you just…" a choked breath "…if you just stay as still as you can, all right?"

No, it wasn't all right, Dylan thought. She felt helpless lying there flat on her back. And she *couldn't see Tristan*.

"That's right, Dylan, just stay flat for now," another voice cut in smoothly. A doctor, stethoscope dangling round his neck, leaned into Dylan's vision on the opposite side of the bed to Joan. He looked as tired as she did, but he smiled. "We need to examine the extent of your injuries before we start letting you move about. You may have a spinal injury, so we have to be very careful."

Sudden panic, as a memory from the train flooded Dylan's mind.

"My legs?" she whispered.

She remembered the agony of lying buried under the debris from the crash, the feeling of fire that had ripped through her legs with every breath, every shift of her weight. Now there was… nothing. A sea of numbness. She tried to wiggle her toes, but it was impossible to tell if they were moving.

"They're still there." The doctor held up both hands in a calming gesture, that same smile fixed on his face. Dylan wondered if he looked like that even when he was giving really bad news. Suddenly it wasn't comforting any more.

He dropped one hand down, resting it on the covers. Dylan couldn't tell if he was touching her or not; if he was, she couldn't feel it.

"I don't… I can't…"

"Relax, Dylan." An impossible order to follow. "There's no reason for alarm. You're on a high dose of painkiller and we had to heavily bandage you because you have some deep lacerations. That's why you don't have much feeling, all right?"

Dylan stared at the doctor for a moment, weighing the truth of his words, then allowed herself to breathe.

"I'll come back in a few minutes when you're taken for X-rays," the doctor added. He smiled and backed out of their curtained section.

"Mum." Dylan swallowed and then coughed a bit. Her throat felt like sandpaper.

"Here." Joan thrust a plastic cup in her direction, the straw just an inch from her lips. Greedily Dylan sucked down the water, although Joan took it away before she was anywhere near satisfied. "That's enough for now."

"Mum," she repeated, a little more strongly. She tried once more, unsuccessfully, to raise her head. "Where's Tristan?"

Joan's lips thinned. She turned her head away slightly, as if she was turning her nose up at some unpleasant smell, and panic coiled heavy and cold in Dylan's chest.

"I thought I heard—" Dylan struggled against the confines of the bed, did her best to lever against the restraints holding her down, "Where—"

"I'm here." Better than just his voice, Tristan's face slid into view on the other side of the bed, as far as possible from Joan – which was a good choice because she was glowering at him with unconcealed suspicion and anger.

Tristan. Relief and joy flowed through Dylan like a river. He was here. He'd made it.

They both had.

Tristan made to reach for Dylan's hand, the one with the drip thrust uncomfortably into her vein, but a sharp noise from Joan stopped him short. Needing his touch, Dylan ignored the discomfort that tugged repulsively every time she shifted her hand, and covered the remaining distance, wrapping her fingers around his.

He squeezed tight and it hurt, but Dylan smiled at him.

"You're here," she whispered.

Then it slammed into her – the memory of saying those exact same words, lying flat on a gurney as two paramedics carried her from the wreckage of the train. The feeling of seeing him there, in the world, alive and solid and real, after thinking that she'd lost him. After thinking that she'd let go of his hand and left him behind. Fresh tears fell down her face.

"You see! You see!" Joan reached across and tried to slap Tristan's hand away, but the waist-high railings and the width of the bed prevented her. "You're upsetting her! Let her go!"

"No! Mum," Dylan tightened her grip on Tristan and used her free hand to bat Joan's arm away. "Stop it."

"Clearly you've bewitched her," Joan spat. "And now here you are, confusing her when she's vulnerable and doesn't know which way is up!"

"Mum!"

Joan totally ignored Dylan, her focus fixed on Tristan.

"I want you to leave," she said firmly. Then she shifted her gaze to beyond the curtain. "Doctor? I want him out. He isn't family, he has no right to be here."

"Mrs McKenzie," the doctor began, leaning in through the curtain, but Joan ranted right over the top of him.

"No. I know the rules. I've worked here for eight years. I don't know who let that young man in, but—"

"Don't go." Dylan was only concentrating on Tristan. He, too, was ignoring her mum, his hand still folded tightly around hers, his piercing blue gaze fixed on her face like he was trying to memorise her features. "Don't leave me."

He squeezed a hairsbreadth tighter, causing a jolt of pain to streak across the top of Dylan's hand, and shook his head imperceptibly.

"I'm not going anywhere," he promised.

Joan was still raving at the doctor, but with Tristan gazing down at her, Dylan tuned her mum out completely.

"I still can't believe you're here," she told him.

"Where else would I be?" He gave her a crooked smile, a puzzled line forming between his eyes.

"You know what I mean." Each time Dylan blinked, she expected Tristan to disappear, to be pulled back into the wasteland, called back to his never-ending duty. It didn't seem real that he could've broken his bond of servitude so easily.

"We're meant to be together," Tristan told her, sliding even closer. "Wherever you are, that's where I'll be."

"Good." Dylan smiled at him, hoping against hope that it would somehow be as easy as he said. She looked over to where Joan stood, hands on hips, face screwed up in anger.

"Mum."

No response from Joan.

"Mum!"

Still no reaction.

"Joan!"

That did it.

Joan turned on her, ready for battle as usual. "Dylan—"

"I want Tristan to stay." Dylan wasn't as stupid as the doctor – she had no intention of letting Joan get started on her. "If he can't be here, then I don't want you to be, either."

Joan reared back as if she'd slapped her. "I am your mother, Dylan."

"I don't care." Not the truth: Joan's hurt expression brought a hard lump to Dylan's throat, but she pushed on regardless. "I want Tristan."

"Well." For once Joan seemed to be lost for words. She blinked furiously, and Dylan was horrified to realise she was near tears. She'd never seen her mum cry, not ever. Seeing it now made snakes writhe in her belly. She fought hard not to back down.

At that moment two orderlies trundled in, oblivious to the tense scene.

"One for the X-ray department?"

There was a moment's pause before the doctor seemed to come to himself.

"That's right," he said, now looking thankful for the timely reprieve. "Dylan here." He waved unnecessarily in Dylan's direction.

The orderlies shuffled round, unlocked her hospital bed's brakes and wheeled her out, drip pole and all.

It was both a worry and a relief to leave Tristan and Joan behind. What might Joan say without Dylan there to act as a buffer? Would she have Tristan thrown out of the hospital? Arrested? One of the orderlies noticed her worried glance and attempted to reassure her.

"Not going far, love, the X-ray department is just round the corner here."

It wasn't enough to calm her. The further she went from him, the more sick and sore she felt. What if he wasn't there when she got back?

No. He wouldn't leave her. He'd promised.

⌐

The X-ray technician was brusque and efficient, and the radiographer didn't even speak to her. Dylan didn't mind; she was focussing all her energy on not throwing up. The pain in her legs was excruciating – she couldn't wait to get some more painkillers when she was back on the ward.

Bizarrely, the trip back through the corridors actually helped, and both her legs and her stomach felt better when the orderlies parked her bed in place.

Joan was there, pacing like a tiger, and, much to Dylan's relief, Tristan was too. He was slumped in a metal chair, looking strangely pale. Joan must have given him hell in her absence. Dylan's eyes met his and he held them with an intensity that revealed his concern.

At least Joan hadn't managed to drive him away.

"Are you all right? Did the doctor say anything?" Joan was straight over to the side of the bed, crowding in on Dylan before Tristan could get up from his chair.

"I didn't speak to a doctor," Dylan answered. "It was the radiographer, but he didn't tell me anything."

"Of course." Joan shook her head at her own stupidity. This was her hospital, Dylan thought. She must know how things were run. "Maybe I'll…" She craned her neck, her eyes fixed beyond the door of the room, and Dylan could tell she was thinking about going to find the doctor, harassing him until he put Dylan at the top of his list. But then Joan's eyes drifted back to Tristan. "We'll just wait, shall we? Won't be long."

Dylan tried to keep the disappointment from her face. She wanted to know what was wrong with her legs, but mostly she wanted Joan out of the room for a few minutes so that she could speak to Tristan. Privately. It still didn't feel real to see him here, in a hospital ward, rather than striding confidently through the meadows and mountains of the wasteland.

Nobody said much as they waited. Joan fussed over Dylan's water, plumped her pillows and tried to detangle her hair until Dylan snapped at her to leave her be. It felt like a lifetime but the doctor finally made an appearance. It was the same one from earlier, looking haggard and harassed.

"Do you have the results, Dr Hammond?" Joan got straight to the point.

He grimaced before smoothing his face back into a professional, reassuring mask. "Well, I've spoken to the radiographer and it's as we thought," he said. "The right leg's broken."

"Is it a clean break?" Joan asked.

There was an ugly pause. Dylan felt a curl of dread in her stomach – that obviously meant no.

"There are multiple breaks, Nurse McKenzie. We're going to have to pin it and insert a brace while it heals."

"An operation," Joan whispered, the blood seeping out of her cheeks.

"Mum?" Dylan whimpered, panic forming at Joan's reaction.

"It's all right." Joan was back at Dylan's bedside in a heartbeat, a smile on her face, though it was strained. "It's only a small one."

"A very routine procedure, Dylan," the doctor continued. "You'll be fine. Although there are further complications…"

"Doctor?" Joan prodded.

"There's also a very fine fracture in your left leg, Dylan. It's not significant enough to need a cast, but you're going to have to keep your weight off it while it heals too."

"Both legs! I'll be an invalid." Dylan shuddered.

"It'll be fine," Joan squeezed her shoulder in reassurance. "I'll be there to help you."

"Tristan," Dylan said. At the edge of her vision she saw him stand, but her focus stayed on Joan. "Tristan will help me too. He can stay with us."

"No!" Joan's response was a bark.

The doctor cleared his throat, clearly keen to extract himself from this discussion. "I'll pop back in a wee while, once I know when we can slot you in for the operation." He slid out as Joan rounded her attention back on Dylan.

"I'm not having *him* in our house. He's—" Dylan narrowed her eyes as Joan visibly collected herself. "We don't need him," she finished with deliberate calm.

Tristan approached the bed, but stood on the opposite side from Joan. "I would like to help," he said evenly. His calm tone and relaxed posture were belied by his white-knuckled grip on the bed railings. Dylan reached out and tugged one hand free, folding her fingers around his.

"No," Joan repeated. "The two of us will be just fine. I'll take some time off work and—"

"Dylan's recovery is going to take weeks, Mrs McKenzie," Tristan interjected quietly. "Likely months."

A tense moment passed as Joan clenched her teeth and Dylan fought to keep the victorious expression from her face. There was no way Joan would be able to take that much time off. Even if the hospital allowed the absence, she knew they couldn't afford to lose Joan's wages.

"Plus, Mum, we live on the second floor of a tenement flat. You're not exactly strong enough to carry me up and down two flights of stairs!" Dylan squeezed Tristan's hand, sensing the inevitable.

After several long, angry seconds of silence, Joan turned to Tristan and spat her words out: "You sleep on the couch. Understand?"

TWO

The man was crying. Susanna watched his face contort and crumple, his hands clenching and unclenching on the handkerchief he carried with him like a security blanket. What was his name again? Michael. His name was Michael.

Michael was crying.

Susanna stared at him and hoped her expression concealed the complete indifference she felt. Michael could continue to cry and plead. He could wail and sob. He could fling himself to the floor and beat on the thin, ugly carpet with his hands and feet – it wouldn't change a thing. He was dead, and that's all there was to it.

She couldn't understand why he was so surprised. He'd been sick a long time and when she came to him at the hospital, he knew. There'd been no need for trickery, no story to spin. She hadn't felt the need to change her appearance to sway him, and continued to look 'herself'. That is, she used the first face she was given when her existence as a ferryman began, when she first saw, thought, felt. The face of the young woman she'd like to be if she could ever really be a young woman. Tall, graceful, dark-haired, dark-eyed. It put her a good decade or so younger than Michael, but he'd made no comment.

He was saving his talk for when they'd started walking. Then it was all: *he wasn't ready. He needed more time. He hadn't done all the things he wanted to do yet.*

Well, tough. He'd had more warning than most people. Susanna knew enough about his life to understand that he hadn't cherished it prior to his illness. If he hadn't put his time to good use, that was his problem.

Still, it had made the first day beyond tedious. Michael had lived in a small community up in the wilds of Canada and he'd succumbed to his disease in the middle of winter. When they took those first few steps outside, the wind howled and snow lay thick and fast on the ground. It hadn't taken long to leave the last echoes of the real world behind and start the trek across gentle hills made mountainous by the heavy drifts that hid the land. Though there wasn't far to travel to the first safe house, they'd barely made it there before dark. *Plod, plod, plod.* Each step a fight against the elements the wasteland had recreated to ease Michael into death.

Susanna didn't really feel the cold, but Michael's constant whining had been a beetle under her skin. Had distracted her from what she really wanted to think about: Tristan.

She'd recognised him as soon as she noticed the ferryman and soul walking determinedly in the wrong direction. She'd have known him anyway – felt the pulse of his energy, the signature that was uniquely Tristan – but he'd been wearing a face she'd seen before. Often. Vivid blue eyes, sharp cheekbones. A slightly stubborn jaw. It was a strong face. Resolute.

He'd gone into the tunnel, right at the fringes of his soul's wasteland, and she hadn't seen him since.

He'd really gone. To the world of the living.

All day Susanna had struggled with that truth. And it *was* the truth, she knew it down to her very bones, but *how*? It should have been impossible for a ferryman. It was, it absolutely was

17

impossible. Even when ferrymen picked up their souls from where they had died, they never went right into the land of the living. They were never able to touch anything or be seen by others who were still alive. The souls had already crossed over at the moment of their death. It was imperceptible, instantaneous. Taking less than the time for a heartbeat – had their hearts still been beating.

So how had he done it? Susanna asked herself that question again and again as she lit the meagre fire in the log cabin that was their first safe house.

Of course, of all the ferrymen it had to be Tristan to do it, to work it out. That didn't surprise her. There was something different about him, something special. He was meant for more than this – this half existence.

Now that he was gone, she felt it. Felt the lack of him. Noticed it all the time. Like a tiny piece of her soul was missing. Which was stupid, because she didn't have a soul. She missed him, though. Missed his presence nearby – he had always been there alongside her as they made their routes through the wasteland: comforting, strong.

So how did he do it?

And… could she follow?

"Tomorrow we have to go faster," she told Michael, cutting over his continuous low-level mumbling and whining. "There are things that lurk out there in the dark, and you don't want them to get you. Trust me."

Beyond the walls of the little log cabin where they would shelter overnight, low moans and wails rose above the constantly blowing wind. Wraiths. They sensed the vulnerable, sensed Michael's weakness, his cowardice, and they were gathering.

THREE

Tristan gripped the handles of Dylan's wheelchair outside their building, as Joan fumbled with the lock, her jangling keys loud in the silence. She was still very angry, Tristan could see, her back ramrod straight. He'd have to be careful.

Joan needed him – for now.

But she wanted him gone.

The hospital waiting room hadn't been the ideal place to make a good first impression. Or the ideal time. He hadn't prepared an explanation for his sudden appearance and, put on the spot, he knew he'd fumbled. There'd be some hard questions later.

Now…

Joan opened the door and he pushed Dylan's wheelchair into the dark tenement hallway. The stairwell loomed above them – they would have to get Dylan up two flights.

"You pick her up – *carefully* – and I'll take the chair."

Feeling Joan's eyes on his every move, Tristan bent down to help Dylan out of her chair.

"Put your arms around my neck," he said quietly. Slipping one hand around her shoulders and the other, very carefully, beneath her legs, he lifted her, and felt the weight pull at his shoulders, his back, as he straightened up.

"Don't drop me!" Dylan squeaked.

"I won't," he promised. And he wouldn't – but either gravity was different in the real world or he'd changed. He'd been strong in the wasteland. Strong enough to fight wraiths, and haul souls of all shapes and sizes across the unforgiving terrain.

Now… he felt like a sixteen-year-old boy with a sixteen-year-old boy's strength. Only pride and the fear of hurting Dylan stopped him from pausing as he took the steps up to the second floor.

Joan followed closely behind with the cumbersome chair, and helped Tristan place Dylan back down before unlocking their flat door.

Tristan had seen Dylan's place, of course, in her memories. But it still felt unexpected: breathing in the faint trace of Dylan and the heavier smell of the damp creeping into the living room. He reached out with one hand and briefly brushed the raised pattern of the woodchip wallpaper lining the hallway. The tips of his fingers tingled. It wasn't any different to any other wall he'd ever touched, and yet it was. It was real. Someone – quite a long time ago, he thought – had once lovingly pasted this onto their wall. Had chosen it from all the other options, to make their home.

He snatched his hand back and coughed as a swell of emotion tightened in his chest.

"Are you all right?" Dylan murmured, when Joan disappeared into the living room, leaving them briefly alone.

"I'm fine," Tristan said. "Don't worry about me."

He was more than fine. He was alive. Blood was coursing through his veins; his heart was beating in his chest. He wanted to laugh, to sing and shout. He wanted to snatch Dylan out of her chair and throw his arms around her, swing her round in circles.

Instead he slowly, carefully, wheeled her into the main room where Joan was waiting for them.

"I need to get some things from the shop," she announced.

"I won't be long." Her eyes narrowed as they flicked from Tristan to Dylan and back again. "Dylan's room is out of bounds when I am not in the flat. No exceptions."

Tristan considered her resolute expression, her clenched jaw.

"All right," he said. He'd no intention of following through on the rule, but if it would appease Joan and give him some time alone with Dylan, he'd agree to just about anything.

Joan seemed suspicious of his easy capitulation, but she swept out without further comment, only pausing to put a gentle hand on Dylan's shoulder as she passed. Dylan wasn't paying attention, didn't see the relief and worry that went into that one small touch, but Tristan did. Dylan had told him that her relationship with her mum was often fraught and tense, but the love between the two of them was palpable.

The moment ended and Joan left.

At last, it was just Tristan and Dylan.

Unable to do anything else, Tristan folded himself over the back of the wheelchair and drew Dylan into a hug. Tucking his face into the crook of her neck, he let himself breathe her in. Feel her skin, warm and alive and in his arms.

"Tristan," Dylan whispered. Her hands reached up to clutch him closer to her. It was awkward – the wheelchair digging into his stomach and his knee pressing into the rear wheel, but Tristan couldn't make himself move. This was perfect. Heaven. He was half-convinced that if he moved so much as a muscle, it would all be snatched away from him. He'd blink and be back in the wasteland. Alone.

He was so lost in the moment that at first he didn't notice the subtle shaking of Dylan's shoulders. It wasn't until he caught the quiet hitch of her breathing that he realised she was crying.

"Dylan? Am I hurting you?" He wrenched away, horrified.

He spun round to the front of the wheelchair and knelt, peering into Dylan's face. Sure enough, tears were streaking down her cheeks. "I'm sorry, angel. I didn't mean to—"

The almost violent shaking of her head stopped his words in his throat.

"It's not that." Her voice was tight and shaky. "I just... I can't believe it. You're here. Really here." She hiccupped a laugh. "You're standing in my crappy living room."

"Well, technically I'm kneeling." Tristan went for a tiny smile, tucking a stray lock of hair back behind Dylan's ear.

"Shut up." She shoved at him playfully, then she leaned forward and planted her forehead on his chest. It was as close as they could get to each other from this angle, with her leg cast sticking out awkwardly in front of her. Tristan rubbed her back gently, making sure to stop well short of her bandages.

She was so battered and bruised. It had been more than he could bear to see her brought out of the train tunnel on a stretcher. Now here he was, whole and well, while Dylan was struggling with injuries that should have killed her. That *had* killed her.

And she'd suffered that for him.

"I love you," he whispered into her hair.

Dylan made an inarticulate sound and lifted her head up to stare into his eyes.

"I love you, too." She smiled, her eyes sparkling. "I told you so."

"What?" Tristan blinked, confused.

"I promise I'll only say it this once – well, twice," Dylan laughed, "but I told you it would work!"

"Oh. Right. Yeah, you did." Tristan's lips twisted into a rueful grin. "On this one occasion, I'm OK with being wrong." His grin stretched a little wider, "And at least you're the only one who'll know."

He looked around the room, took in the slightly sagging couch jazzed up with new cushions.

"Let's get you out of the chair."

"All right." Dylan put both hands on the arm rests, ready to lever herself upright, but Tristan halted her with a hand on her shoulder.

"I've got you," he told her.

"I know," she replied, smiling.

Once again, lamenting his new human body, he strained every muscle to lower her slowly, gently, down onto the cushions. He moved to straighten up, but Dylan snagged his hand and tugged him down to sit beside her.

He didn't fight the pull – there was nowhere else he wanted to be. The closer the better.

"How do you feel?" Dylan asked him quietly.

"How do *I* feel?" He shifted round to shoot her a quizzical look. "I'm not the one who was just in a fatal train crash!"

"I know," Dylan waved a hand in the air as if that didn't matter. "I mean, how do you feel *here*? Is it any different? Do you… do you feel solid?"

The hold she had on his hand squeezed a little tighter, as if she also believed he might evaporate out of existence. He squeezed back reassuringly.

"I feel solid," he agreed. "And…" He frowned, really considering it. There was a tightness at his temples, a heaviness behind his eyes. And a gnawing sensation in his stomach. "Tired, I think. but my stomach… I guess I'm hungry." Another pang twisted. "Really hungry. God, that's a horrible sensation."

"You'll have to wait till my mum gets back for anything decent," Dylan said, "but there's probably some biscuits or something in the kitchen."

Following Dylan's instructions, he managed to locate Joan's old-fashioned shortbread tin above the microwave. He brought back as many as he could fit in one hand and passed half the stack to Dylan.

"Chocolate digestives," Dylan wrinkled her nose. "These aren't the best biscuits, but they'll fill a hole."

She stuffed an entire round into her mouth, chewed quickly and swallowed. Tristan watched her, then looked down at the three biscuits in his own hand. The chocolate coating was melting against his fingers.

Dylan watched him with interest before finally speaking. "You didn't try eating in the hospital?"

Tristan shook his head slowly, his gaze still on the food.

"Your mum offered but I was just… I was too worried about you to think about it. I had some water but—"

"Do you know how to do it?" A sharp glance up assured him Dylan wasn't making fun of him, that it was a genuine question.

"I know how to do it," he said. "It's just—"

"It's a big moment," Dylan finished for him. The left side of her mouth quirked up. "Sorry it's not something more impressive than a McVities."

"This is great," he said. "And anyway, I've heard lots of good things about chocolate."

Not wanting to put it off any longer – because then he'd be forced to admit to himself that he was a little bit apprehensive – Tristan lifted the biscuit to his mouth and bit off a chunk.

It crumbled against his lips. When he began chewing, sweetness burst across his tongue. Saliva pooled and mixed with the pulped-up food until he felt the need to swallow. He paused, expecting to feel the lump in his throat, odd and uncomfortable, but there was nothing except the demand for more. Before he realised it, he was licking the remnants of chocolate from his fingers.

"Well…?" Dylan prodded, watching him carefully.

"I think I like chocolate."

That made her throw her head back and let out a peal of laughter.

"We should have started you on something more boring. Everything else is going to be an anti-climax now." She tilted her head to the side, a tiny furrow between her eyebrows as she considered. "I think you'll like pizza, too. And crisps. Crisps are amazing."

A moment of silence passed before Dylan reached out to take Tristan's hand again. "Are you glad you're here?" She paused. "Did we do the right thing, do you think?"

"Is that a real question?" Tristan waited until Dylan met his gaze. She gave him a hesitant nod. "There is nowhere else I'd rather be, Dylan. I swear it to you."

She rewarded his words with another sweet smile, the one she always gave him when she forgot herself. It was a while before she spoke again.

"What have you said to Joan? About us, I mean. When I was having my X-ray?"

"I said I was your boyfriend," Tristan replied. "She asked why she'd never heard of me and I kind of mumbled something about you not being ready to tell her yet. She wasn't happy."

"She won't let it go, you know," Dylan said. "She'll push and push until she gets proper answers from us. I don't know what to tell her. I mean, what the hell do we say? The truth? Can you imagine?"

"Shhh," Tristan soothed. He could see that Dylan was getting upset, agitated. "Angel, it can't be the truth – you know that. We'll think of something. It'll be all right."

"Promise?"

"I promise." Tristan drew her to him, resting his forehead against the top of her head. "We'll figure it out later. Right now, I just want to hold you."

"Is that all?" Dylan breathed. She twisted, lifting her face, and Tristan was already dipping down to meet her when pain ripped through her expression.

"What's wrong?" Tristan pulled back, his eyes raking over Dylan's body, searching.

"It's nothing," Dylan protested, though her face was bone white. "I'm fine."

"You're not fine. You're injured and you need to heal. Here." Rising, he rearranged the cushions on the sofa and gently pushed Dylan back onto them. "Rest."

"I don't want to rest," Dylan pouted. "I want you to kiss me."

"I will," Tristan said. "When you're better."

"That'll take ages!"

He laughed. "I'm not going anywhere. We have all the time in the world now."

Dylan's disgruntled snort, the adorably put-out look on her face, almost had him giving in, but at that moment Joan came banging back into the flat. She appeared at the living-room door a heartbeat later, her face flushed like she'd run the whole way.

Her eyes narrowed as she took in the two of them on the sofa.

"You," she barked at Tristan. "Help me with the groceries."

❧

"...I just don't think it's the right time ... No, I think you're being selfish ... Do you have any idea what she's been through? ... Don't you dare turn up here! You can't just force your way into— No, I don't care that she contacted you before; things are different now ... She is not old enough to make that sort of decision, she's only fifteen!"

Dylan hovered in her wheelchair outside Joan's bedroom,

listening to her mother hissing quietly into the phone. It wasn't hard to work out who she was speaking to.

James Miller. Dylan's dad. The man Dylan had been heading up to see in Aberdeen when she was in the train crash that took her life… then gave it back again. She remembered how she felt when she got on the train; nerves and excitement had been champagne in her blood. What would he be like? What would they do together? Would Dylan be able to see echoes of her face in his?

She hadn't gotten any answers that day. Instead, fate had sent her on a completely different adventure – one that had taken her to Tristan, so she couldn't regret it, not even for a moment. Now, several days after her return home from the hospital, she was left feeling… a sense of loss at not having reached her dad that day. She'd fought hard to get so far on the journey to meeting her dad, had to work to break down the barriers Joan had thrown in her way, and she needed to finish what she'd started.

Seized by a sudden rush of determination, she wheeled her chair into Joan's room, bashing the half-open door out of her way with her plaster-clad foot.

"Dylan!" Joan jolted out of a reverie where she sat on the bed.

"Who was that?"

"What?" Joan blinked, blindsided.

"Who was that on the phone?"

Her mother cradled the phone to her chest. "Just a friend from work."

"Liar!" Dylan used her hands to shove the chair further into the bedroom, cursing as she scraped the knuckles of her left hand against the doorframe.

"I beg your pardon?" Standing, Joan braced herself. "Just who do you think you're talking to, young lady?" She shifted her narrowed gaze over Dylan's shoulder. "Where's Tristan?" Joan avoided saying Tristan's name as much as possible – in the same way that she did her best to avoid looking at him or speaking to him – and she spat it out now.

"He's in the living room, watching the telly."

"He's supposed to be helping you, that's why he's here, staying under my roof."

That was another dig Joan had never failed to get in during these first few days. *He's staying under my roof. He's eating my food.* And, the one that somehow angered Dylan the most, *I put the clothes on his back.* Her snide little comments never failed to rile Dylan, but this time she refused to be side-tracked.

"You were talking to my dad, weren't you?"

"Dylan—"

"Tell me. I know it was him!"

Backed into a corner, Joan came out fighting. "And if it was?"

"What did he say? Why was he calling?" Dylan leaned forward hopefully. "Does he still want me to come up and visit?"

"As if you're in any fit state to be doing that!" Joan made to sweep past Dylan, but the wheelchair was too wide. She put her hands on her hips and stared her daughter down, waiting for her to move, but they'd been fighting since Dylan could remember – she wasn't going to be cowed by Joan's angry face.

"I could manage if Tristan came with me."

"Absolutely not!" Joan's snapped. "You and that boy are not disappearing anywhere!"

That boy. Her usual way of referring to Tristan.

"Well, my dad could come here then."

A flash of something in Joan's eyes.

Dylan immediately jumped on it. "That's it, isn't it? He wants to come here."

"Now wait—"

But Dylan was right, she knew it. "When's he coming?"

"There aren't any plans for that right now, darling." Joan's voice had dropped from sharp anger to coaxing, almost pleading. "It's not something that can just be organised overnight."

"Yes, it is! He's only in Aberdeen, not the other side of the planet." Dylan stared at Joan accusingly. "You told him not to come!"

"Yes." At least she didn't deny it. "You've been through a massive trauma. You just... you need a little time to heal, Dylan. We'll talk about your dad – I promise we will. After."

Dylan considered her mum's words for the length of several fast, angry heartbeats. "No."

"Dylan—"

"No. I don't want to wait any more. If you won't invite him down, I'll do it myself."

Quite how Dylan would do that she wasn't sure, as the only contact number she had for him was in the phone she'd lost on the train. She held her mum's gaze, in case she called her bluff.

Seconds ticked by at half speed. One, two, three, four...

"Fine." Growled out from between lips tightened in fury, letting Dylan's heart soar. "Fine, I'll ring him. But you won't be meeting him alone. I'll be going along with you, and that's non-negotiable, Dylan."

"Fine." It was, actually. Because while she was looking forward to meeting her dad, looking forward to it desperately, there was no small amount of nerves mixed in with that excitement. With some fumbling, she shifted her wheelchair so her mum could exit. Joan swept past with as much dignity as she could muster.

"Mum," Dylan called after her. Joan inclined her head, but didn't turn back. "Thank you."

A sigh, then she did turn to face Dylan, her smile a little watery. "You're welcome, sweetheart."

FOUR

"Are you ready for this?" Tristan paused across the road from the school gates, causing an obstruction on the pavement so that the hordes of pupils behind them had to step out onto the road to pass. When Dylan didn't answer, he reached forward to squeeze her shoulder.

"I hate this thing," she muttered, slapping her hands on the large wheels of her chair. "Everybody's looking at me."

And they were – craning their heads to get a glimpse of the invalid in the wheelchair. Dylan scowled at every curious pair of eyes, trying to ignore the rapid flutter of her pulse and the tight, ugly feeling in her chest.

Joan had been surprised when Dylan had wanted to come back to school so quickly, but the woman was driving her crazy. Fussing over her, watching every move Tristan made, suddenly appearing any time the two of them moved even close to Dylan's bedroom. Did she honestly think that they were going to be up to no good with Dylan's right leg in plaster up to her thigh and her other leg and lower back a mass of bandages and dressings?

Dylan had to get out – anywhere was better than being at home.

At least, that's what she'd thought until the hideous concrete block that was Kaithshall Academy had come into view. Now she was remembering all the reasons she hated this place…

starting with the idiots that were risking getting run over so that they could nosey at her broken leg. Well, she admitted grudgingly, they weren't only looking at her.

"Are *you* ready for this?" she asked.

It was Tristan's first day of school. Ever. Getting him enrolled had been a dicey process, as he had no records, no ID, no name, no history. As far as the system was concerned, he was a ghost. Of course, it had been harder trying to convince Joan that he was a real person than it had been to convince the school, but Joan was the queen of interrogation. Once they'd persuaded her that Tristan – Tristan Fraser – had left a violent home somewhere in the outskirts of Glasgow and didn't want to talk about it, she began to ease off, even felt sorry for him. Well, a little bit. She agreed he should be in school at any rate, and had spun some lies about his identity to the headmaster. Dylan couldn't believe she'd done that, but then Joan probably figured it would keep him out of trouble. Keep them both out of trouble, because where Tristan went, Dylan went – and vice versa. They hadn't spent more than an hour apart since Dylan had woken up in the hospital.

Of course, Joan didn't know that; she still thought Tristan slept on the couch.

"I'm fine," he said.

Dylan twisted her head round in the chair to look at him, but his face betrayed no more emotion than his voice did. He looked calm and cool, returning the prying stares with disinterest. He was as unruffled here as he'd been in the wasteland, even though Dylan had pulled him completely out of his element. She thought about how she'd been when faced with his world – a crying, frightened mess – and felt embarrassment creep round her neck.

In fairness, though, there weren't any wraiths here. The biggest danger was that the idiocy of the rest of the student population might be catching. A prime example was coming their way.

"Oh my God, Dylan! I heard what happened to you and I totally didn't believe it!" Cheryl McNally, as orange as ever and dressed in a ridiculously short skirt and high-heeled ankle boots, was stalking towards them. "Look at you!" She screeched the last bit, to attract the attention of anyone who wasn't already gawking in their direction.

"Hi Cheryl," Dylan forced through gritted teeth. She knew exactly what Cheryl was up to. The bottle-blonde airhead made no secret of the fact that she didn't like Dylan, had been instrumental in multiple humiliating episodes at Kaithshall – like the time she shoved Dylan in the cafeteria so that she spattered spag bol all over her shirt and ended up looking like a murder victim. But the train crash, and the stupid wheelchair, meant that Dylan was going to be the centre of attention for a few days, and Cheryl just had to be where the attention was. Plus…

"Is this your cousin?" Cheryl neatly side-stepped Dylan's chair so that she was standing next to Tristan, her smile wide and beguiling. It was all Dylan could do not to spin the chair round and ram her out into the traffic – Cheryl would definitely be the centre of attention then!

Unfortunately, she hadn't quite mastered manoeuvring the chair enough yet to swivel on the spot like that. Even more unfortunate was the answer she had to give Cheryl.

"Yes." The word left a nasty taste in her mouth. "This is Tristan."

It was part of the story they'd concocted with Joan: the family connection an excuse for her to assert guardianship over Tristan, to allow her to get him into the school. Dylan supposed Joan took some enjoyment in doing this, as it meant they couldn't act like a couple, and she had to sit in the stupid wheelchair while Cheryl ran her hand down Tristan's arm and purred, "Welcome to Kaithshall."

Bitch.

"Thank you." Tristan nodded and stepped neatly away from Cheryl's touch, his tone cool.

That made Dylan feel instantly better, but Cheryl showed her usual lack of insight, completely missing his subtle signals. She wobbled closer on her ridiculous heels to nudge his shoulder with hers.

"I can show you around if you like, Tristan." She speared Dylan with a pitying glance, "You won't be able to, hen, not with your chair."

"I'll manage," Dylan ground out.

"You shouldn't push yourself, not with your injuries." The concern on Cheryl's face was as fake as her tan.

"I'm not pushing myself," Dylan responded tartly. "I have Tristan to push me."

Cheryl blinked, trying to work out Dylan's words, while behind her Tristan laughed.

"There are traffic lights at the junction," Dylan said to him, pointing to a set a hundred yards down the road. "It'll be easier to cross there. Bye, Cheryl."

Much quicker on the uptake than Cheryl, Tristan took the hint, wheeling Dylan away without another word. Several seconds later, Cheryl's warbled "Bye, Tristan!" floated after them.

"You need to push the button," Dylan reminded Tristan when he paused by the crossing, staring at the traffic whizzing past.

It was funny, he knew so much about the world, but little things – like knowing how to call up the green man at a pedestrian crossing – were missing from his knowledge. Tiny gaps that betrayed him, made him stand out as different. Odd. Dylan was doing her best to plug them where she found them.

"She's a friend of yours?" Tristan asked while they waited.

"I told you," Dylan said, squirming uncomfortably in her chair, "I don't have any friends here."

"Yes, you do," Tristan corrected, placing his hand on her shoulder. "You have me."

Dylan didn't reply. Her throat was too tight and she didn't want him to hear the waver in her voice.

Though there were plenty more stares, Dylan and Tristan made it into the school without being interrupted by any more nosy 'well-wishers'. They stopped at the office so that Tristan could pick up his timetable – identical to Dylan's – and get the obligatory welcome from the headteacher. Dylan had to sit outside for that, parked in an unobtrusive corner of the administration corridor, and she fretted and fidgeted the entire time Tristan was out of sight. After what felt much longer than ten minutes, the door opened and Tristan walked out. His face was inscrutable as ever; the headmaster's, though, was distinctly thoughtful. He stared after Tristan as he walked away, a pensive frown creasing his brow, then shrugged and closed the door.

"All right?" Dylan asked.

"Fine," Tristan responded. "Where to?"

"Registration," Dylan sighed glumly. "We'll have to take the lift up, it's on the top floor."

The lift was rickety and cramped. The sixty seconds it took to groan its way up the three floors stretched painfully for Dylan, and she was relieved when the doors opened again to spit them out.

"The end of the hall," she pointed needlessly down the length of the corridor. "Miss Parsons' room."

It was early, the start of registration still ten minutes away, but she hadn't wanted to get caught in the mad crush of the warning bell. Though it was protected by a plaster cast, even slight jolts to her leg caused shocks of pain.

Miss Parsons was writing on the board when they entered the room, and, after a brief annoyed glance, she shifted the desks at the front so Tristan could manoeuvre the wheelchair in. Unfortunately, that meant every pupil in the class would parade past them.

Their eyes roved the lines of Dylan's wheelchair, the stark white of her cast, sticking out awkwardly into the room. A few people smiled sympathetically, but most just stared. That is, until they shifted their gaze to the new boy sitting beside her.

Dylan tried to see Tristan as they would. Tall, broad, he looked too old to be in fourth-year. He was, technically, by a few centuries, but given that he didn't have any formal education it didn't really matter where he began. He'd refused to cut his sandy hair, ignoring all of Joan's increasingly pointed hints, and it fell over his eyes. He wore the school uniform – white shirt, black trousers and a green-and-red tie – and Dylan couldn't decide if it looked ridiculous on him... or gorgeous. Given the looks the girls were giving him, it was the latter. He outshone the boys in her class, emphasised how runty, immature and gormless they all looked.

Judging by the mutters that were rumbling at the back of the room, the boys knew it too.

"Who is he, anyway?"

"It's Dylan's cousin."

"He looks like my dad with his tie done up like that! Mammy's boy!"

Tristan, who'd been ignoring the less that discreet murmuring, turned his head at that last one.

"Ignore him," Dylan said softly. "That's Dove MacMillan. He's a moron."

35

Tristan didn't say anything, but he still stared hard in Dove's direction. Dylan winced, waited for it. It didn't take long. The scrape of a chair sliding back as Dove got to his feet.

"What you lookin' at? Eh?"

"Tristan," Dylan reached out her hand to keep Tristan in his seat, but he showed no signs of getting up. He just kept that hard, impassive look on his face. Dylan hunched her shoulders, waiting for Dove to stomp over and start a fight. He didn't, though, and when Miss Parsons snapped "David, sit!" a moment later, he did.

Eyebrows raised, Dylan stole a look behind her. None of the boys were looking in their direction. Dylan was careful to keep the smirk off her face until she was facing the front again.

They were scared of Tristan.

If only the girls were similarly affected.

⌐

The tie was killing him. Tristan sat squashed into the corner of a history classroom beside Dylan and tried not to haul the thing from around his neck.

It was ridiculous. The whole thing was ridiculous. Pretending to be a child, a clone of the immature, irresponsible idiots that surrounded him. It had been the same in French, but this history class was even worse: the teacher was wholly incorrect in his description of the Battle of Culloden. Tristan may not have been there himself, but he had a first-hand account from a boy of thirteen who'd paid with his life.

Tristan tried to whisper that to Dylan as they sat there, composing answers to the inane questions listed on the worksheet, but she shushed him.

"Just write down what the teacher said," she hissed, eyeing their neighbours to make sure their conversation was going unheard.

"But it's wrong," Tristan protested.

"It doesn't matter," Dylan barked back. "He's the one who's going to mark this, and these are the answers he wants. That's how school works, all right?"

No, it wasn't all right. It was stupid, regurgitating inaccuracies as if they were fact. Pointless. He had to remind himself he was doing all this to please Dylan. This was her world. He needed to fit in, even if it was senseless.

To be honest, he was a little relieved that he could even do the work at all. He hadn't known he could read and write, but when Dylan had plucked a book from the shelves of her bedroom and shown him a random page, the lines of letters had simply made sense. In just the same way that he'd been able to speak in any language to any soul.

Later that afternoon, English class was more bearable. The poem the teacher read to them moved Tristan, the words beautiful and evocative. Then she spoiled the whole thing by insisting they annotate it, line by line, dissecting it like a wild creature on a butcher's table. What had begun as a fluid, graceful thing became heart, lungs, bones... nothing but cold dead pieces.

Tristan kept his thoughts to himself because, unlike with every other subject, Dylan seemed to like the softly spoken poetry assassin.

Maths up next, though. What the hell was the point of maths? Unable to resist any longer, squashed again next to Dylan's wheelchair, he reached up and grabbed at the school tie that Dylan had painstakingly knotted for him that morning. It resisted, somehow tightening and strangling him even further.

"Tristan!" Dylan's hiss jerked him out of his thoughts.

He looked at her and she motioned her head towards the front of the class. A woman stood there, mousy in a woollen pink cardigan and tortoiseshell glasses, next to their balding maths teacher.

"Tristan Fraser?" she called again, her tone making it obvious that this wasn't the first time she'd called him.

"That's you!" Dylan whispered furiously.

"I know," Tristan whispered back. While Tristan was the name he'd always chosen when taking a generic male form, he was still getting used to having a surname. "I can't leave you." She'd be completely helpless, her arm strength not enough to manoeuvre the heavy chair. And now he'd met some of her fellow pupils, he was loath to abandon her to their nastiness.

"You'll be back well before lunch," Dylan told him, pushing at him now with her hand.

"And if I'm not?"

"Tristan Fraser!" He didn't like hearing his name in that harsh, snappish voice, and Tristan sent the woman a sharp look. It didn't deter her. "You're needed in the office." She gestured at him with her hand and Tristan reluctantly stood.

"I'll just wait here for you," Dylan promised. "Go!"

Tristan forced himself to smile at her, then left, following docilely behind the admin woman. He still didn't want to leave Dylan, but he had to play nice, he reminded himself. He was a teenage boy, a pupil. He had to do what he was told.

Especially because his place in Dylan's flat was precarious at best. Joan didn't trust him, didn't like him – and wanted him out. He doubted Joan believed the story they'd told her about his past. Only her need for someone to care for Dylan in her absence had convinced the woman to give him a chance. Any slip up, any tiny blemish on his record – in the flat or at school – and he was out. Tristan was resolved to give her no reason to act on her threat.

It chafed, though.

A tight feeling gripped his chest as the woman led him down the corridor. When they hit the stairwell, the feeling dropped into his gut, churning and twisting. *She'll be fine*, he told himself. She'd survived this soul-rotting place for three years without him. There were no wraiths here to hurt her, no monsters to slay. The only danger was a slow, painful death through boredom. Still, when he descended one flight of stairs and then the next, the feeling only grew.

By the time he hit the ground floor, Tristan knew that it was more than simply concern for Dylan. He couldn't breathe. His lungs were working frantically, but he was getting light-headed, feeling weak. He stumbled after the woman, using the wall for support. Every step he took, the debilitation only intensified. By the time they reached the main office, Tristan felt like he was going to die. He leaned heavily against the doorframe, knowing that if he moved, he'd fall. Shards of agony were searing up both legs.

"I just have to ask you about your doctor and emergency contact," the admin assistant said breezily, seeming unfazed by his tardiness and his current condition.

"I don't have a doctor yet," Tristan forced the words out, struggling to focus through the bone-deep pain that was wracking his body. "But it'll be the same as Dylan's. My cousin," he added. "The emergency contact will be the same too. Her mum, Joan McKenzie."

"Her phone number?" she asked, a form up to her nose, eyes squinting through her glasses.

"I don't have it memorised yet – can't you get it from Dylan's file?" he asked, temper colouring his own words. He couldn't take much more of this. It felt like his organs were being crushed by steel hands, shredding them to mincemeat. He *had* to get back to Dylan. Now. He'd die if he didn't get back to her.

"Very well." The woman pursed her lips in clear dissatisfaction.

"Can I go?" Tristan managed to hold onto enough reason to remember he had to ask permission to leave. He gripped the door handle to keep his feet rooted to the spot until the woman said he could.

She sighed, rolled her eyes "You still need to sign this."

"Fine." He all but fell across the room. Snatching the pen from her hand – and causing a censorious tut from her – he scrawled the signature Dylan had helped him design – and lurched away.

Run. He needed to run. And he would, if he could just make his legs work. Tristan lumbered down the corridor, bouncing from wall to wall. He slammed through the double doors guarding the stairs and used his hands to propel him upwards. With every step he took, the agony dulled, the panic diminished, until he was able to pause at the entrance to the maths corridor and collect himself.

Head down, hiding his face from view, he took several deep breaths. The post-pain nausea that gripped him now was a mild irritation by comparison. He had to see Dylan with his own eyes, check she hadn't suffered as he had.

One look at Dylan's ashen complexion told him she'd felt it too. Worse, she hadn't been able to hide it. The teacher was hovering worriedly over her chair, one hand on her shoulder, and every pair of eyes was fixed in her direction.

"Tristan." The maths teacher caught sight of him, waved him over. "It seems Dylan's not feeling well, but she didn't want to leave without you."

It was obvious from the man's relieved expression that 'not feeling well' didn't come close to describing Dylan's state. But even in the few seconds it took Tristan to cross the room he could see colour coming back into her cheeks.

"I'll take her home," Tristan said, angling his body so he could squeeze past the desk and grip the handles of her wheelchair.

He wanted to touch her – run his fingers over her hair, knock the teacher's hand away and rub her shoulders.

"Absolutely." The teacher helped them pack up their things and smiled as he ushered them out the door. It showed just how much he wanted them out of the room in case something really was wrong with Dylan. "Take Dylan to the office and phone home, see if someone can come and get you."

"Right." Tristan had no intention of stopping in at the office or asking anyone's permission to take Dylan anywhere, but she insisted they at least signed out properly.

At last, Tristan was able to push Dylan out into the fresh air. They didn't talk until he'd negotiated the uneven pavements to the nearby park, wheeling Dylan over to a bench and angling the chair so that he could sit close enough to grip both of her hands. The air was chilled, but he suspected that wasn't why her fingers were frozen.

"What happened?"

"I don't know." She'd lost the pallor to her skin, but not the frightened, haunted look in her eyes. "I started feeling weird pretty much as soon as you left. I think something like this happened in the hospital when they took me for X-rays. But this time, it just got worse and worse... then suddenly it was better. I was almost feeling all right when you appeared back in the doorway."

"Weird?" he prompted.

"Weird," Dylan agreed. "At first it was like I couldn't breathe, and I started to feel sick. But then... God. It hurt so bad. My legs felt like they were breaking again, and my back felt hot and wet. Agony, like it was bleeding."

"Let me see," Tristan said encouraging her to lean forward so that he could gently lift the back of her school jumper. He didn't need to peel back her shirt – small dots of red patterned the fabric where blood had seeped through her bandages.

"Just like on the train," Tristan murmured.

"What?"

"Your injuries on the train. Your legs were broken, and you had gashes across your back, remember?"

Dylan nodded, wide-eyed.

"Why did it happen?"

"I don't know." Tristan took a deep breath. "But Dylan, the same thing happened to me."

Dylan gaped at him.

"The further away from you I got, the worse it was. When I was down in the office with that stupid woman," he scowled at the memory, "I thought I was going to die."

Dylan's horrified look made him sorry he'd been so candid.

"What do you think it means?" She squeezed his hands and hunched over, looking for comfort, he realised.

He couldn't hug her, not with the bulky chair and her plaster-cast leg, but he shifted position so that she could rest her head on his shoulder, although probably not comfortably. She nestled closer regardless, and he realised just how afraid she must have been.

"I think it means we're not supposed to be apart from each other," he told her gently. She sucked in a deep breath, but she didn't argue. "I'm not supposed to be here..." he went on.

"You are," she interrupted. "You're meant to be with me."

"I am," he agreed. "You and I, we're supposed to be together." He huffed a laugh. "And I guess we're going to have to take that literally from now on."

Dylan lay quietly against him for a long moment, her head tucked under his jaw.

"Oh well," she said, a good minute later. "That's not exactly going to be a hardship."

"No," he said. "It isn't."

FIVE

It wasn't evening, not even close, but it was getting dark. The day had started cloudy, a match to Michael's mood, and as they'd traversed the unforgiving landscape of his snow-covered wasteland, those clouds had gathered and grown. Now a storm broiled above their heads and the snowflakes that had been drifting all day were falling thicker, faster. The wind was picking up, burning their exposed faces and hands. Susanna gritted her teeth and resisted the urge to move quicker than Michael could handle.

It wasn't physical – *nothing* was physical for Michael any more – it was all in his mind. It was a subconscious delaying tactic. Susanna had seen it a thousand times. Souls dawdled in the wasteland because they were afraid to step into the unknown. A single step that took a lot of courage, courage the likes of Michael simply did not possess.

Susanna could see herself shoving this soul across the line herself. It wouldn't be the first time.

"Come *on*," she snapped at him, turning to where he was stumbling behind her. "We have to get to the next safe house as soon as we can."

She didn't like the way the weather was turning, didn't like the depth of shadows that were forming as light was sucked from the sky. And she definitely didn't like the hisses and low snarls that were *not* the wind creaking over the land.

"I'm trying," Michael whined, his face pale except for an ugly red windburn splotch that spread across his nose and cheeks. "I hate this. I hate the snow. And I'm *cold!*"

Susanna pursed her lips unsympathetically. She didn't like it either, and she was tempted to point out that it was all Michael's fault – that his mood affected the weather – but to be honest, she simply couldn't be bothered with the explanation. It was her job to protect him. If that meant getting tough with him, so be it.

"We need to move faster," she urged. "It's dangerous out here."

"Dangerous?" Michael coughed, glaring at her. "There's nothing here!" He threw his hand out in a wide gesture: snow, snow and more snow, topped by an ugly grey sky. Only a few hardy trees and the black of rock scoured clean by the wind interrupted the endless white. It looked utterly empty, desolate.

Susanna knew better. "We aren't alone out here."

At that moment, the wind dropped. Right on cue, the wraiths that had been mewling menacingly to Susanna throughout the day chose to roar. A shrieking, growling, multi-layered rumble of sound. Susanna wouldn't have thought it possible, but Michael paled even further, his face bleaching of all colour and turning his chapped nose a darker red.

"What's that?"

"You don't want to know."

The wraiths sang again, sounding so eager, so bloodthirsty, even Susanna felt the hairs on her nape prickle. Without another word, Michael started forward, practically running even though each step sank his foot deep into the snow.

Satisfied, Susanna followed. But her relief was short-lived. The safe house wasn't in sight. It wasn't even over the next rise, or the next one. They had a long way to go, and the wraiths sounded impatient. They were hungry, and it was as if they could already taste Michael's flesh. One quick glance at the sky told her the heavily laden heavens were only getting darker. They were going to have to fight.

Michael didn't strike her as much of a fighter.

Blowing out a breath, Susanna stared off into the landscape. For a moment she let the expanse of white drain away to see the wasteland as it truly was underneath Michael's projection. Heat–blasted hills, drenched in blood-red colour, and a thousand other souls making the crossing with their guides. An army of ferrymen but still no Tristan. She felt alone. Lonely.

Without Tristan, her world was a different place. But who in their right mind would come back, having left this behind? She didn't blame him, but at moments like this, oh how she missed him. Blinking once, she let the chill of snow settle on her once again, the wind biting into her face before she'd even opened her eyes.

Back to work. She needed to *focus*.

Trotting to catch up with Michael, she took a firm grip on his arm and tugged him along faster still. It was hopeless, but it was her job. If they couldn't outrun the slavering beasts that were stalking them, she'd have to fight them. It was a losing battle against a creature – *creatures* – who couldn't be killed.

They crested the next small hill. Michael paused, gasping, looking for a break, but Susanna couldn't let him have it.

"Come on. It's not far."

It was far, but there was no sense telling him that. It might even make him throw in the towel. And here was not a good place to quit. It was too open, the wraiths could come at them from all sides.

They started down the hill, snow tumbling away from their sliding feet. Susanna behind Michael, the scruff of his jacket firm in her hand so she could steady and push him at the same time. Still, it wasn't enough to hang on to when he suddenly dropped like a stone.

One of his legs sank thigh-deep into the snow and the other

buckled, unable to support his whole weight. As soon as Susanna felt the fabric tear from her fingers, she reached for him, but it was too late. He was tumbling, twisting, flailing down the hill, gravity speeding him away much faster than she could hope to follow.

"Michael!" she yelled, rushing down to him as fast as the deep drifts would allow. He lay slumped twenty metres below, face-down, body unmoving. "Michael!"

He needed to get up. He needed to get up *now*. If he just lay there motionless, he was a gift for...

Even as the thought flew through Susanna's mind, the perfect white snow that surrounded Michael began to bleed an inky, evil black. Curls of smoke rose from the frozen ground, coalescing into shadows clothed in rags, gaping maws snarling and screeching.

Wraiths.

"Michael, get up!"

He jerked this time, lifted his head, but he made no move to rise, to defend himself. He just gaped at the hissing demons that were circling him in swooping, swirling dives.

Susanna was close. Ten metres. Five. Three.

Close enough to see the utter terror on Michael's face. Paralysed. Helpless. An easy meal for the wraiths that surrounded him. They were cackling – gleeful at their find.

"No!" Bracing herself, Susanna threw her body over Michael as they descended en masse. The air was forced from her lungs as claws pierced her clothes and skin. She cried out as pain flared through her shoulders, her hips and her legs, but she didn't move from Michael.

Holding him with one hand, she lashed out with the other, tearing a wraith free of her leg. Blood spurted from a series of long, deep furrows, painting the pristine snow in jagged drops of crimson.

The wraiths went wild at the iron scent of Susanna's blood.

It didn't matter to them that ferrymen weren't food; they liked to *hurt*, too. The creature she'd thrown free clamped itself to her foot again as Susanna struggled to dislodge a pair that were working at her shoulders, trying to get at her vulnerable neck.

Her hands were numb with the cold, fingers wet with melted snow. Below her, Michael was whimpering and moaning, but at least the wraiths couldn't get to him. Their angry screams and wails revealed their growing frustration, as did the relentless slashes of their teeth and talons as they tore at Susanna.

It hurt. Susanna clenched her jaw and scrunched her eyes closed, trying to shut out the pain. No matter what, she couldn't let go. The soul was paramount. Her life, her pain – inconsequential. She repeated that in her head as a wraith snuck under her heavy jacket and tore right into her side, slicing through flesh like butter.

You can't die, she reminded herself. *You'll be all right. Just breathe.*

The wraiths changed tactics. Instead of trying to cut through her to the soul they were so hungry for, they dug in to her jacket – shoulders, waist, hood – and pulled.

Susanna flew backwards and up, high into the air. The wraiths carried her writhing and struggling body until Michael was just a dark blob down below. A dark, unmoving blob.

Then they plummeted, pushing her ahead of them.

The white ground rushed up to meet Susanna, so fast she could only shut her eyes and take one quick, stunned breath before she was thrust deep, *deep* into the snow. It frothed up past her until it was over her head, dropping down on top of her. Surrounding her. A prison of icy white.

It shifted like liquid when she tried to fight against it. Susanna raged for a moment, until she realised she was alone. The wraiths had abandoned her. Why?

Seconds later, she had her answer. Michael started screaming.

SIX

"I've been thinking," Tristan said suddenly, looking up from the wildlife book he was reading, showing the jungles of South America – his favourite landscape to ferry souls across. They were in the library, taking a 'free period' instead of PE, which Dylan clearly couldn't do.

"Yeah?"

"I reckon we should experiment."

"Experiment?" Dylan stared at him, not following at all.

"We need to know just how far apart we can go before we start feeling, you know—"

"Like we're dying?"

"Exactly."

Dylan considered that. It was a sensible enough suggestion, but one worry drowned out all the other thoughts in her head.

"You want to get away from me?" She tried to make it a throwaway comment, a joke, but failed miserably. She'd slept awfully the night before, tossing and turning as much as she was capable of doing with her leg in plaster. It had ached the whole night and Tristan wouldn't let her take any more than the recommended number of painkillers. The cold, uncomfortable sensation she now felt was clear in her voice. Tristan must have heard it too, because he was out of his seat like a shot, perching on the edge of Dylan's desk.

"No," he said, tugging on the tendrils of her ponytail a little harder than he normally would. "That's not it. Why would you say that?" He waited, but all Dylan could do was offer an embarrassed shrug. She'd die before she'd admit what she was really thinking. He went on: "We need to know where we stand. Or," an amused grin, "how far away we can stand. Think about it, do you want to have to come with me every time I need to go to the toilet if it's more than a room away? Or into the boys' changing room in PE?"

"Well," Dylan said huskily, trying to swallow down her ugly feelings, "that one might not be so bad."

She received a playful shove for her efforts before Tristan's hand lifted to wrap warm around her nape.

"You'll want some independence," he said. "You won't want me there every second. We need to know how far is safe. Yeah?"

He was right, she knew. She didn't want to go through what had happened in maths class the day before – that sense of dying all over again – so long as she lived. Which, hopefully, would be quite a long time. "All right," Dylan conceded.

"Do you have any walkie-talkies?" Tristan asked.

"What?"

"Walkie-talkies."

"No." Dylan raised a playful eyebrow at him. "I'm not ten. Or a boy. What do you want walkie-talkies for?"

"We can speak to each other then, monitor how we feel. As soon as you start to feel bad, we'll stop."

Oh. That made sense. "I think in this century mobile phones will do the trick," Dylan laughed. "And we won't look stupid."

This time the tug on her ponytail was enough to make her squeak.

Tristan wheeled Dylan right to the back of the library, into the warren of tall bookcases holding the reference books that nobody ever used. It was the only way to keep the beady-eyed librarian from seeing them dig out their mobile phones. Dylan had a brand new smart phone – a present from Joan to replace the one she'd lost on the train; Tristan had a crappy old pay-as-you-go Dylan had unearthed from one of her drawers at home.

"Ring me," Tristan said. "We'll see how far we can go."

"About five metres," Dylan snapped. She took a deep breath, still trying to get a handle on her temper. Despite Tristan's reassurances earlier, she was still feeling delicate, and wasn't looking forward to the physical battering she was about to get from being apart from Tristan.

"Come on, angel," Tristan said, hunkering down in front of her. He took her free hand between his, tickled the tips of his fingers across her palm.

And pathetic as it was, that was all it took.

"All right," she drawled. "Let's get it over with."

He rewarded her with a quick kiss before tapping her phone and straightening up. "If you need me to stop, just say." He started backing up, his gaze fixed on her face.

At first, Dylan felt absolutely nothing – except for a bit stupid, sitting there all alone. Tristan kept going until he was right at the edge of the stacks.

"Well?"

She raised her voice as loud as she dared. "Nothing. You?"

"I feel fine."

He backed up a little further, until his back touched the double doors leading out of the library. Dylan could only just see him, thanks to the tall bookcases, and she smiled as he raised his eyebrows questioningly at her.

She shrugged. She felt… OK. A little twinge of discomfort in her chest, perhaps, but that might just be apprehension.

Sure enough, a heartbeat later, when Tristan slipped quietly through the doors, she felt it. Panic. Nausea. The pain in her leg increased, the almost-healed gashes on her back beginning a slow burn. With trembling fingers, she scrolled quickly through her phone contacts and smacked her thumb down on Tristan's name.

"I feel rubbish," she told him as soon as he answered. "My chest is tight and I feel sick."

"Your leg?"

"It's... bearable." Ish. She wanted to ask him to stop, but she held it in. They needed to test this, it was important. "Where are you?"

"I'm literally right outside the library door."

"Oh." Dylan chewed on her lip. "I thought you'd gone further than that."

"Nope." She could sense Tristan's disappointment through the phone line.

"Try and go a little further," she urged.

A pause, then, "You're sure?"

"Yes." *No.* "Do it."

"I'll just go to the end of the corridor," he assured her.

She listened to the sound of his black school shoes slapping against the hallway floor. *He's there*, she told herself. *You can hear him, you know where he is.*

It didn't help – the tightness in Dylan's chest intensified, making her fight for every breath. Her head started to pound, her stomach rolled. But she could handle that. What she couldn't handle was the feeling that every wound she'd experienced in the train crash was being made anew. The bones in her leg felt like they were bending and snapping, the skin of her hip and lower back felt like it was being peeled open to expose the flesh within. She felt faint, weak. Like her life was draining away with every footstep Tristan took.

"Too far," she gasped. "Come back."

"Dylan?" Tristan's voice came through the receiver as a crackle. "Are you OK?" A pause. "I feel... I think this is far enough." He swallowed tightly, the sound a sharp click in Dylan's ear.

"Come back," she repeated.

"I will," he promised. "Just... hold on a few more seconds. Let's see if it eases after a while."

Dylan concentrated on breathing in and out. *It's not real*, she told herself. *It's in your mind. It's not real.* But it was useless. Rather than ebbing, the pain just seemed to intensify. Dylan was alarmed when she found her head weaving and bobbing, her vision blurring.

"I can't, Tristan." She reached down and clawed at the cast that seemed like it was squeezing her leg in a vice. "God, it hurts."

"A few seconds?" Tristan repeated.

"I think I'm going to black out," she whispered down the phone line.

"Dylan? Angel?" Panic in Tristan's voice. That, and pain. "I'm coming."

The flat, heavy sound of running jerked Dylan back to consciousness. Her whole arm felt numb, her head too heavy to lift. Unexpectedly, another voice echoed through the speaker.

"You – stop running!"

Thomson. Only the crotchety old Assistant Head had a bellow like that. But Dylan could still hear Tristan running. That was a very bad idea.

"I said stop!"

Thomson would put Tristan in detention, and she wouldn't be able to come with him. That separation would last a lot longer than their little experiment.

"Stop, Tristan," she whispered into the phone.

She heard the angry growl of Tristan as he skidded to a stop, and a muffled, "Sorry, sir." He must've pocketed his phone.

"What's the rush, boy?"

"I've left my cousin in the library and she's in a wheelchair. She can't really get around on her own."

"Dylan McKenzie survived a train crash – what do you think is going to happen to her in the library?"

A heavy pause, and then, "Book avalanche?"

Despite the hideous combination of panic, nausea and pain still swimming around her body, Dylan barked out a laugh before she had the sense to clamp her hand over her mouth and smother it.

"Do you think you're funny, boy?"

Dylan did. Unfortunately Thomson didn't have a sense of humour.

"No, sir." Smart answer.

More silence. One one thousand, two one thousand, three one thousand.

"Get out of my sight!"

Quieter footsteps, walking fast. The squeak and scrape of the library door pushing open.

Tristan was coming. Dylan sat back up and tried to get a handle on herself. She still felt off, but the pain was receding. Just a few more seconds and he'd be in sight… She blinked rapidly and tried to focus.

"Tristan!" A female voice, a horribly familiar female voice. From the muffled sound of it, Dylan suspected Tristan still had the phone in his pocket. She heard him mumble a quiet reply, then the female voice came again – much closer.

"Have you got a free period?" Cheryl's sugary-sweet tones were probably meant to be seductive – to Dylan they sounded like nails on a chalkboard. "Steph, remember I told you *all* about Tristan?"

"Hi, Tristan." Steph Clark. Famous for the things she did out back by the generator – and for being thicker than Cheryl McNally, which was quite a feat.

"You know," Cheryl went on, "This is the first time I think I've seen you without your cousin."

There was way too much emphasis on the word 'cousin' for Dylan's liking. What a stupid idea that had been.

"We're really close," Tristan said, his voice low and defensive. That mollified Dylan somewhat.

"Plus, you know, she's an invalid," Cheryl added. "It must be so hard, having to look after her in that chair."

"It's fine," Tristan replied shortly. "Look, I have to go—"

"Wait!"

Stuff that. Dylan was going to go over there. She'd show Cheryl how much of an invalid she was when she rammed into her. Ending her call – they were in earshot now anyway – she gripped the two large wheels and started shoving. The chair inched forward. Grunting, Dylan shifted her hand position and tried again.

"What are you doing after school, Tristan?"

"What? Why?"

Was she going to ask him out? Dylan pushed harder, getting the wheels to roll across the carpet at last, but her aim was off. The chair was coasting sideways on a collision course with a bookcase full of autobiographies.

She wrenched harder with her left hand, trying to alter her trajectory, but her stuck-out foot glanced off a hardback of *Churchill: The Life*. Agony rocketed up her leg. All she could do for several seconds was sit there and gasp, and listen to the girls chat Tristan up through the bookcases.

"But you don't have to stay in, just because she does..."

"No, I don't." Tristan again. Was that anger in his voice? "I'm staying in because I want to."

"Well, I'm having a party a week on Saturday," Cheryl began. "Why don't you come?"

No answer. Which meant he was thinking about it. If it wasn't for her throbbing broken leg, she could march over there and punch Cheryl's lights out. And maybe Steph's too.

"I'll see what Dylan thinks about it."

The tight knot of anger in Dylan's chest released, a little bit.

"Oh. Well. I mean—" Cheryl stuttering and spluttering. "What with her chair and everything, she probably won't want to..." she came to a faltering stop and Dylan knew exactly how Tristan had made that happen. That look on his face had shut her up more than once in the wasteland.

"If Dylan doesn't go, I don't go," Tristan replied coldly.

Seconds later Tristan appeared at the end of the row of bookcases. He looked annoyed, and worried.

"Are you OK?" He dropped to his knees beside her, reached out and cupped her face with both hands, forcing her to look at him. Dylan didn't want to. Ugly, angry feelings were bubbling up inside her. She wanted to find Cheryl and Steph and make them *hurt*. And Tristan, too. She knew that wasn't fair – but her heart wasn't interested in being rational right now.

"I'm all right," Dylan mumbled, trying to keep the resentment out of her voice. She forced herself to give Tristan a proper answer. "The pain was... it was manageable, then all of a sudden—"

"I know, I felt it too." He rocked closer, pressing his lips to hers.

"Tristan," Dylan whispered warningly. "If anyone sees..."

"I don't care," Tristan whispered back. "I'm so sorry, Dylan. I shouldn't have suggested the experiment. Never again, all right?" Another kiss. "I promise."

Though it was the last thing she wanted to do, Dylan forced herself to tug her face out of Tristan's grasp. If anyone saw, it would not go down well for Dylan to be caught kissing her cousin.

"We had to test it," Dylan reminded him. Then she offered a lopsided grin. "Once."

Tristan flashed a quick smile in response, but his face was thoughtful. "Out of sight."

"What?"

"As soon as we were out of sight of each other, that's when it amplified."

"But that doesn't make sense," Dylan shook her head. "I knew where you were. Don't you think we just reached some sort of barrier?"

"Maybe." Tristan's face was sceptical. "But it got so much worse, so much more quickly."

Dylan tried to see where he was going with this. "So you're saying it's psychological?"

"In part."

"But we've been out of each other's sight before. Every time we go to the bathroom, for goodness sake!"

"It's your flat though," Tristan reminded her. "It's your space, it's familiar. You know I'm definitely coming back to you."

"You think I'm scared you're going to run away from me?" Dylan didn't even try to keep the outrage from her voice.

"No," Tristan denied it quickly. "It affects me too, remember?"

"Well, what then?"

"I think we've created a connection with each other in order to both be in this physical world. If we try and separate that bond, well, reality reasserts itself."

"Reality where I've died." Dylan nodded. The way her leg seemed to re-break, the way her wounds seemed to slice open…

"If we can see each other, or if we're in a safe space," he dropped his hands to her knees, squeezed. "Then we know we're OK. Out of sight, the connection tries to force us together again."

There was silence as Dylan considered Tristan's words. "But, you're just guessing at this, right?" she said at last. "You don't *know*."

"No, I don't know," he agreed. "It's not like this has ever been done before."

"So," Dylan huffed a laugh she didn't feel. "You really are stuck with me. *For ever*."

A joke, but she watched Tristan's reaction like a hawk. If he grimaced, if she saw even a flicker of aversion in his eyes, well she didn't know what she'd do. She couldn't bear the thought that he might be bound to her by compulsion rather than need, desire. Love.

He smiled, though, the expression lighting up his eyes. He leaned forward to plant one more kiss.

"That's the best news I've ever had, Dylan."

SEVEN

Michael was dead. Susanna supposed she should feel bad about that. She searched her feelings, hunting for a hint of grief, but all she felt was tired. Cold, and bone-tired.

It was his own fault, anyway. She'd done everything she could to protect him. She'd urged him to be faster, but he couldn't do it. He'd been sick, his body couldn't take the sudden physical activity. He needed to rest. Just for a minute. And then a minute again.

Well, he'd rested too long. He should have listened to her, believed what she was saying. He wasn't sick and his body didn't need to rest any more. It was all just his mind, clinging on to the form it knew.

They hadn't even made it to the valley. Perhaps that was something to be grateful for. Susanna couldn't imagine trying to brave it in a blizzard. He'd never have made it the length of that death trap – and if, by some miracle, he had, the lake would have finished him off. Still, it rankled Susanna's pride a bit that they hadn't even got past the 'easy levels'.

That's how a boy had described it to her once: like the stages of a video game. Beginners started off easy, with simple terrain and manageable 'baddies'. Then, when they had learned the basics, they moved up to intermediate. That was where things got more challenging – testing the mettle of the player. Survive that and you graduated to 'expert'. The final levels, where the 'big baddie' lurked and had to be defeated in order to complete the game.

Susanna had to admit that his analogy fit neatly into the trials of the wasteland crossing, but still it made her uncomfortable. Because it wasn't a game. Winning was the difference between life and death. Well, survival and extinction. If you died in the wasteland, you couldn't go back to the beginning and start again. You were just... gone.

She didn't say that to the boy, however. He'd been ill his whole short life, a rare condition forcing him to spend his time indoors, away from the world and all its germs and viruses. Computer games *had* been his reality. He'd seen almost as little of the real world as Susanna had – and she'd made damned sure he made it through every level of the wasteland, past the 'big baddie' and safely to the finish line.

Perhaps if she'd tried that hard with Michael, he'd have made it too.

Sighing, Susanna turned from the spot where the wraiths had dragged Michael's soul under, the snow churned up and stained pink with blood – both hers and his – and began to walk away. As she moved, the crunching snow beneath her feet began to evaporate and the dour grey sky brightened. For a short moment everything glowed a blinding shade of white – Susanna was heartily sick of that colour – then gradually the world began to reform. She was walking on a narrow dirt road beside a river. Vast rice paddies extended out into the distance, their green stalks vibrant in the sun. Not far away, a small village nestled in the hill. Her destination.

As she walked, Susanna felt her hair growing, sliding further down her shoulders until it tumbled along her back. Her strides became choppy as her legs shortened and her reed-thin body thickened. By the time the transformation was complete, she felt awkward and clumsy. She pursed her lips in annoyance. This new form was squat and round, would be unwieldy and cumbersome if they had to run, or fight.

The house was smaller than most, a squat little single storey dwelling with a tiled roof that seemed to dip slightly in the middle. The doorway sat back from a wooden porch, etched and painted with swirling designs so faded Susanna could barely make them out. It had the look of a place that had been well kept, but recently neglected. Flowers fought with weeds in carefully built beds, and the grass had grown until it drooped over the flat stones on the path to the door. Inside, the air smelled like incense, acrid and slightly overwhelming in the small space. An alcove halfway down the hall held a half-dozen incense sticks, blackened on a ceramic burner before a small statue of Buddha, his belly fat and eyes smiling.

The bedroom at the back remained dark despite the warm sunshine outside. Entering, Susanna stared at the small figure on the bed for a heartbeat, then rounded the heavy wooden footboard and opened the curtains. Outside, the real world and the wasteland blended seamlessly together. Though she stood in the wasteland – the curtains in her hands a figment of the woman's imagination – the world she could see beyond was real. And so close.

The window wasn't large, but enough light filtered through to reveal a faded yellow colour on the walls, a delicate flowered covering on the bed.

"My Lian doesn't visit me any more," a low, warbling voice said, and Susanna jumped. Her gaze flitted to the face of the woman on the bed. Xing You Yu. She wasn't still asleep, as Susanna had thought, but watching her with calm brown eyes.

"But I am here, Grandmother." Susanna smiled, taking on the role she'd been assigned.

"Yes, you are here," the old woman said, shifting to a seated position with a groan. "But you aren't her."

"Grandmother?" Susanna frowned prettily, smiling in feigned confusion. She was an exact copy of You Yu's granddaughter, she knew. Right down to her eye colour, every detail would be perfect.

"Don't lie to me," You Yu chided. "I know Death when I see him."

Susanna said nothing, a bit taken aback.

"You wish me to go with you, I suppose." The legs that swung round to land on the carpet were as thin as a bird's, and the arm that reached out to grab the robe slung over the footboard was frail.

"Yes, Grandmother," Susanna tried again. "I've come to take you out for a walk. It's a beautiful sunny day."

"*Don't* call me that!" The old woman snapped, eyes sharp on Susanna. "You are not my Lian." Her eyes ran the length of Susanna and the harsh expression softened. "I told you, she doesn't visit me any more. It makes her too sad. And me too, I suppose." She sighed. "But it is nice of Death to wear such a familiar face. You'll give me time to dress?"

Susanna nodded mutely.

They left a short time later, You Yu – as she had instructed Susanna to call her – in sensible walking boots with a simple tunic and sturdy trousers dyed a heart's blood red. It was too warm outside for the dark green wool-lined jacket she'd also donned, but Susanna didn't comment, knowing how quickly the weather could change in the wasteland. A drop in You Yu's mood and they would be facing bitter winds and driving rain.

But the sun still shone as they walked back down the little path. You Yu stopped halfway and drew a deep breath into her lungs, tilting her deep-lined face up to bask in the brightness.

"Emphysema," she said quietly. "That's the first full breath I've taken in…" a shake of her head, "I don't know how long."

Hands on her hips, she gazed before her, and Susanna looked too. Though the village square was peaceful, there was still a quiet life about the place. An old man bent over a hoe in his garden to their left, and a young couple with a baby in a pram were walking slowly towards them.

"I shall miss this place," You Yu said quietly. "I have lived my whole life here."

"Perhaps you'll see it again," Susanna offered.

"You don't know?" You Yu asked, raising a questioning brow in Susanna's direction.

"No," she answered honestly. "I am only your guide for this part of the journey."

"Hmmm," was You Yu's only response. Then, after one last, lingering look, "Well, lead on."

They took to the road, and You Yu didn't seem to notice that the gardener didn't respond to her wave, or the young couple to her smile. They were real, they were there – it was You Yu who wasn't. She was a hairsbreadth to the left, a step out of time. When they left the village, the road would seamlessly blend into the first tracts of the wasteland. That they were so close to the real world, yet utterly out of reach of it, was still hard even for Susanna to comprehend, and she'd been doing this for... well, she didn't know exactly how long, but it seemed like forever. The world, reality, *life*, was so close here. Within touching distance.

Gripped by that thought, Susanna did something she'd never, ever attempted. As they passed by the young couple, who were pointing out what a shame it was that You Yu's beloved garden was being allowed to fall into disarray, Susanna reached out. She let her fingers trail through the air by the woman's arm, searching for the soft stroke of the lemon-coloured cashmere cardigan she wore.

Nothing. Though she searched with her heart and soul as well as her hand, she felt nothing. The veil between the wasteland and the world might be so gossamer-thin as to be invisible, but it held.

"Did you just mark that woman for death?" You Yu asked quietly as the young parents continued their walk unaware.

"No," Susanna replied honestly. "I couldn't touch her."

She did her very best to keep the bitter gall of disappointment out of her voice. How had Tristan done it?

How?

Because if he could do it, maybe she could too. Maybe she could be with him again.

EIGHT

Dylan was a sulker. She denied it vehemently whenever Joan accused her of it, but she knew it was true. She tried her best not to let the angry, resentful feelings bubbling inside her bleed into her conversations with Tristan, but it was hard. Rather than let her feelings come through her words, she often ended up saying almost nothing.

Sulking.

It took until that evening, with ready meals on their knees because Joan was on a backshift and Dylan was too aggravated to cook, before the burn began to fade.

"Do you want to go to this party?" she asked Tristan, keeping her voice even but stabbing at a lump of chicken with unnecessary vigour.

"What?" he looked away from the news report he'd been watching – he couldn't get enough of the news – and stared at Dylan, who shovelled several mouthfuls of tikka masala into her mouth before she could bring herself to voice the question again.

"Cheryl's party. Do you want to go?"

He continued to gaze at her, as though trying to work out what it was she wanted. Dylan carefully kept her face blank.

"Do *you* want to go?" he said at last.

"I'm not bothered." Liar. "If you want to go, we can."

Tristan went back to eating, eyes on his dinner and then the television screen. Sixty long seconds later he finally spoke: "I don't have any desire to hang out with them, but they're your friends, so—"

"They aren't my friends, you know that!" Dylan said quickly. Then, because she'd given it away now, "I don't want to go."

"Why didn't you just say so then?" Frustration coloured Tristan's words.

"Well," a pause, and then everything came tumbling out, "I don't like them, but that doesn't mean that you can't be friends with them – and even though Cheryl's thick as two short planks, boys seem to like her and they think she's pretty, and I don't know. I mean, do you think she's pretty?"

The question hung there in the air. Dylan bit her tongue, forcing herself not to make it worse by saying more. Eventually Tristan scowled, a deep groove between his eyebrows.

"You're serious?"

"No," Dylan replied, because it seemed like the right answer. Then, very quietly, "I don't know."

"All right," Tristan said, setting aside the remains of his tikka masala, "All right. Let me be crystal clear. I go to that school because you have to. You are the only person there who's even remotely tolerable." A small grin that Dylan did her best to return. "I have no interest in Cheryl McNally, or Steph whatever her name is, or anybody else. Only you."

He used the knuckle of his index to gently chuck her under the chin.

"All right?" He was still there, earnestly looking into her eyes. It was too close, too intense. Dylan leaned back slightly, mortified that he'd seen her insecurities so easily. There seemed to be only one way out.

"Not even Mrs Lambert?"

"Which one is she?"

"The librarian." The one who liked to wear cardigans that clashed horribly with whatever fifties dress – as in, bought in the fifties – she had on that day. The librarian who had sprouted several long, grey hairs on her chin. Amusement sparked in Tristan's gaze.

"She is tasty," he agreed, then his mouth stretched into a grin. "But I'll stick with you."

"Well, if you don't want to go to Cheryl's thing, there's always the Halloween Dance…" Once again Dylan feigned disinterest.

"What's a Halloween Dance?" He looked at her in utter bewilderment and Dylan shifted uncomfortably on the seat.

"It doesn't matter. It's fine. I just thought you might want to – have another real human experience. Or something." She looked away. Her face was burning and she didn't want Tristan to see. She felt him nudge her wrist, a gentle request for her to look at him.

"Let's go to the dance," he said. "Together."

Dylan lifted her head at that. He was smiling calmly back at her.

"You want to go to a Kaithshall Academy Halloween Dance?"

"Yes." He shrugged. "It'll be an experience. You don't want to go?" A quick grin. "What are they like?"

"I don't know," Dylan answered honestly.

"You don't know?"

"I've never been to one before."

"Why not?"

Why did she bring this up? What was she thinking? *Stupid, Dylan.* "Just… you know." Her turn to shrug.

"No," he said slowly. "I don't." A quirk of humour in his lips. "I'm new here."

"Shut up." Dylan punched him lightly in the arm. He was still waiting for an answer, though, and she knew he wasn't going to let it go. "I just never had anyone to go with before. I mean, I had Katie, but these things are like, couples' dances." She muttered the last bit under her breath.

"Great," he said quickly. "I want to take you."

Dylan's heart wrenched at the sheer sincerity in his voice. It was embarrassing, having him know how desperately – secretly – she wanted to go to one of the stupid dances, be a part of things. But it was also incredible that he knew her so well. She grinned at him, then winced.

"Of course, I'll be going to the dance with my cousin," she reminded him.

He looked unconcerned. "I'm sure we can find a dark corner somewhere if we need some privacy."

Dylan blushed at that. He kept her gaze, searching her face, but embarrassment still made her want to squirm away and hide. "Your dinner's getting cold."

"It is," Tristan agreed, not moving, "But I doubt it'll make it taste any worse."

He grinned at her, blue eyes sparkling. This ethereal being who had guarded her soul against annihilation in the wasteland was teasing her, laughing like it was the most natural thing in the world. Sitting here beside her, on their crummy sofa, like he belonged. It was amazing. *He* was amazing. Dylan fought to keep the wonder from her face.

"Hey!" she shoved at his shoulders, pretending to be outraged. "I microwaved that ready meal to perfection. You *have* to like chicken tikka masala if you're going to live in Scotland. It's practically our national dish."

"My apologies then." But he didn't go back to his dinner. Instead he drew himself closer to Dylan. Her stomach tightened with apprehension and her heart beat faster. He pressed his mouth to hers once, twice. Dylan caught spicy tomato sauce on his lips, infinitely more appealing when tasted this way. God, she'd missed this. Through Tristan held her every night, he had been treating her like she was made of glass ever since she came out of hospital. Like her bones would shatter if he so much as squeezed her.

Dylan leaned into his kiss, eager for more, but all too soon Tristan flopped back into his spot on the sofa. Picking up his dinner, he winked at Dylan then turned back to the TV.

Dylan looked too, taking in the reporter's miserable face as he stood hunched against driving wind and rain. Behind him the landscape was a muddy wash of browns and dulled greens, lit by the harsh glare of the red and blue lights of emergency vehicles. It was barren and ugly – and eerily familiar.

"Tristan," she said. "Turn that up."

He did as she asked, and the reporter's voice floated into the room.

"…the bodies were found earlier today when a quantity surveyor arrived to look at the damage to the roof of the tunnel. It is understood that all four men were the victims of some kind of attack, and although police have not yet stated the causes of death, they are treating them as suspicious. What has been made clear is that this was not an industrial accident – but mystery surrounds the facts. When questioned, officers on the scene refused to confirm or deny that wild animals may have had a part to play. Autopsies are to be carried out on all of the bodies, and the families of the dead men may finally get some answers as to what happened in the dark of the train tunnel. Back to you in the studio."

Dylan reached for the remote and paused the report just as the news journalist was nodding his goodbye.

"Is that—" It couldn't be. "Is that the tunnel, Tristan? *Our* tunnel?"

The angle of the camera wasn't good, focussing on the melée of police cars, ambulances and a solitary fire engine, but train tracks stretched across one corner and there, almost out of sight, was the gaping back hole that Dylan would never forget.

"I don't know," he said, leaning forward to squint at the screen. "Rewind it."

They went through the report again, glued to every word. Annoyingly, they couldn't see any more of the scenery, even though Dylan tried to crane her neck to the left, as if that would magically let her see beyond the framing of the shot.

"It looks the same," she maintained. "And the reporter said the site of the crash – how many other train crashes have you heard about recently?"

Tristan shook his head slowly. "It has to be."

He turned back to the screen and played it once more. Dylan's gaze fixed on the tunnel that had so drastically changed her life. As the reporter spoke, certain phrases jumped out at her, seeming louder than the rest: *wild animals*, *perished* and, the worst, *mystery*.

Four men murdered. Four ordinary men, just doing their jobs, murdered at the exact spot she and Tristan had defied nature and broken back through to the land of the living. Dylan's stomach twisted. It reminded her of the sick feeling she'd had as a child when she'd secretly given her younger cousin – her *actual* cousin – a haircut. She'd accidentally snipped the cartilage on the top of her ear, and had never forgotten the feeling. It felt like that now – the guilt, the responsibility, the horror of blood on her hands – but a thousand times worse.

"Do you think that has anything to do with us?" she asked in a strangled whisper.

"How can it be?" He hesitated. "It must just be an accident, a terrible tragedy." Tristan sounded sure, but actions speak louder than words. He took the video back to the start and watched it yet again, this time with the sound muted.

"The police said it was suspicious," Dylan reminded him.

"Suspicious doesn't mean—" He broke off, clearly not believing his own words.

"Do you reckon... do you reckon they died because I lived? Like, yin for yang? Balance or something?"

"It's possible."

"But that isn't what you think." Dylan made it a statement, sensing Tristan's scepticism.

"No," he replied, his face drawn in thought.

"Well, what *do* you think?"

"I don't know," he said. "It's... We need to know more. We need to know how they died."

"You mean, we need to know what killed them?"

"Yeah," he replied. "That's exactly what I mean."

NINE

For an old woman, You Yu was spry. She swept along the narrow dirt road they were following, barely batting an eye at the flat, verdant fields that hemmed them in on either side. Arms pumping, her strides were long and purposeful, and it was Susanna, with Lian's short, chubby legs, who was left breathless and struggling to keep up.

"What's the rush?" she panted, almost jogging beside the older lady.

You Yu tipped her head Susanna's way and smiled, but she didn't let up her ruthless pace.

"I haven't felt this good in a long, long time," she said. "No aches, no pains. It feels amazing, I feel… alive." She barked out a laugh. "Isn't that ironic!"

Susanna shook her head in wonder. She couldn't ever remember a soul taking to the journey with such vigour, such enthusiasm. She'd known exactly who Susanna was, despite her exact resemblance to You Yu's granddaughter; she'd come without any complaints or protestations; she'd taken to the idea that her body and all its limitations had been left behind, and was barrelling along like a sixteen-year-old. Not to mention – and this was the kicker – the sun was shining down on them from an unrelenting blue sky. It was almost as if You Yu was happy to be dead!

"There's a hut not far ahead," Susanna told her, "We'll stop there for the night."

"Oh, we shouldn't bother with that," You Yu waved the idea away. "Let's sleep under the stars."

Susanna shook her head. "No," she said. "You don't want to do that."

"Yes, I do."

There seemed no point hiding the truth, not from You Yu.

"No, really. There are... things that come out in the darkness. They're evil, and if they take you, they'll tear your soul apart, force you down into the ground and feast on you until you become like them."

You Yu's stride faltered for a heartbeat, but then she gathered herself and began soldiering on.

"I see," she conceded, "But it seems silly to stop so soon. The sun's still right overhead."

"It can get dark very quickly," Susanne countered. "But there isn't another safe place within reach today. We'll have to bunk down at the hut."

They marched along in silence for a little longer, then You Yu sighed. "All right."

For the first time, Susanna was grateful to arrive early at a safe house and have a little rest. Ordinarily, she liked to get there as close to dark as possible so that the soul would be tired, lulled to sleepiness by the encroaching night, and less keen to interact. But her legs were aching, her heart was pounding and she was drenched in sweat. When the little wooden hut came into sight, she could have wept with relief.

It had earthen walls packed into a slightly higgledy-piggledy wooden frame, with a thick and moulding thatch roof. There was only a small window at the front and a single, low door. The whole thing had a weather-beaten look to it and the facilities inside were basic as usual, but it would keep the wraiths outside, and that was all that mattered.

"This is nice." You Yu smiled as she walked in the door. "My grandfather had a little place just like this. He used it for fishing and hunting, and getting away from his wife." She hiccupped a laugh. "At the time, I hated it. There was no hot water and only one small bed, just like this," she patted the bamboo-framed single bed, "so I'd have to make do with a pallet on the floor. I couldn't understand why he liked it." Hands on her hips, she surveyed the small room, taking in the sink with its pump-action faucet, the rugged fire pit and handmade table and chairs. "I do now."

It was still light outside, but Susanna busied herself with the fire. The air inside was chill and slightly damp, and Susanna wanted to get it going before the shadows started to gather. While she worked, You Yu took one of the stools and sat it in the doorway, watching the sun dip down towards the horizon.

"Do you hear that?" she asked suddenly, and Susanna paused, tilting her head to listen. At first all was quiet, but then she caught it. The high-pitched, eerie keening that always sent chills down her spine.

"I hear it," she said.

"There are no wolves in this countryside."

"No," Susanna agreed. "There aren't."

"It's those creatures you spoke of?"

"Wraiths." Susanna nodded. "Yes, it's them. Don't step beyond the doorway."

As she'd predicted, the sun had dropped with unnatural quickness and dusk was bleeding into twilight.

"I don't think I believed you," You Yu mused. "Well, no, I did believe you, I just didn't understand." A pause, then a cheerier tone.

"I know you said I don't need it, but it feels strange not to be preparing for supper. I'm not hungry, I just feel like I should be doing something."

"That takes a while to go away," Susanna said. "So I'm told."

Confident the fire wouldn't burn itself out, she flopped down on the narrow bed and moaned. Her muscles hurt. Her bones hurt. Even her *hair* hurt.

"Are you all right?" You Yu was watching her with amusement.

"Sorry." She sat up but couldn't hold in her groan.

"Aren't you used to this?" She was mocking her, and with good reason – Susanna had been out-walked by an old woman.

"I am," Susanna admitted, "But I'm not usually…"

"Not usually carrying an extra forty pounds around, you mean?" You Yu raised her eyebrows, but then waved Susanna's sheepish expression away. "I told her! I told her she was too heavy. My granddaughter is too fond of sweets!" A snort, then she gazed at Susanna, a look on her face that was both sad and wistful. She seemed to snap to just a moment later however. "You are stuck in this form while you're with me?"

"Well, not stuck. But it's—"

"Change it." You Yu cut right over her explanation. "I know why you do it, but like I told you before, I know you are not my Lian. It's nice to see her pretty face one last time, but it's you I see staring out through her eyes. Change it. What do *you* look like?"

The thought of ditching Lian's too short, too unwieldy form was too much to resist. Between one moment and the next, Susanna let herself take on the appearance she thought of as her true self. The one she chose on those rare occasions she had the freedom to choose. She stretched and slimmed, her hair slid up towards her jaw and darkened. The cheekbones of her face became more angular and her chin sharper.

"Much better," You Yu complimented. "Now your personality matches your face, if you know what I mean."

Susanna didn't exactly, but she felt instantly more comfortable, though her muscles still ached.

"Come sit with me." You Yu motioned to the other stool and Susanna hoisted it over to sit next to the old woman in the doorway. The world beyond was a writhing mass of darkness, the wraiths quietly swooping and diving.

"You are very accepting of all of this," Susanna said, after a long, peaceful moment.

You Yu shifted her weight on her stool, shrugged shoulders softened by the thick fleece that now protected her from the cold night temperature. "Well, there is no point protesting or complaining, is there? It won't change what has happened. Besides," a pause, "I'm not sure that I would change it even if I could."

"You wouldn't?" That surprised Susanna.

"I was old," You Yu reminded her. "My body had shut down, some days I couldn't even get out of bed. And I was lonely." This last word was said on a gusty sigh.

"You had your granddaughter," Susanna said gently.

"I did," You Yu nodded slowly. "But like I said, Lian didn't like to see me like this, you see? It made her sad."

"You didn't have anyone else?"

"I had my Hui," You Yu said. "I haven't seen him for a long time, but I won't have to wait much longer."

Susanna knew what she meant – had heard many people say something similar. "When did he die?" You Yu's flinch made Susanna wince. She hadn't meant to blurt it out insensitively.

"Eleven years ago," You Yu said softly. "That's how long he's waited for me."

"How do you know you'll see him again?"

You Yu turned, and the light from the fire lit up the frown on her face. "You truly don't know where you're taking me?"

Susanna chewed on her lip, then shook her head.

You Yu gave a half-shrug. "It doesn't matter. I believe he will be waiting for me, just as I would wait for him. However long it took."

I hope you're right. The words floated in Susanna's head, but she didn't give voice to them. She didn't want to cast any doubts over You Yu's beliefs, because she wanted them to come true.

"You don't have someone?" You Yu asked. "Someone who would wait for you, however long?"

No, she didn't. Ferrymen don't get that. Not like You Yu meant. She'd felt something, though. Companionship, connection. A sense of not being quite so alone. Now he was gone...

"I don't have anyone."

You Yu patted Susanna's knee in a grandmotherly gesture. Such affection was almost totally alien to Susanna. It made tears sting her eyes as she stared out into the twilight. It was a calm, peaceful scene, but it was still a lie. All Susanna had to do was close her eyes briefly, adjust her perception, and when she opened them again, the true wasteland lay before her.

Even in the growing dark it was easy to make out the myriad shades of red that swept across the landscape. The molten black serpent that imitated a pleasant stream in You Yu's countryside. The souls, transparent and flickering, nearby and – the only redeeming feature of this view of the wasteland for Susanna – all the other ferrymen. They were stars, always twinkling in the mire. She could look at them and pretend she wasn't alone.

But she felt it.

To her left, another safe house sat quiet and quiescent. No ghostly soul, no glowing ferryman guide. Tristan's safe house. His route through the wasteland closely matched Susanna's, their safe houses nestling side by side almost the entire way. Many nights she'd sat just like this, staring out of a window or through an open doorway, and seen him doing the same. They hadn't communicated, hadn't called out to each other – that wasn't allowed – but they'd been there. Their eyes had shared more than they could have said aloud.

That connection was gone now. All she could do was sit and stare at the spot where he'd been. Wonder what he was doing now. Did he ever spare a thought for her? Still here, still trapped.

Unable to bear the sudden feeling of aloneness, of abandonment, Susanna imagined Tristan sitting right there, where he always had been. She moulded his features, drawing them exactly from memory: his brooding, penetrating gaze so easy to recall. Would he smile, maybe, if he saw her again? Would his eyes light up, giving Susanna a glimpse of the sparkle that she hadn't seen for so long?

It didn't matter, because he wasn't coming back. With a blink, Susanna erased the ghost-like image she'd created.

She was truly alone now. And it was heartbreaking.

TEN

"Well, this is it." Susanna stood at the line with You Yu and found that she was the one who was stalling.

They'd crossed the wasteland with next-to-no difficulties, only flirting with danger in the valley where the shadows had narrowed the path to a thinner ribbon than Susanna had ever seen it. They'd have been fine, but the sheer walls and majestic shape of the mountain crags had captivated You Yu and she'd dawdled, forgetting how the sun could plummet in the wasteland.

Even then, the wraiths hadn't gotten close enough to mar the soft, lined skin that wreathed You Yu's smiling face.

Instead of running and fighting, they'd spent their evenings watching the stars – because there were no dark, brooding clouds in You Yu's wasteland. Susanna could almost believe this place was the real world, looking at where they stood now, neatly tilled green farmers' fields stretching flat as far as the eye could see. And peonies. In You Yu's wasteland there were peonies.

And now it was over. You Yu would be going on, and Susanna would begin all over again. How long would it be before she found another soul so contented, so wise as You Yu? The thought was a depressing one.

"You're not even remotely tempted to try and go back?"

"What, after we've walked all that way?" You Yu laughed, then her expression became serious and she shook her head. "No. Not for all the world would I make my Hui wait for me any longer."

That was what Susanna thought, but she had to check. She'd come up with a new theory during the long nights that she and You Yu had spent in the quiet dark of the huts.

Susanna had a sneaky feeling that she knew how Tristan had gone back into the world. That the soul he was guiding had found her way back through, taking Tristan on her coattails.

So maybe Susanna could do that too... only she'd need a soul who wanted to go back. You Yu would have been perfect – wise, kind and trusting. But she was right, she'd little to go back to – her body an aging husk betraying her sharp mind – and everything to look forward to.

A husband. A love that had made her willing to face the uncertainty and dangers of the wasteland with no fear. Susanna couldn't ask her to abandon that. She wouldn't.

"I'm sorry I won't get to meet your Hui," she told the old woman. "He must be quite a man to have earned the love of a person like you."

You Yu smiled, then she reached out and embraced Susanna, holding her tightly as if she would miss her. It made tears spring to her eyes again.

"Bless you for taking care of me on this journey," the old woman said, then she turned and walked straight over the line. No hesitation, no looking back.

Susanna waited – for what she wasn't sure, but she couldn't quite make herself leave. Before long, however, the urge, the command to turn around and collect the next soul became too strong to ignore. Wiping away a solitary tear, Susanna gazed once more at You Yu's beautiful peonies, then turned away and let the tranquil vista pale around her.

The world that rebuilt itself in its stead was a very different place. Tall blocks of flats, ugly and worn down. The road was hemmed in by cars, most of which were in a poor state of repair. There was litter, graffiti… Susanna knew nobody could hear her, see her or touch her but the soul she'd come to collect, but still, she felt unnerved.

Her body, too, underwent a transformation, although that one was much more subtle. Her skin remained unmarked by age, her hair still dark, though straighter, with a thick fringe draping down to her eyebrows. She slimmed, but not by much, and she doubted there was an inch difference in her height. That pleased her – her face might be different, but she felt like her still.

The soul she'd come to collect lay in an alleyway. He'd died in a pool of his own blood, courtesy of a knife to the gut, and was currently curled up in the foetal position, unconscious. He was tall, but skinny. Like he'd shot up and hadn't had a chance to fill out yet. He wouldn't now. The dark denim jeans and black t-shirt he wore hid the blood that had saturated the fabric, but his fingers were stained with the viscous liquid, near black against the pale white of his skin. His hair was dark, flopping over his forehead. Beneath it, his eyes were closed, his expression peaceful. He had a young face, Susanna thought, gazing down at him. Unlined, unmarked, cheeks still with a hint of baby fat.

She crouched down beside him, awkward in the heels she was now wearing. Tentatively she reached out – long, glossy red nails? Really? – and grasped his shoulder. She shook gently and the soul, Jack, groaned. Groggily, he fluttered his eyelids then sank back down into oblivion. Pursing her lips, Susanna rattled him harder.

"What?" he batted at her hand, though his coordination was off. Susanna kept shaking. "Get off me!"

Irritated into opening his eyes fully this time, Jack peered around at the gloomy alleyway. He was having trouble focussing on her.

"Jac—" She didn't even get his full name out before he was in motion, exploding upwards and throwing her against the brick wall. Before she could catch her breath, he had an arm across her throat, cutting off her airway.

"Who are you?" he snarled. "What the hell's going on?"

He might have a young face, Susanna thought, but those eyes were old. No sixteen-year-old should have eyes like that.

"Jack!" Susanna managed to squeeze the word past her constricted vocal cords.

Instantly the pressure eased and Susanna gulped in a lungful of air.

"Sammy?"

Sammy was his ex-girlfriend. The most positive influence in his life so far, from what Susanna could gather. Sammy wasn't in the picture any more, but she lingered in Jack's heart, along with a heavy dose of wistful longing that might've made Susanna feel guilty. Once.

"It's me." Not a lie, not really. Susanna didn't like to lie to the souls. It made it that much harder for them to listen to her later, to trust her. And that's when the wraiths got them.

"Man." He rubbed at his face and took in his surroundings. "I feel like I've had a right doing. What happened? What are you doing here? Where are we?"

"An alleyway," Susanna offered, choosing the easiest question to answer.

Jack snorted. "You don't say. Come on."

He grabbed her hand and hauled her out into the street, then jerked to a stop when he saw where he was. Remembered why he was there.

He'd been running away. Susanna saw Jack's final memories – the confrontation with his stepfather, his mum crying in the background, her eye already puffy and swelling; storming out of the council flat. Travelling as far as he could on a bus, meeting a group of boys he didn't know, who didn't know him and didn't like him in their 'patch'. A fight, a flick knife. A moment's pain and then... panic. Footsteps pounding away from him. He'd dropped to the ground in the alley, and that was where he'd died. Susanna saw it all, saw the senseless waste of it. A life less than half-lived.

Jack scowled at the darkened street, empty now except for a solitary car. He fidgeted, shifting his feet, clearly thinking hard. What to do, where to go?

Susanna knew she needed to take charge, get him moving to the first safe house, but with his violent display in the alley and the casual aggressiveness of him – a complete contrast to You Yu's quiet gentleness – she was wary.

"I'm not going back," Jack said suddenly. "If that's why you're here, you can forget it. I've had enough, I'm not going back to Stirling." He looked sideways at Susanna, belligerent. "I'm not."

"All right," she answered, thinking fast. "I'm coming with you, then."

That made Jack pause. He stared at her, a half-smile lightening his features. "You serious?"

"Yeah." Susanna licked dry lips.

He cocked his head, eyeing her. It was easy to read the hope in his eyes. "You said we were done."

"I know but... you were right, what you said." The raw, painful memory of Jack and Sammy's last conversation rang in Susanna's ears. "We can't trust anybody else. You and me, that's it now."

He grinned at her, sixteen again. Happy. A twinge of remorse twisted in Susanna's stomach.

"I don't like it here, we should go."

Jack nodded. "Yeah, before the wrong person sees us. I'm in no fit shape for another fight." He rubbed at his stomach, the exact spot where the knife had pierced down to his organs, though there'd be no trace of that now. "I was gonna head for Glasgow. Find a squat or something."

"We could do that." Susanna chewed nervously on her bottom lip. "But it's too late to get the bus. We'll have to walk a bit."

"This day just keeps getting better and better." Reaching out, he snagged Susanna's hand and started hauling her along.

Given that he was going in the right direction, Susanna let him lead. It was obvious he was used to doing so, his stride long and sure, shoulders rolling in a pronounced swagger. She had a horrible feeling this soul was going to be a tricky one to control. He was cocky. Volatile. Too much confidence – nothing like Tristan, whose easy self-assurance was understated. Tristan. From him her thoughts naturally led to the girl who'd gone with him into the tunnel. Was that the key?

Instantly her mind rejected the idea. It was wrong, wrong, wrong. Once you were dead, you were dead. There was no going back. That's what she'd told a hundred, a thousand souls. She didn't even have to think about it – as soon as the soul asked (and they always asked) the answer was just there. No.

She'd never questioned it until Tristan had vanished.

Right now, there was nothing Susanna wanted more than to turn around and follow Tristan to the world of the living. Instead, she let Jack tug her deeper into the wasteland.

ELEVEN

Much sooner than anyone had anticipated, Dylan's dad was heading to Glasgow. He had rearranged his plans to come down as soon as he could, and his imminent arrival distracted Dylan from the men killed in the train tunnel.

This was her dad, and finally she was going to meet him. James's sudden visit hadn't pleased Joan one bit – she'd had to shuffle about her shifts at work. Dylan had tentatively suggested that Tristan could come with her instead, but Joan had shut that down straight away.

Which left Dylan in a bit of a pickle. Joan had said outright that she didn't want Tristan at the meeting – which was happening at a coffee house in Royal Exchange Square – because it was a 'family thing'. Dylan's response that she considered Tristan family was met with a derisive snort and a flat-out 'he's not coming'. There was no way Dylan and Tristan could cope if he stayed at home. It might kill them… literally.

Dylan whined and pleaded, shouted and sulked, all to no avail. It was Tristan who saved the day. A compromise, he suggested. He'd be there, but not. Tristan was going to sit on the steps of the Gallery of Modern Art, so close it was within sight of the coffee shop, and wait.

Joan didn't like it, Dylan could tell by the stiff way she held herself, a muscle in her cheek tensing as she clenched her jaw, but she gave in. With exceedingly bad grace.

The accessible taxi dropped them near the coffee shop. It was a bit awkward getting out, even with the wider doors of the black cab and the special ramp for her chair. The driver was at least seventy years old, and Joan was forced to admit that it was just as well that Tristan was there to help get Dylan out safely.

Dylan checked her watch as Joan paid the fare. They were early, by more than half an hour.

"Do you want to look around the shops?" Tristan asked.

Dylan shook her head. "Too nervous. Let's… let's stay around here, get some fresh air."

It wasn't a warm day, and Dylan was too jittery to stay in Royal Exchange Square – where the tight confines felt claustrophobic. Joan refused to go, saying she'd save a seat in the coffee shop, but Tristan dutifully wheeled Dylan along Queen Street for a short distance until they reached George Square. He parked her in the wide pedestrian area in the centre and for a little while they watched the traffic's sluggish flow around the busy junction. It didn't seem like anything was going to calm Dylan's fluttering pulse, so she asked Tristan to take them back.

"Oh God," she whispered as they approached the coffee shop. "He's already there!"

She could see him, sitting in the window on a low leather couch. Joan was perched, upright and stiff, on the one opposite, a rectangular table creating a physical barrier between them – as if the cold radiating off Joan wasn't doing the job.

Dylan couldn't focus on that, though. Her eyes were glued to her dad, James Miller, drinking him in for the first time.

It was hard to tell, hunkered down in the sofa as he was, but he looked tall. The stretch of his arm across the back of the seat, the sprawl of his legs around the table, made her think he must be at least six foot. He had dark hair, the same as Dylan, but peppered with grey.

"Are you sure you'll be OK on your own?" Tristan's concerned voice floated over her shoulder. "I can still come with you."

"Mum would be mad."

"I don't care what your mum thinks, I care about you."

Dylan thought about it, beyond tempted. Joan wouldn't want to say anything to cause a scene in front of Dylan's dad – but they'd pay for it later.

"No," she said. "I need to do this by myself."

Tristan was silent for a moment. "All right," he said at last. "Will you at least let me wheel you inside?"

"Yes," she said. "Thank you."

There was no way she'd manage the door by herself anyway.

Tristan started forward again, and Joan caught sight of them. A second later, Dylan's dad turned too. He searched for the space of three frantic thumps of Dylan's pulse, then their gazes caught. Held.

Dylan's breath blew out in an astonished rush: "He looks like me!" They had the same green eyes and the same too-rounded nose. The same wide mouth. The same pale skin that blushed far too easily, which Dylan was doing right now. She just – she just couldn't stop staring. That was her dad. The man who made up half of her.

As they approached the door, a pair of shoppers darted in front of her chair and broke the spell. Dylan's dad disappeared. She frowned, blinking rapidly at the empty space, a sudden irrational terror striking her: had she imagined him? Time froze, but then it started again as the coffee shop door was flung open... and there he was.

"Dylan!" He strode towards them and crouched down beside her. The position put him level with her and his eyes drank in her face, staring at her just like she'd been staring at him. Did he see the resemblance too? She hoped so. "There you are," he murmured. Then a broad grin. "Hi."

"Hi," Dylan said breathlessly, with not a clue what to say next.

Her dad let her off the hook, breaking her gaze to look up at where Tristan hovered protectively behind her. Dylan thought she saw something briefly cloud her dad's eyes. "You must be the boyfriend."

"I am," Tristan confirmed. "It's Tristan."

They shook hands and Dylan had the impression that her dad was doing his best to break Tristan's fingers. If he was, Tristan didn't let on, offering James a reserved smile in return. Dylan wondered what Joan had told her dad about Tristan – and grimaced.

"I'll take her chair from here," James said firmly, and he nudged Tristan out of the way to take control of her handles. "Let's go and get better acquainted, eh?"

Her dad's attentiveness warmed Dylan just as much as it sent butterflies fluttering again. Feeling slightly panicked, she looked over her shoulder to where Tristan watched her go.

"I'll stay in sight," he mouthed, pointing to the steps of the art gallery, where several students were already lounging. That made her feel slightly better as she waved goodbye. Then before she knew it, she was parked in an awkward sandwich between her dad and Joan on their leather sofas.

"All right?" Joan's frosty demeanour had thawed – now she just looked worried. She reached out and squeezed Dylan's hand comfortingly.

"Yeah." Dylan had the urge to twitch her hand away – she didn't want her dad to think she was a baby – but she forced herself not to. It would hurt Joan's feelings. A second later, Joan let go and settled back.

"What would you like Dylan? A juice?" He huffed a quick laugh. "*I* know!" He stood up, a triumphant expression on his face, "Hot chocolate! Complete with whipped cream and marshmallows. I don't know a teenage girl in the land that would say no to that."

Dylan didn't particularly like hot chocolate, but she found herself nodding, not wanting to disappoint him when he was clearly trying so hard.

"Sounds good."

He disappeared towards the counter, as tall as she had thought, the top of his head easily visible above the throng of customers. Then she whipped her eyes around, searching for Tristan. She knew he had to be close; there was a tightness in her chest, but it felt more like nerves than the excruciating pain of distance.

At first she couldn't find him, and for an instant the tightness became immeasurably worse… but then her eyes picked out his flop of sandy hair, head bent low over the tablet she'd lent him. She breathed out. He was there. Of course he was.

As if he felt her gaze on him, Tristan lifted his head, stared in her direction. It seemed unlikely that he could see her through the reflective glass at that distance, but she felt better all the same. Taking a deep breath, she turned back to Joan.

Her mum was drinking some fancy frothy coffee in a large mug. It looked expensive, and if James was buying, that's likely why she'd picked it. Normally, Joan was a straightforward tea drinker. She had also opted for a piece of gingerbread, again unlike her, which she was delicately nibbling.

"We can leave any time you like, you know," she said abruptly. "Just say the word."

"All right," Dylan replied. She didn't bother to add that she wouldn't want to go any time soon. She wanted to sit and talk with her dad for hours. Then again, she'd only ever had one phone call with him. She knew she might find that the time it took to drink a hot chocolate was about as long as she could keep up a conversation with this relative stranger. "He looks like me."

"He does," Joan agreed, her tone carefully blank.

"Does that... I mean—" She stopped, chewed on her lip. "You've had to look at me every day. And you don't like him. You must have thought—"

"You can stop right there, Dylan." Joan pinned her with her gaze. "When I look at you, I see you. End of story."

And end of conversation. They didn't talk again until her dad came back, placing a tall thin mug topped with a mountainous swirl of whipped cream and little chocolate shaves in front of her. "Ta da!"

"Thank you." She managed to eke the words out through a throat that was suddenly desert dry.

"Well." Her dad threw his big body down and leant forward, his hands clasped between his knees. "At last, here we are!"

"Yeah," agreed Dylan. At last.

TWELVE

Four times. Susanna had already used her little mind control mojo on Jack four times. And they weren't even at the first safe house yet. He was a thug, uneducated and unpolished, but he seemed to have the ability to fight off her hypnotic commands with startling speed. Which was unfortunate as he wasn't the type of boy to take orders.

Especially not from a girl.

"Just trust me," she said, trying to hide the exasperation in her voice, instinctively aware that it would only rile him further. "I know where I'm going."

She was trying to wheedle and cajole him along, because each time she forced him to come with her – four and counting – he was throwing it off quicker and quicker. She was getting nervous that soon it wouldn't work at all. And they had a long, long way to go.

"Sammy," he smirked at her, "you couldn't find your way out of a paper bag. I'm seriously supposed to trust your sense of direction?"

"I know where I'm going," Susanna repeated. She took his hand and plastered on her most winning smile. "Come on."

His scathing expression softened a little bit and to Susanna's surprise he let her tug him along. It only lasted a handful of steps, though. After that, he had to take over, upping his pace so he was the one in the lead.

She was already counting the days until she could shove this particular soul across the line. And, an insidious thought crept in, if the wraiths got him earlier than that – well, she wouldn't lose too much sleep over it.

Not that she slept.

Susanna had never purposefully failed in her role as a ferryman, in fact she couldn't. It was coded into her every thought and action: protect the soul at all costs. Even above her own pain, her own suffering. But if souls were stupid, if they didn't listen, her best efforts weren't always enough.

Jack was a classic example of the type that fell victim to the wraiths' insatiable hunger.

"So," he said in her ear, pulling her out of her thoughts. "You want to tell me how you found me?"

"Somebody saw you get on a bus," she said, quickly flashing back through Jack's final memories, hunting for a cover story. "The 47. I got the same one."

"Right." A drawl, and Susanna sensed danger. "And how'd you know when to get off, eh?" A sharp tug on her belt loop at the end of Jack's question.

"It was the same driver. I asked him and he remembered you, he told me where you got off."

He hauled her to a dead stop, whirled her to face him.

"Really? That sounds bloody convenient." He stared down at her and Susanna forgot she was looking up at a sixteen-year-old boy. Her heart started to pound in fear. It was the way he could switch from playful to predator between one breath and the next.

"How else could I have known where you were?" she asked. She added a mental push, a strong one, to make him believe her.

He did nothing but stare back: no tell-tale dilating of his pupils, no relaxation in his tense stance.

"That's the question, isn't it," he whispered. "Why else would you be there. It's a long way from home, Sammy."

A pulse started thudding in Susanna's throat. How the hell had she gotten herself into this situation? Why – *why* – had she been matched with this particular soul? The powers that decided these things were usually smarter than this. Jack should have had a male ferryman. Someone it wouldn't smart his pride to follow. Not her.

Definitely not her.

"Are you seeing someone else?" he asked her softly – but not gently. Threat underlay every word. "Are you going with some boy from round here now?"

"Don't you trust me, Jack?" Susanna kept her face carefully blank of every emotion except hurt. She buried her fear as deep as it could go.

That did the trick. He looked down at her for one more long moment, then he smiled, and for a heartbeat she saw what must have attracted the foolish Sammy to this particular bad boy.

"'Course I do," he said, dropping a surprisingly tender kiss on her nose. "You're my girl."

Danger past, Susanna got him moving again. They were almost at the first safe house. Given that his murder had happened at night, she'd expected to see the odd wraith coasting hopefully along, looking for easy pickings. But the first miles of the wasteland were empty of the vile, scavenging creatures. She didn't pause to wonder why that might be, or trust her luck to hold. She just wanted to find their first shelter so she could get herself together, come up with a better way to manage Jack before he got her hurt… and himself dead. Forever this time.

"You know, I've got a friend who lives round here," she said.

"Who?" Instant suspicion – the heavy weight of jealousy.

"Marcy," Susanna said, plucking the name from nowhere.

"Marcy?" Jack snorted. "You've got a friend called *Marcy*?"

"Yes. Anyway… she's away on holiday. She lives on her own, so the place'll be empty. We could probably squat there tonight. It's late, and I'm getting tired." Susanna cracked her face into a wide yawn. She felt stupid doing it, but she needed Jack to fall for her ruse. Besides, even though she didn't get sleepy – ever – the yawn helped stretch her clenched jaw muscles.

Jack shot her an incredulous look and she was pretty sure he was going to argue – was it worth risking another push? Maybe she should just clobber him over the head? – but then he grinned wickedly. "This place have a bed?"

"Yeah…"

"Then let's go."

OK. That was easy. Susanna shook her head, confused, but for once Jack wasn't fighting her so she let it go.

In Jack's urban sprawl of wasteland, the first safe house was on the ground floor of a tall block of flats. The place had an apocalyptic feel – broken windows, boarded up doorways and smoke damage to several walls. Glass littered the building entryway, but inside the flat itself was sparse and clean.

"Your friend lives here?" Jack asked, eyes on the lobby and the lift doors that were buckled and bent as if they'd been rammed by a bull. Or maybe a herd of bulls. Susanna shut the door, turning a sugar-sweet smile on him.

"Yes. It was her gran's, but the old woman died and left her it."

"I bet she was really pleased," Jack said, voice laden with sarcasm.

"The place is set to be knocked down," Susanna continued, ignoring him, "but she's hanging in for the compensation money."

Her little book of lies was filling up, but with Jack somehow resistant to her hypnosis it was her only option. She would deal with the consequences later.

"Your friend got any food in the place?"

"I doubt she left any lying around." Susanna searched around for an excuse that would stop Jack from attempting to eat – because he couldn't. "There's a mouse problem." She offered him a tentative smile. "I'm not really hungry anyway."

She'd like to be, just once. To know what it felt like. Not pleasant, probably, but alive. Real. But that was just one more entry on an endless list of things that had been denied her.

"Fair enough," Jack agreed. Then that devilish light came back in his eyes. "Where's the bed, then?"

"There's a bedroom through there." Susanna pointed to the only door. There was no bathroom – because Jack wouldn't need that the same way he wouldn't need a kitchen. The safe houses were nothing if not efficient.

"Come on, then." Grabbing her hand, he hauled her through to the tiny bedroom with him.

There was a double bed, a faded floral bedspread pulled flat across its surface, the top barely rising over two flat pillows. It didn't look comfortable, but Susanna had spent countless nights on the floor pretending to sleep, to fool newly released souls. It was nothing she couldn't handle.

Not that she was planning to sleep in there – not with Jack. There was a perfectly serviceable, if grubby, couch in the living room, thank you very much.

Unfortunately, Jack had other ideas. Keeping a firm hold of her hand, he gripped her waist with the other and lifted her through the air. Susanna hit the mattress with an audible 'oomph' that was cut off when a heavier weight landed on top of her.

"This was a good idea," Jack grinned down at her, right before he dropped his head and started kissing her neck.

"Jack!" She pushed ineffectually on his shoulders. "Stop!"

He didn't stop, but he did raise his head for a short moment to mumble, "What's the matter babe?"

"I don't…" she tried to shift away from the heat of his mouth on her collar bone. "I'm tired."

"Uhuh," he murmured between little kisses. "I bet I can keep you awake. I've missed you."

One hand dropped to her waist and started easing under and up the long-sleeved top she was wearing. Susanna had had enough.

"Sleep!" she commanded, putting every ounce of will she had into the command.

And Jack dropped like a tonne of bricks above her.

"Brilliant, Susanna," she muttered. "Just brilliant."

Slowly, carefully, she eased out from underneath him. Then, sitting on the side of the bed, she looked down at him. In sleep, with those cold eyes closed, he looked almost innocent. Sweet sixteen.

Susanna blew out a breath, relieving the tension that had gripped her more and more during their first few hours together. If only she could fast forward several days… But then, she'd just get another soul, and another. The truth was, she'd had enough. She didn't want to be here any more, didn't want to do *this* any more.

That had been true for a long time, but now, knowing Tristan was someplace else, in the *real* world, it hit Susanna like never before. She wanted out. Now. She wanted to be where Tristan was.

To her utter astonishment, Susanna realised there were tears on her cheeks. Tears.

Shaking her head, she wandered out to the sagging leather sofa to wait out the night. Closing her eyes, she imagined it. The fantasy she had been nurturing since Tristan left. Him and her, in the world. Doing things, seeing things. Living. Sharing experiences, not just the secret, silent smiles they'd exchanged across the short span between their safe houses. Sharing touches.

What would it have felt like if it had been Tristan, putting his mouth on her neck like that?

What would have felt like if it had been his fingertips sliding up her side?

She could almost see it, almost feel it. Almost.

THIRTEEN

In the bustling Glasgow square, Tristan tried to focus on the tablet in front of him, but his attention kept wandering. He didn't like that Dylan was out of sight. He knew exactly where she was, but he couldn't see her through the glare of the coffee shop's window. Which meant he couldn't monitor how she was feeling, how she was handling the tumult of emotion he'd seen building over the last few days.

She had her phone, though. She could ring him or text him if she needed him. He checked his one more time, just in case. Nothing.

Placing it back in his pocket, he went back to Dylan's tablet, using the coffee shop's free Wi-Fi. It was amazing, the internet. He'd known of it, heard about it from the more recent souls as they talked about their lives – but the exhilaration of actually having all the knowledge in the world at his fingertips was something he was still getting used to. That, and fruit. And sleep. And holding Dylan in his arms…

Focus. Jabbing his way into the news app, he skimmed through stories until he found the one he wanted. The headline ran boldly across the top of the page, but it was the picture that drew his eye. Taken from a different angle than the television report, this one showed the heart of the tunnel, one man –

one body – on a stretcher being carried out of the tunnel's gaping mouth. It was definitely the same place.

And no matter what he'd said to Dylan, it could not be a coincidence. Something they'd done had caused those deaths, he was sure of it.

Skimming through the article, he searched for more information. They'd released the names of the four men, but he wasn't interested in that. He needed to know how they'd died. Reaching the end, he frowned in dissatisfaction.

Tristan tried three more news sites, but came up with the same brick wall. The deaths were suspicious, but the police weren't saying anything. Investigators had ruled out accidental death. But nothing concrete.

Cursing, he gave up on the official news pages and started scrolling through forums. There was a lot of stupid stuff – conspiracy theories and trolls who just wanted to stir things up – but then he stumbled on a blog and hit gold.

It was someone claiming to be one of the emergency services workers at the scene. As soon as Tristan started reading, he knew his suspicions were right.

And he knew he was in big, big trouble.

```
I've never seen anything like it. At first
we reckoned it had been some sort of animal
attack, because they were seriously scratched
up. But I don't know any wildlife around here
that can do that kind of damage! Besides the
scratches, they had… holes in them. Like
someone – something – had just punched right
through them. One guy had one through his
chest, another one his stomach. You could see
the tunnel floor through their wounds.
```

I don't know where the guts and organs ended
up. Maybe whatever it was ate them.

The worst thing though, the thing that'll
stick with me forever, was the look on their
faces. Like they saw the face of the devil
and just died of sheer terror. I've attended
traffic accidents where there's been nothing
left of a person but jam, so trust me that I
know what I'm saying when I tell you that this
was seriously messed up.

"Bloody hell," Tristan whispered. "Shit, shit, shit."

He went back and read the account over and over again, until
he knew every word by heart. Each time his heart sank a little
lower, because he knew what had caused those deaths. Knew what
could scratch and claw, swoop and dive, terrify its victim, and
plough straight through them.

Wraiths.

Wraiths had somehow managed to find a way through the
barrier between the real world and the wasteland. It didn't take
a genius to figure out why it had happened right where Dylan
dragged him through. There was only one possible explanation:
they must have made a tear in the veil between life and death. One
that remained open. The wraiths had found it, and now they were
free to feast on abundant human flesh there was no way they'd
return to the wasteland, scratching out a survival on the wisps
of souls.

No, now that they'd had a taste, there was no way the demons
wouldn't want more.

What had he done?

Guilt rose in his throat like vomit. Four lives. Four lives had been prematurely ended because of his selfishness. And if some wraiths had found their way through already, how many more would follow?

There wasn't time to dwell on the consequences of his actions however, because the coffee shop door opened once more and the wheels of Dylan's chair burst through the gap. He could see James struggling to hold the door and steer the wheelchair at the same time, and Joan rushing to help, looking vaguely annoyed. Tristan guessed the man had refused her help getting Dylan out of the tight and awkward space.

Flicking off the tablet's screen, Tristan rose and walked quickly over to the trio.

"… really so pleased you got in touch. I can't tell you how many times I thought about it, but I—" Dylan's dad broke off, either because of Tristan's rapid approach or the absolutely molten look from Joan.

"I suppose you'll be heading back up to Aberdeen, then?" Joan asked, subtly shifting her position so that her back was to Tristan. He suppressed a smirk. She thought it bothered him, the cold-shoulder treatment, but the truth was he was happy to deal with her as little as possible. So long as she didn't interfere with Dylan and him.

"No, I'm not heading back." James's reply caused gasps of surprise in both Dylan and her mum – for different reasons.

"You're staying down here?" Dylan asked.

"I can work from home, so I decided I'd just make this home for a little while. My neighbour is looking after my dog and I've rented a place, so I'll be here for the next month at least." He took a deep breath. "I wanted time to really get to know you."

Dylan's cheeks pinked and she gave him a shy smile. "That sounds good."

Tristan tried his best not to feel jealous – or at least, not to show it. This was her father, he wasn't a threat. Although if Tristan ever had to shake his hand again he wanted to put on a gauntlet first.

"What are you doing tomorrow?" James asked.

"Homework," Joan interjected. She sounded stern, unyielding. "You have that modern studies project to hand in, and I know you haven't finished it."

"That won't take all day," Dylan protested.

"It's all right." James broke in, to save them both some energy. "We can do something after school one night next week, maybe. Go and get dinner." He looked up, caught Tristan standing there. "You can bring your boyfriend and we can get to know each other too."

That appeased Dylan somewhat, but she still sent a stinker of a glare towards Joan before surrendering.

"I should go." James pulled his phone out of his pocket. "I know you have a new number, Dyl. Why don't you give me it and I'll call you?"

Joan opened her mouth to squelch that idea, but Dylan was already rattling her digits off. Promising to call by Monday at the latest, Dylan's dad bent down and kissed Dylan's forehead. He gave a nod to Tristan and, after a short hesitation, bussed Joan's cheek. Both Dylan and Joan watched him stride off until he was swallowed by the milling shoppers.

Tristan moved forward to grip the handles of Dylan's wheelchair. They were warm from the heat of her father's hands, and for some reason Tristan disliked the feeling.

"Are we going home now then?" Dylan asked.

"Yes, well," Joan was still looking off to where James had disappeared. She had a strange look on her face, a mix of anger and something else that didn't seem to be sitting easily with her. "You go." She dragged her head round to smile at Dylan. "I'll give you money for the taxi, and a bit extra. You can get a takeaway from the chip shop for tea."

"Where are you going?"

"I've just got something I've got to do in town. A bit of shopping, that's all."

Tristan raised his eyebrows. He'd no interest in where Joan was going – though he had a good idea it wasn't shopping. Dylan didn't seem to pick up on it, though. She just shrugged and mumbled, "OK."

They waited while Joan fished a couple of notes out of her purse, then headed for a taxi rank. They spent most of that time in silence. Tristan figured Dylan was likely mulling over the meeting with her dad – he'd ask her about it when they had a hint of privacy. His own thoughts, however, were much darker. And he couldn't decide whether or not to share them with Dylan.

She deserved to know, but it would hurt her.

"So," he said once they had found a taxi and were crawling slowly through the thick city-centre traffic. "Do you want to tell me how it went?"

"Good," Dylan said. "It was good." For a moment he thought that was all she was going to say about it, but then the details came flooding out. "I mean, at the start it was really awkward, you know? It would have been easier if Mum hadn't been there, but then I'd have been on my own and that would have been really scary."

"I'd have been there," Tristan reminded her gently.

Dylan reached out and gave his arm a quick squeeze before continuing. "I wasn't really sure what to say, but he asked lots of questions and once I got going it was pretty good. He's funny." A lopsided smile. "And he looks like me. Did you notice he looks like me?"

"You're prettier," Tristan offered. That earned him a full-on grin.

"I think… I wish I knew what happened between him and my mum to make her, you know, hate his guts."

"Mmmm." Tristan thought about the way Joan had stared after Dylan's dad as he left. She'd been so desperate to get away – to go after him? – she hadn't even thought about the fact she'd be leaving Tristan and Dylan alone together. "It's probably more complicated than that."

"You think?" Dylan blinked at him, then carried on telling Tristan the details of their chat.

Tristan let her words wash over him, let himself bask in her innocent excitement, and realised he couldn't lay the heavy burden consuming him around her neck. Not when she was so excited, so happy. He would – he promised himself. He'd tell her everything. But not yet.

She'd been through so much, she was so young. This was a burden he could shoulder for her, and he'd find a way to fix their terrible mistake himself.

FOURTEEN

"I'm dead? What the hell do you mean, I'm dead?" Jack grabbed an old glass tumbler, cracked and dirty, and hurled it against the wall, where it smashed into a thousand pieces. "Shit, Sammy. What the hell are you playing at?"

Susanna stood her ground, fighting the urge to cower away from Jack's anger. Three days in the wasteland, that's how long she'd managed to keep it a secret from him – the remarkable absence of wraiths had kept his questions at bay. But the little mind-control tricks she'd been using had stopped working by the second day, and she'd had to resort to pleading and coaxing to get him to the second safe house, a battered-looking caravan, in time. Now, a bare hour into day three – they hadn't even left the caravan yet! – he was back to fighting her. So out came the truth.

Unfortunately, it hadn't done much for his temper.

"I'm not Sammy," Susanna said. "I'm your guide across the wasteland."

"Don't be so bloody stupid," he growled. "Are you out of your mind?" He took a menacing step closer. "What the hell is wrong with you?"

Quite a lot, Susanna thought, though she fought not to show it. "I'm not Sammy," she repeated, knowing this was the one thing that would convince him. "Look."

She changed before his eyes. A tiny adjustment in height and weight, the fringe disappearing – she wouldn't miss that – and her hair thickening and curling slightly. She felt a tingle in her face as her features rearranged themselves. Then she was the 'true' Susanna again.

Jack paled. Swayed. For a second she thought he was going to fall, or vomit, but he pulled himself together. She'd shocked him into silence with that shape-shifting move. He looked around the caravan, then staggered over to the short sofa built into the wall – the sturdiest bit of furniture in the safe house – and collapsed down onto it.

"It's true?" he croaked, making it a question even though it was clear he believed her.

"It is," she agreed, then added, "I'm sorry", because she felt she should.

"How?" Then understanding dawned. "The alley."

"Somebody stabbed you," Susanna said.

"One of those boys," he glowered at her. "Which one did it?"

"I don't know," she shrugged helplessly. "I don't come along until afterwards."

"This is," he put his head in his hands and stared down at the floor. "This is… it's absolute shit! No way, no goddamn way!"

With each curse he got louder and louder, his hands clawing his skull. Susanna started backing away, sensing an explosion, but when it came, it still shocked her.

He erupted off the seat and then started destroying everything he could lay his hands on. He wrenched the door to the tiny wardrobe off its hinges, battered at the window over the sink with a frying pan until it caved in and cracked. He tore the curtains off the rails, ripped the sofa from the wall and started smashing the drawers beneath until there was little left in the caravan that resembled furniture. Then, finally, he just stood there, breathing heavily amongst the wreckage. And his eyes settled on Susanna.

She took a cautionary step backwards, but she was already against the wall. There was nowhere to go.

Watching him lose control, she couldn't help but compare him to Tristan. He was his polar opposite in every way. His rage, his indignation. He'd been stupidly reckless with his life and now here he was, complaining about the consequences. He didn't know what it was to truly suffer, like she and Tristan did. Going around and around, with no right to complain, no freedom to change. They hadn't asked for the hand fate had dealt them, had done nothing to deserve it. Not like Jack, wandering stupidly down dangerous streets in the dark, picking fights. Tristan had been just as unhappy as Susanna, she was sure – she'd *felt* his pain and dissatisfaction – but did he lose it like this? Yell and throw things? Destroy everything in his grasp? No. He soldiered on, stoic and resolute.

God, she needed that sense of purpose, of calm, right now.

"No," Jack finally spat at her. "I don't accept it. You can take me back." He advanced a step, then two. The caravan was a tiny space and one more step would put him within arm's reach. Susanna would not cower and whimper, *she would not*, but she was frightened.

"What?"

"Take me back, whoever the hell you are. *You* took me out of there, *you* can take me back."

"No, I—"

"Didn't you hear what I said? Take. Me. Back."

Susanna had heard those words spoken countless times by innumerable angry souls. She'd very rarely been frightened as she was now. And she'd never, *ever* responded as she did.

"I can try."

Because what Jack was demanding – it was what she wanted, wasn't it?

"What?" She'd surprised him. His eyes widened, then narrowed into suspicious slits. "Is this one of your little tricks? I know you've been messing with my head all this time. Do it one more time and I'll bloody smash you in! You're not Sammy – you aren't even a real girl. I could pulverise you and not feel a thing."

"You couldn't," Susanna told him, shaking her head earnestly. "You can't kill me. I'm a ferryman, Jack, I'm an immortal being."

"Oh come off it."

"You want proof?" Susanna's fear had turned to rage. She strode to the caravan door and flung it open. "Listen."

The sun hadn't yet risen, and the sudden movement from the caravan caused an instant rise in noise from the wraiths. Jack froze, and for the first time genuine concern crossed his pale face.

"Is…" Jack swallowed. "Is that what I've been hearing at night?"

Without answering, Susanna stepped onto the faded grass, tempting the hungriest, most frenzied of the nearby wraiths to swoop towards her. Writhing, screaming, twisting closer and closer. Before it reached her, Susanna took a calm step back into the caravan and shut the door. She'd never done anything so brazen, and the wraiths were furious. Their hisses and snarls filled the air outside.

"What the hell was that?" Jack croaked.

"Wraiths. People who don't make it. Starved, crazed souls, and you'll become one of them if they get you. It's my job to protect you from them."

"Take me back." Jack's voice was low. "I don't want to be here."

"I'll try. But I can't promise it, remember it's only a chance – I've never attempted it before."

Jack looked thoughtful for a moment, and Susanna hoped that her little show had impressed him enough to kerb his attitude. Then he advanced on her.

"Why not?" She could feel the distrust and hostility rolling off him in waves. "Am I supposed to think I'm special, that you would try this with *me* and no other soul ever? You're lying!"

"I'm not," she said quickly. "I'm not. I didn't know it could be done until recently."

"How?" The question was thick with suspicion.

"I saw someone else doing it, another ferryman. I watched him take his soul back across the line. But..." She licked her lips. Her heart was pounding with hope and fear. "But you'd have to take me with you. Otherwise it won't work."

She didn't know if that was true or not, but that was the price for her help.

"And then what?" Jack's abrupt, clipped question made her flinch a little. "I take you with me and then what?"

"Nothing," she promised. "I give you back your life, you take me out of the wasteland. Then I'll leave you alone. You'll never have to see me again." Straightening her shoulders, Susanna swallowed against the knot in her throat. She held out her hand. "Do we have a deal?"

He took the hand, grabbed it, and hauled her towards him. Dark, angry eyes glared down into hers. Whatever he was searching for, he seemed to see it. .

"Deal."

FIFTEEN

Dylan really hated the hospital. She, Tristan and Joan were there again, waiting to see the doctor, to check how her leg was healing. Her appointment time had come and gone twenty minutes ago, though the awkward silence made it feel more like an hour. Finally, a squat, grumpy-looking nurse appeared at the ward door and hollered Dylan's name.

"You can wait out here," Joan told Tristan when he rose with her.

Tristan opened his mouth, then seemed to think better of it. He looked to Dylan.

"I want Tristan," she said simply. "He helps keep me calm."

That wasn't a lie exactly.

"The doctor doesn't need a crowd when he's trying to look at your leg, Dylan." Joan was using that deliberately reasonable voice that always set Dylan's teeth on edge.

"You're welcome to stay here then, Mum," Dylan offered, saccharine sweet.

"Oh, for goodness sake." Joan rolled her eyes and marched off in Nurse Grumpy's direction.

Dr Hammond was seeing them again. He greeted Dylan warmly and offered Tristan a wary nod. He likely remembered the tension from before. He explained that he was going to be removing the cast today.

"Is it not too soon, doctor?" Joan asked, in her best nurse voice.

"Well, ordinarily it would be," he agreed. "But I want to make sure that the bone is healing straight and that none of the wounds are becoming infected. Better to know now than later, when the bone can't take her weight."

Dylan only vaguely heard him, her attention was focussed on the tool in his hand which looked like...

"Is that a circular saw?" It came out as a panicked squeak.

"Well, yes. In essence, but it's very safe." Dr Hammond held it up for Dylan to see. "Don't worry," he joked, "I haven't been making any garden furniture with it." He grinned at her cheerfully, then hit the power button for the mini-saw with his free hand. He looked like a horror-movie psycho. Dylan watched the little spinning disc get closer and closer to her leg, but at the last minute she caved, turning her face away. She squished her eyes together and waited for the pain.

"It'll be fine, Dylan." Tristan was suddenly there, clasping her hand.

She felt the vibration and heard the change in noise as the saw began to slice its way through the plaster. It created a weird tingling itch down the front of her shin and she wanted to jerk her leg away. Only the images of blood spurting across the sterile white room stopped her.

Less than a minute later the buzzing stopped. Dylan eyed her limb through half-closed eyes. Her leg looked like a prop from a Frankenstein movie. There were long red lines where her skin had been sliced to insert the pins, and these were crosshatched with thick black threads. Most of her flesh was a mottled purple colour. Most embarrassingly, however, was the two weeks' worth of leg hair that dappled her skin.

"Don't look," she ordered Tristan.

"Well," the doctor was frowning down at her leg. "These look, these look…"

"Gosh." Joan was peering over his shoulder.

"What?" Dylan's stomach was a pit of dread.

"It looks remarkable," the doctor admitted.

"I've never seen anything like it," Joan echoed.

"Your leg is healing very quickly, Dylan – and cleanly too." He reached out and began to palpate Dylan's knee and the muscle of her calf. "How does that feel?"

"Fine," Dylan answered honestly.

"Hmmm. I think—" he stepped back. "I think we'll do an X-ray, just to see what's happening."

It took less than an hour for Dylan to be wheeled round to the X-ray department, Tristan and Joan trotting behind her, and for the radiographer and her technician to get the shots they wanted of her leg. The longest part was hanging around in the waiting room for Dr Hammond to come back with the results.

He did appear at last and, though it was Dylan's leg that was the one in question, it was Joan that Dr Hammond engaged in conversation, drawing her over to a PC in the corner. Tristan hovered behind them briefly, then returned to Dylan with a grim expression on his face.

"What is it?"

He didn't answer at once.

"Tristan?"

"Your leg," he said, nodding down her naked limb in all its multihued glory. "It's…"

"It's what?" Dylan asked. She really wished she could cover it, hide the hairs that she swore were growing longer each time she looked at them.

"It's healing too fast," Tristan said. "Did you hear what the doctor said?"

"Well, isn't that a good thing?" Dylan asked. "Maybe I can keep the stupid cast off and you won't have to push me everywhere."

"I like pushing you," Tristan told her with a smile. "No, it's… you're healing like me."

"What?"

"In the wasteland, when I was hurt, it didn't take me long to recover. Do you remember?"

Did she remember? That memory was burned onto her brain. She'd thought Tristan had died. He'd been caught by a whole swarm of wraiths because she'd been too slow, too clod-footed. And when she saw the damage that the wraiths had done to him, she thought she'd die of shame.

Then, in the morning, she'd been shocked by the improvement. As if he'd spent a week healing rather than just a handful of hours.

"You think?" Dylan asked. She looked down at her leg. The purple bruising and angry red scars looked plenty bad to her.

"Dylan," Tristan reminded her quietly, "Your fibula and tibia were like a jigsaw puzzle, they had to put in multiple pins. You don't recover from that in a fortnight."

"Let's just see what the doctor says," Dylan replied.

As if he'd been waiting for her cue, the doctor chose that moment to show her the X-ray picture on the screen, not that it made much sense to her. She could make out the harsh white lines of metal where they'd braced her bones together, and the slightly curved lines of the bones themselves, but she'd no idea if they looked good or bad.

"Well, I didn't really believe what the radiographer said, but I have to say," the doctor said, "this is remarkable. If it hadn't been me who performed the surgery on you initially, Dylan, I'd have said the consultant exaggerated the extent of the damage."

"Really?" Dylan asked. She ignored Tristan's *I told you so* look.

"Really." Dr Hammond smiled at her. "Your bones have fused and, though we don't want you putting too much pressure on your leg, I think we can dispense with the cast. We'll just strap it up to give it a bit of support."

"I can get rid of the wheelchair?" Dylan asked, hardly daring to hope.

"You can get rid of the wheelchair," the doctor confirmed. "Although, you'll have to have crutches and you might find them hard going at first." He nodded at her lower body. "Let's have a look at the gashes on your left leg and lower back. It wouldn't surprise me if they'd healed completely!"

⌒

The next day, Dylan and Tristan took a taxi to school. When it stopped outside the entrance, Dylan got out on her own two feet. She had to lean heavily against the side of the vehicle while Tristan dashed round with her crutches, but she was standing. It was enough to make her grin up at the three-storey concrete monstrosity of a building.

She could get about pretty well now, but Tristan still insisted she use the lift. Strangely, it seemed even more tight and cramped than it had before – possibly because she was much more aware of how it lurched and juddered as it hauled them to the top floor.

"I hate this thing! Every time we get in I think it's going to break down and trap us. Or the cables will snap and send us plummeting to our death."

"It's only three floors," Tristan said. "That's hardly plummeting."

"It's far enough to die," Dylan told him acidly.

"I tell you what," Tristan said, moving closer in the cramped space. To Dylan's surprise, he dropped both their bags and leaned in so that he was sandwiching her between his body and the wall. "I'll distract you."

Dylan opened her mouth to speak and Tristan took advantage, covering her lips with his. She let out a startled squeak – they were in the *school lift!* – but the threat of being caught wasn't enough to make her put the brakes on.

Tristan hadn't kissed her like this since they'd left the wasteland. Not a proper, no-holds-barred kiss. He'd said she was too delicate, that she was healing. It had frustrated her no end, but he was making up for it now and no power in the world was going to stop them. Except, perhaps, the need to breathe.

Gasping, Dylan broke away. Dropped her head back against the wall of the lift and tried to calm her racing heart.

"See," Tristan whispered into her ear. "That sped things up a bit."

Dylan let out a strangled laugh that settled into a happy little sigh. Tristan gave her a chaste final peck on the cheek then collected her crutches from the floor – she didn't even remember dropping them – and handed them to her. Then he stepped out into the heaving corridor, cool and nonchalant. The only hint he gave that he was as affected as she was, was a happy little wink before he turned to clear a path for her through the crowd.

Not even the thought of two periods in the freezing portacabin with Miserable Monkton after registration could dampen her mood.

When they got to the hut that served as Monkton's teaching lab, the teacher was nowhere in sight. That wasn't unusual. What *was* unusual was the excited buzz in the air. Dylan halted on the threshold, taking in the animated faces with no small amount of confusion.

"What's going on?" she asked Marie Cummings, who was the only person not involved in the small huddles dotted around the room. Another social outcast like herself, Marie had been Dylan's seating partner in several classes before Tristan's arrival. That was probably the reason behind the slightly miffed look Marie gave her, but apparently the gossip was too good not to share, because she couldn't hold on to her snit.

"A murder!" she said, eyes flashing behind heavily framed glasses.

"Is it somebody famous?" Dylan asked. OK, a murder was a terrible thing, but it didn't usually have everybody up in arms. The pupils of Kaithshall were not particularly known for their social conscience.

"No, it was a construction worker," Marie said with relish.

Dylan's thoughts immediately went to the tunnel. "So why is everyone...?" she gestured at the room.

"There's footage!"

"Of the murder?"

"No, the victim. The person who found the body videoed it and posted it online. You can see *everything*! He was, like, eaten or something."

Dylan looked at Tristan, who had turned whiter than her during this conversation. Not wanting to hear any more, she shuffled past on her crutches, negotiating the tables until she and Tristan could hide away at the back of the classroom.

"Can you believe that?" she asked him as they sat back down. "D'you think it's another worker from the tunnel?"

Dylan could see the mobile screen in the centre of each group. Her eyes rested briefly on Dove MacMillan, who was grinning broadly and acting out a dramatic reconstruction of the poor man's death.

Tristan's whisper in her ear made her jump. "Have you got your phone?"

"Yeah. Why?"

"I want to watch that video."

"What! Why?"

Monkton chose that moment to wander into the classroom, so Dylan had to wait while he handed out some worksheets and told them their task for the day. She grabbed the chemicals they were supposed to be mixing, and as soon as Monkton was occupied elsewhere, she elbowed Tristan in the ribs.

"Well?" she hissed. "Why the hell do you want to watch that grotesque video?"

"Because," he gave her a look that told her he thought she was being extremely thick, "your friend said it looked like he was *eaten*."

As he spoke, he ran his thumb over the screen of her smart phone, loading up the video. In the pit of her stomach, Dylan knew what was coming.

"You think... you think it's related to the deaths of those four workers?"

"I think it *is* one of them."

"What?"

"Well, one of the paramedics on the scene said something similar about the bodies in the train tunnel. I think maybe it's his footage of one of those guys."

Dylan tilted her head and just stared at him for several long seconds. Then she couldn't hold it in any longer. "What?!"

Tristan squirmed, looking distinctly uncomfortable. It wasn't a look she was accustomed to seeing on him. She didn't like it.

"When you were meeting your dad," he began, "I did some searching on the internet and found a blog—"

"That was almost a week ago!"

"Miss McKenzie!" Monkton hollered across the classroom at her. "Is there a problem?"

"No, sir," Dylan ground out, forcing her furious gaze away from Tristan. "Sorry, sir."

He humphed, which Dylan took as an acceptance of her apology. Teacher appeased, she went back to glowering at Tristan.

"Why didn't you tell me what you found out?" she muttered furiously under her breath. Glancing at the worksheet, aware Monkton was still watching her, she snatched up a hazardous-looking bottle of liquid. Pouring a healthy glug into her dish of white powder, she watched it all turn molten green. How exciting. "Well?"

"Because I didn't want to upset you. What was done to the bodies, it made it pretty obvious who killed them."

He held her gaze, as if trying to establish how determined she was to hear the answer. She was very determined.

"They were clawed," he said. "There were gouges on them made by long talons. And the bodies had holes in them, like—"

"Like something had punched its way right through them," Dylan finished for him. She felt the blood drain from her face. "Wraiths."

Tristan took a deep breath. "I think so." He winced. "No. I know so. They were killed by wraiths."

"But how could wraiths be here?" She tailed off under the steady look he was giving her. "We let them in. When we came back, we let them in, didn't we?" Her hand crept up to cover her mouth. She thought she might vomit. "Shit! This is my fault."

"This is why I didn't tell you," he said. "Dylan!" He reached out to grip her shoulder, gave it a gentle shake. "This isn't your fault."

She threw him a disbelieving look, though it was quickly replaced with horror, tears bleeding into her eyes.

"It isn't," he repeated. "We couldn't have known what would happen – and if it's anyone's fault, it's mine."

She could only stare at him, the tears building until they spilled in hot streaks down her cheeks. Catching sight of Monkton out of the corner of her eye, she ducked her head and used her hand to cover her face. There was no way she could manage any expression but horror right now, imagining their mangled bodies. Flashbacks burst across her mind, memories of the swooping, clawing wraiths as they'd surrounded her.

They had utterly petrified her – and because of her selfishness four innocent men had had to face the same terror in the real world. Had had to die that way, only to find them in the wasteland too – if they even got there.

She couldn't breathe. If she opened her mouth, she'd be sick.

"Would you care to tell me what the issue is?" Monkton asked Tristan, ice in his voice.

"Dylan's upset, sir. I think she's in pain since the cast came off. I'll take her for some fresh air."

Vision still blurred by tears, Dylan let him lift her off the stool and lead her away. Monkton stood firm in their path, his arms crossed over his chest, and for an instant Dylan thought that Tristan would march right through him. Thankfully, they were saved by an almighty bang as Dove's workbench exploded in a cloud of billowing smoke and test-tube shards.

Monkton's hollered "MacMillan!" and the screams and excited cries of the rest of the class provided enough cover for them to sneak out unchallenged.

There weren't many private spaces at Kaithshall Academy, but Tristan managed to find one. He led Dylan to a bench in an alcove around the side of the main building that provided a break from the wind. He held her while she cried into his shoulder, her face pressed into the fabric of his school sweatshirt to muffle the sounds. It was a long time before she was able to lift her head. Though humour was the furthest thing from Dylan's mind, she snorted when she realised where he had taken her.

"You know this is where Dove brings his conquests?" she asked, raising one eyebrow.

Tristan's focus changed from caring to indignant.

"Has he ever brought you out here?" he asked hotly.

"Are you kidding?" she gaped. Tristan waited. "No." She rolled her eyes, then sobered. Felt her eyes prickle anew with tears.

"*Wraiths*. You really think they were killed by wraiths?"

"If I see the video, I'll know." He had the smart phone in his hand, but he waited, eyes on Dylan.

She didn't want to watch. She *really* didn't want to watch it, but Tristan was right, they had to know. "Go on then," she said. "Let's see."

It took a moment to find, and achingly long seconds to load as the towering school building hampered their signal, but then the hoarse, gasping breaths of the man who found the massacre could be heard. Tristan lowered the volume until the curses and oaths were barely audible.

"I can't see, Tristan," Dylan pointed out quietly.

He glanced up at her, and reluctantly adjusted the angle on the screen so they could both watch. He'd been unconsciously protecting her still.

At first there wasn't much *to* see. It was dark, the flickering light of a torch giving relief in flashes too quick to focus on. Then the torch settled on white skin rent in deep gashes. The lower half of the torso was nothing but a purple mass of torn-up flesh and empty space. A hole, like something had ripped right through.

"Shit, look at his face!" An exclamation could be heard from the video, even though Tristan had the sound so low it was almost on mute.

Dylan couldn't help but do as the voice commanded – and then really wished she hadn't. The horror and violence of his death was painted across his features.

"God," Dylan whispered. "He looks so terrified."

The video ended and, though Dylan got the feeling that Tristan would have liked to watch it again, he looked up at her and then pocketed the phone.

"There can't be any doubt." Tristan shook his head. "Not after that. Wraiths are here. They're coming through the way we did."

"What are we going to do?" Dylan whispered.

"I don't know," Tristan said. "I still need to think about it."

"People have died," Dylan reminded him. "Four of them – that we know of. It could be more." She swallowed back her nausea again. "We've brought it into the world, and it won't stop. Will it, Tristan?"

"No," he said, shaking his head. "It won't. I just... I think maybe I need to go there, as soon as possible. See what I can work out."

"By 'I' you mean 'we', right?" Dylan scowled at him.

"Dylan, no way! You're injured, and it could be dangerous. I'm not letting you—"

"Letting me?" He wisely didn't respond. "I'm coming with you, Tristan. You can't go without me at any rate."

He considered her, measuring the strength of her resolve. Dylan stared right back until he conceded with a sigh.

"All right." He bent forward and touched his forehead to hers. "I'm sorry." Dylan knew he wasn't just apologising for wanting to visit the tunnel alone. "I'm really sorry, baby. I should have told you, I just..."

"You just what?" Dylan prompted when it seemed he wouldn't go on.

"I couldn't do it to you. Lay this on you. Not after all you've suffered."

"We're in this together," she reminded him. "You and me. You should have trusted me."

"I know," he said. "I forget sometimes how strong you are. I mean," he offered her a crooked smile. "You're the girl who faced the wasteland all alone to come back for me." A gentle kiss that soothed Dylan's heart. "You're the one who saved me."

SIXTEEN

"I can't believe I'm back here."

Dylan stood knee-deep in thick grass verge and stared down at the black gaping maw of the tunnel. Police tape fluttered in the wind and the mouth had been roughly covered by a large sheet of metal with the sign:

NO ENTRY
POLICE INVESTIGATION

They must have just finished clearing the crash site when the murders had taken place. It occurred to Dylan that perhaps it was only when they had taken away the lanterns and construction lights that a wraith had dared to creep through.

It was mid-afternoon. The bus driver had looked at them as if they were mad when they'd asked him to drop them off at the side of the road in the middle of nowhere, but, by Tristan's estimation, it was the closest spot to the tunnel that public transport would reach.

From there, they'd had to slog three miles down single-lane country roads and through fields. This had almost done Dylan in – despite the speed at which her leg was healing. The going was rough and uneven on crutches, a test even for her good leg.

She was still a little upset with Tristan. He should have told her what he'd discovered, when he discovered it. But now that they were here, their spat didn't seem quite so important. Tristan must have thought so too, because he inched over and started rubbing at the tension that had suddenly formed between her shoulders, understanding how difficult it was for her to come back to this spot. The place that had killed her.

For that alone, she forgave him.

What would it be like down there? Her memories of being pulled out of the train were hazy at best. All she remembered was darkness, flashing lights. And pain. The tunnel was silent now, empty. Well, except for a doorway to the wasteland.

Dylan swallowed, her throat tight. Would she be able to see the hole they'd made through from the wasteland? A small, irrational part of her was terrified that she might not see it, that she might fall in.

Well, they'd soon find out.

"You don't have to go down there," Tristan reminded her, breaking into her thoughts. "In fact, I'd rather you didn't."

"I'm going, Tristan."

"It's treacherous," Tristan argued. "You could snap your leg again. It's not exactly crutch-friendly."

"Fine then, I'll leave them here." Dylan shifted both crutches from under her arm and balanced them against the barbed wire fence she'd torn her jeans getting over. Apparently it was as sharp in real life as it had been in the wasteland, though at least she hadn't cut her hands this time.

"You know that isn't what I meant." Tristan marched over and picked her crutches up, went to hand them to her and then thought better of it. Hanging both supports over one shoulder, he threw his free arm around her back and grabbed hold of her jeans at her opposite hip. "Lean on me," he ordered. "If you're determined to go, I'll help you."

It was said with extremely bad grace, but Dylan decided a meek "Thank you" was the smart response.

Once they were down on the train tracks, the going was easier, though Dylan's crutches sank into the thick layer of stones that formed a bed for the sleepers. At the entrance to the tunnel itself, she paused. Tristan had moved the NO ENTRY sign and was ripping off the police tape which had been stretched across the opening, but that wasn't why Dylan stopped. Now she was here, she wasn't entirely sure she could go back into the tunnel's inky depth. Memories crowded in from last time, before she realised she was dead. Waking utterly alone, deafened by the silence. The tumble of seats, strewn all over the place. Those suspiciously soft, spongy objects, the slickness she'd slid across, then smeared on her jeans. Clawing her way out of the chaos then stumbling down the long, lonely length of the tunnel.

"Tristan," she whispered.

He looked up from where he was rolling the blue and white tape into a sticky ball. He read the emotions on her face and his lips pressed into a thin line.

"Stay here," he begged.

Perversely, that was the spur Dylan needed to free herself of her paralysis. "No. Let's go."

She left one crutch leaning against the wall beside Tristan's wad of tape, keeping the other on her bad side. Tristan used a torch app on her phone to illuminate the way forward. It was a cold light, making the grey stone of the walls seem like the bowels of some medieval dungeon, but it was better than nothing.

Though the crashed train carriages had been removed, there was still a lot of debris littering the ground. Further up the tunnel, the crash had dislodged some heavy wooden sleepers and twisted up the metal train lines. In shifting flickers from Tristan's makeshift torch, hampered by her stupid crutch, Dylan had to edge along gingerly.

"Wait up, Tristan!" Dylan called. "I can't— Gah! My stupid leg!"

Tristan stopped, turning to flash the phone in her direction to better light the way, but Dylan still felt the need to hurry. She didn't see the hunk of broken metal in front of her, but she felt it when it skittered out from underneath her feet.

Falling, Dylan braced against the wall with her free hand. Her nails dug in valiantly, but she toppled forward, scraping her hand down the brickwork and landing in a tangled heap.

"Dylan!" Tristan was at her side in an instant, lifting her up to a sitting position and collecting her crutch. "Are you OK?"

"Yeah." She grimaced, lifted her palms up. In the pale torchlight, they were bloody and raw.

"Let me take you back," Tristan pleaded.

"No." Dylan shook her head. She wasn't leaving until this was done. "We're almost there now. Help me up."

Tristan sighed, but he grasped Dylan below the elbow and hauled her to her feet. "Will you let me carry you, at least?"

"No, you might need both arms free."

Tristan stilled at her words. "Dylan," he said carefully, "If I thought there were wraiths in here, I wouldn't let you anywhere near the place. End of story."

Dylan opened her mouth to argue – who the hell was he to let her anywhere? – but before she could get the words out he held up her crutch. "You ready?"

As ready as she'd ever be. Dylan nodded and Tristan proceeded back down the tunnel, slower this time, making sure Dylan could keep up with his long-legged strides.

It was obvious when they came to the exact spot, the place where her life had ended. For one, the area was cordoned off by yet more police tape and there were chalk markings on the wall and across the ground, along with what looked like dark pools of dried blood, and a heavy, raw smell. Worse, though – from Dylan's perspective – she *felt* it.

A coldness in her chest, a weakness in her limbs – like the life was being sucked out of her again. Or like her soul was trying to leave her body. She stepped back, suddenly afraid of exactly that.

"Here," Tristan said unnecessarily. "This is where we came through."

"And where those men died," Dylan agreed.

"Come here," he said, hunkering down to inspect something on the ground. "Look at this."

Dylan took one step forward, then had to stop. She had that feeling again, deep in her chest. Like her heart was made of iron and there was a powerful magnet pointed right at her. Pulling, dragging.

Panicking, she shuffled quickly backwards and almost fell over again.

"Dylan?"

"Don't you feel it?"

"Feel what?"

"That pull. God, it's like something's trying to tear out of me."

"Like your soul?" Tristan's eyes widened in terror. "Back! Back, Dylan!" Not waiting for her to move under her own limping steam, he leaned down and gripped her round the waist, lifting her off her feet and hustling her backwards.

Heart still pounding, like it was fighting to stay in the protective cage of her ribs, Dylan didn't feel like arguing with him. She expected him to drop her after several feet, but he kept going, the crutch squashed between them uncomfortably, his arms a steel band around her middle.

"Tristan, put me down," she said.

He ignored her. "Should never have brought you here. Don't know what the hell I was thinking."

"Tristan," she tried again to get his attention. "It's fine. I don't feel it any more, you can put me down."

"When we're out."

"Tristan, please, this is really uncomf—" she cut off the rest of her complaint, eyes focussing on something in the dark. "Tristan!"

"No, Dylan!"

She started struggling in earnest, eyes still fixed over Tristan's shoulder. "Put me down! Put me down, now! Seriously, Tristan, you have to! It's—"

A wraith. It was a wraith, swooping and swirling down the tunnel like it was tasting the air, its looping pattern circling closer and closer in their direction. Dylan was astonished that it wasn't making a beeline straight for them, but it seemed confused. Disoriented.

"Tristan!"

"I know, Dylan," he ground out. "I can feel it."

Tristan hustled Dylan over to the tunnel wall and dumped her down, forcing her body into the corner between the wall and the pebbled floor. Then he spun round and stood guard over her, tense and ready.

"Wait!" Dylan squealed, struggling to stand up.

"Stay down," he ordered.

"No, Tristan. Wait!" She tugged hard on his sleeve, then realised how stupid that was – he needed both hands free. Instead she thwacked him frantically on the thigh. "This isn't the wasteland! You're real now, a person. If that thing gets you, you'll die!"

"Shhh!" He pushed her hand away, his attention on the wraith.

The light streaming in from the tunnel entrance, just ten or fifteen metres away now, made the creature harder to see. It clung to the shadows, advancing then retreating.

"What's it doing?"

"It doesn't understand where it is," Tristan murmured. "They're stupid, wraiths. They hunt as a pack, can't think for themselves."

"A pack!" Dylan exclaimed. "We should run, Tristan!"

Never mind that she couldn't. She'd manage. And if her leg broke again, well, it healed fast the last time. Better in plaster than dead.

"Shhh!" Tristan hissed again, turning for an instant to glare at her. "It's only one. Don't. Move."

"Tristan!"

"Maybe it'll ignore us. It keeps being drawn back to the blood stains at the back, then catching something else out here. It can't decide. We might be able to just slowly—"

"Tristan?"

Tristan stopped speaking at the same time Dylan softly called his name. He turned round and stared at the hands that Dylan had lifted. The same thought had crossed their minds at the exact same time.

Dylan's bloodied palms.

"You," he whispered hoarsely. "It smells your blood."

"What wins out," Dylan asked, trying to tamp down on her panic, "Old blood or fresh?"

It might've been her imagination, but it seemed as if the wraith caught her question, locked on to it. And decided.

"Dylan? Dylan, get up!" Tristan moved forward a few inches so that Dylan could climb up his body like it was a ladder. "Go," he said once she was up. "Get out of here."

She wanted to tell him no, to forget it, that she wasn't leaving him, but she was a handicap to him and she knew it. The stupid crutch, her pathetic leg. She wasn't fighting fit, and even if she had been, she'd no experience fighting wraiths. Hating it, but knowing Tristan was right, she started to hobble away.

It was agony, leaving Tristan. But if she saw he was in trouble she'd lose the will to flee – and likely fall flat on her face again.

She fell anyway.

Her bad leg crumpled – this time with a hideous flare of pain – and she sank down, slamming onto her hip then clocking her head on a dislodged sleeper. She couldn't breathe, she couldn't move; not even to look at Tristan and the wraith. All she could do was lie there, trying to gather her scattered thoughts.

"Tristan!" She tried to scream it, but nothing came out. "Tristan!"

"Dylan, go!" He sounded breathless, afraid. That gave her the impetus to galvanise her stunned brain, marshal her battered body. She wriggled onto her side and heaved herself up. But what she saw made her heart stop.

Tristan was fighting the wraith – with nothing but his bare hands. He had one clenched in the ragged black wisps of the wraith's body, and with his other he was trying to rip and tear at its face. The wraith was twisting this way and that within his grip, slashing teeth searching for purchase. Talons curved forward from beneath its body, hacking at Tristan's arm and chest. The light blue jumper he wore was already torn and Dylan could see blood blooming down his sleeve.

The only consolation she had was that he'd obviously kept some of his abilities from his experience in the wasteland. He could grip them, unlike her when she was on the other side.

Suddenly the creature jerked backwards, freeing itself from Tristan's iron grip. It plummeted again, but lunged to evade Tristan's hand and dive right at Dylan! She had time to draw one startled gasp and lift a hand to protect her face.

Evil, venomous eyes fixed their sights on her…

And crashed to the ground just short of their target, Tristan's broad hand crushing down on its skull. He held it there, though the thing thrashed and scrabbled frantically to get free. Adjusting his grip slightly, Tristan put his full weight onto the thing and there was a sharp crack. The wraith slumped down, unmoving. It didn't so much as twitch when Tristan lifted his hand away.

"Shit!" Dylan found her voice at last.

She reached out to touch it – a black mass, edges blurred, shape still indefinable – but Tristan slapped her hand away.

"Don't touch it!"

"It's dead, isn't it?"

"It was already dead," he reminded her. "I don't know what it is now. It was never meant to be here." He snorted. "Like me."

"It's smoking," Dylan pointed out.

The feathery, wispy outline of the wraith seemed to be evaporating into the air, in thin tendrils of acrid smoke. Grabbing a twig, Dylan poked at it, and it exploded in a ball of noxious black gas.

"Don't breathe it in!" Tristan warned even as Dylan jerked herself out of range. She forced herself not to take a breath until the dark fumes had dissipated.

"God!" Dylan waved at the air, even though it was clear once more. "Did you know it was going to do that?"

"No." Tristan shook his head, blinking rapidly. He looked at her, but didn't seem able to focus. For the first time Dylan realised his eyes were glassy, his skin pale and waxy.

"Tristan?" She reached for him, just able to catch him as he slumped to an awkward sitting position. "Are you all right?"

Awkwardly, she got him to lie down, urging him over a bit so he wasn't lying on the spot where the wraith had been. In the dim light, she could make out deep scratches that ran down his throat, with two on his chest where his jumper had been ripped open. His face, apart from its pallid complexion, seemed untouched. What concerned her was the growing red stain on his sleeve. Grabbing his jumper at the neckline, Dylan pulled at it until it split down the seam.

When she pushed the fabric free of Tristan's shoulder, blood surged freely down his side and onto the ground. She blotted it with her own sleeve and caught a glimpse of mangled muscle and sinew beneath, and something off-white that looked suspiciously like bone.

"No," she breathed. Not knowing what else to do, she put her sleeve-covered hand back over the wound and pushed down, hard.

You're not in the wasteland any more, an insidious little voice whispered inside her head. *You're in the real world, and in the real world, people die.*

Pressing down still, Dylan stared down at his pallid face, features slackened, and fought panic. Tristan was so still and lifeless beneath her, he could be dead. The thought made nausea rise up her throat. No, she couldn't lose Tristan. Not now, not after everything that had happened. She just couldn't.

"Tristan!" she sobbed. "Tristan! Please be all right. Please. I *need* you!"

Fumbling on the floor of the tunnel with her free hand, she found her smart phone still shining its torch. It was low on battery and there was no signal, but when she rang 999 anyway, it somehow managed to connect.

"Emergency. Which service do you require?"

"Ambulance," Dylan blurted. "I need an ambulance!"

SEVENTEEN

"This is it," Susanna turned a corner and swept her hand out. "This is the street where you died."

Jack stared down the road, a jumble of high rise flats and short rows of terraced houses. There were no gardens to speak of, no trees to line the road. Just ugly concrete and rusting vehicles. A lot of the buildings had their windows boarded up, any empty walls tagged with graffiti. It was a miserable place, made even more so by the darkness that shrouded it. In the last hour, the mid-morning light had steadily dimmed until the sky above them was as dark as it had been the moment he'd died.

"I should never have come here," Jack scuffed his worn trainer against the kerb. "It was stupid, wandering around on my own."

"Why did you?" Jack hadn't shared much about himself – and what he had shared Susanna hadn't particularly liked, so she hadn't asked too many questions.

Jack shrugged. "Didn't have enough money to go any further."

"Why did you leave if you couldn't afford the trip?" Susanna had seen enough of his memories to know he'd planned to go to Glasgow, lose himself in the city.

"What do you want me to say?" he asked, suddenly defensive.

He did that a lot. Sometimes all she had to do was look in his direction, and he'd get defensive.

Defensive, angry. Aggressive. Was it really any wonder that he'd ended up stabbed to death in an empty alleyway at just sixteen?

"I had to get away," he said suddenly. "My stepdad was... And my mum. She's useless. She never stands up to him. I'd had enough."

Susanna clamped her lips shut and just nodded. No need for Jack to know that she'd seen him cowering in his room while he listened to his stepdad laying in to his mum – whether she stood up to him or not.

He took a deep breath, rocked back on his heels with his hands stuffed firmly in his pockets. It struck Susanna suddenly that he was nervous. Frightened, even. The attack must have been agony, and then there was the trauma of lying helpless in an alley while his blood slowly leeched out of him. Still, he faced his fear the same way he'd faced everything else in his too-short life: with a scowl.

"Let's get on with it."

As they traversed the long street, the edges of the wasteland began to blur into reality. Nothing about the scenery changed – Jack's wasteland had been designed to exactly mirror his place of death, at least at first – but signs of life began to materialise. Traffic appeared on the road, people emerged from doorways and walked down the pavement.

They didn't touch or look at Susanna and Jack – they couldn't. But several days in the wasteland had accustomed Jack to silence, to emptiness. And his small encounter with the wraiths had obviously affected him. He gave each person they passed a wide berth and flinched at every car noise. Then he caught himself doing it, and worse, realised Susanna had too. For the final few hundred metres, he deliberately walked in a straight line, not deviating for anyone. He stormed right through a couple of young girls, one of whom shivered.

At last, they came to the alleyway.

Jack stood and stared at the place he'd died. His jaw was clenched, as were his fists. Susanna stood just behind him, looking over his shoulder, seeing what he saw.

A body. Without the air of violent energy about him, it didn't really look like Jack, but it was. He lay curled up, one arm reaching out, the other pressed to his gut. Near his hip, his jacket lay abandoned where it had fallen from his grip. On the ground beneath him, blood spread out in a wide pool, and more of it was splattered up the brick wall to his left. Litter lay strewn across the cracked concrete around his body.

It was a sad final place to lie. He made a tragic figure splayed there amongst the rubbish.

"How do I do this?" Jack asked, his throat tight, the words coming out scratchily.

That was the question, wasn't it? Susanna had no idea. She stood there, thinking fast, then panicking when Jack turned on her. "Well?"

"You need... you need to reconnect with your body. I think, I think you need to climb back in."

"Climb back in?" He raised his eyebrows at her in disbelief. "It isn't a hatchback!"

"You know what I mean," Susanna frowned at him. Another idea occurred to her. "When you do it, try to think about how much you want to go back."

"Wish myself alive, you mean?"

"Well, yeah."

He snorted. "This is ridiculous."

Defensive herself – because she really didn't know what she was doing – Susanna glowered at him. "I can always take you back across the wasteland if you'd rather stay dead."

"No." He shook his head at once, something like panic on his face. It was the first time she'd seen real fear in his eyes. He was good at hiding his emotions. Well, emotions other than anger – he had no problem displaying that one. "No, I'll do it. All right, then." With his usual lack of hesitation, he approached the body – *his* body – and started to crouch down. One hand reached out, ready to link around his own cold, dead fingers.

"Wait!" Susanna's frantic yelp made him snatch it back. "You've got to take me with you."

She held out her own hand and Jack stared at her.

"Otherwise it won't work!" she added hastily, in case he didn't believe her.

He grabbed it, squeezing hard. So hard it hurt. Susanna didn't protest – at least she knew he wasn't planning to let go.

"Let's go," he said, and without warning he toppled forward into his own corpse.

Susanna felt the jerk on her hand as he dropped towards the ground, then a much harder pull coming from the very centre of her. It gripped her hard and yanked. She looked down, convinced her organs were being ripped from her body, a cruel punishment for daring to defy nature. She saw nothing, blinded suddenly by pain. Deafening pain. Taking over every nerve and making them scream.

She couldn't breathe, she couldn't move, she couldn't think.

She couldn't stand another second of it.

Then, just as quickly, it was over. Susanna found herself on her hands and knees, palms pressed into the rapidly cooling puddle of Jack's blood. Shaking her head to clear the remnants of pain, she blinked and looked around her.

The alley.

Jack!

She reached for him, planting her palms on his chest. Warm

beneath her touch – and moving. His breaths were laboured, slightly ragged, but he was breathing.

"Jack!" She shook him gently by the shoulders. "Jack, can you hear me?"

It was like a replay of their first moment together, only this time he still clung to life. This time he had a chance.

Susanna lifted his t-shirt to look at the wound and breathed a sigh of relief. It was seeping blood, but only a steady trickle rather than the gush she expected. She rolled up the bottom of his t-shirt and pressed firmly against the gash – and he exploded into consciousness.

"Get off me!"

Just like in the wasteland, he launched himself upwards and pressed her up against the wall. His eyes were dazed, a frown of utter confusion pasted across his forehead. He squeezed the hand that gripped her, trapping her breath in her lungs.

"Jack!" she croaked. "It's me. It's Susanna."

He narrowed his eyes, thinking, searching his mind. The moment recognition flashed in his eyes, he let go of her and immediately crumpled to the floor. He started gasping, grabbing at his side.

Susanna leaned over him, her hand at his stomach. "Jack, we made it!" she said. "Stay with me. Stay awake."

"Oh my God!" The voice came from over Susanna's shoulder. It was high-pitched and female. Susanna turned and saw a girl, still in her school uniform, a satchel over her shoulder. Her eyes, surrounded by heavy make-up, were wide and shocked. "Do need help?"

"Yes!" Susanna said, feeling a rush of relief. Jack's injury far too serious for her to deal with herself. "Get us an ambulanc

"No." Though she thought he'd slipped away again, the ha

that wrapped around Susanna's arm was firm in its grip. "No ambulance."

"Jack!" Susanna turned back to him. "You need medical help."

"No!" he ground out, shifting to glare at the girl.

"You call an ambulance and you're for it!"

She paled and dropped the phone down to her side.

"Get out of here!"

"Wait!" Susanna called after her, but she was already running away, school bag bouncing against her shoulder. Susanna rounded on Jack. "Why did you do that? You're really injured, you need medical help." A pause. "Do you want to die again?"

"Just listen to me, will you?" Jack continued his efforts to get up. "Stupid cow. Do you know who comes along if you call for an ambulance?"

"Paramedics?" Susanna said, confused.

"The pigs!" Jack groaned as he shifted his weight. "Are you really this stupid? The police! Look, just get me up."

Wrong-footed by her incomplete knowledge of how things worked in the real world, Susanna did what he said, bracing his arm at the elbow and hoisting him to his feet. He cried out in pain, then turned the air blue with a string of bad language.

"Jack, that's really serious." Susanna pointed at the wound he was covering with one hand, his body hunched over to ease the pull on his muscles. "You need to get it dealt with."

"Can't trust the police. I'll patch it up at home." Jack ignored Susanna's dubious look. "Just get me out of here."

That hadn't been their agreement. The deal they'd made was that Susanna would help get Jack back into his body – alive – and then they'd both be free. Their bargain was over, but Susanna couldn't escape her feeling of obligation – her instinct as a ferryman – to keep him from harm.

Plus, now that she was here, Susanna had no idea where to go, what to do. How to find Tristan. She didn't like Jack, didn't trust him – was even a little afraid of him – but right now, he was all she knew.

And he knew this world a lot better than she did.

"All right," she said. "I'll help you."

Following his snarled orders, Susanna flagged a taxi and gently lowered him in, hoping it was still too dark for the cabbie to see the blood on their clothes and hands.

"What's wrong with him?" the driver snapped. "He's not going to puke, is he?"

"He won't be sick," Susanna reassured him, patting Jack's arm sympathetically, making him wince at the movement. "I promise."

"Aye, right. Where to?" the cabbie asked, although he still sounded unhappy.

Susanna looked expectantly at Jack. She had thousands of memories in her head, knew all about his life, but she had no clue where he wanted to go.

"Stirling," Jack muttered. "Vincent Street."

The cabbie pulled away from the kerb without further comment. Susanna stared out of the window, watching as the street sped by. She was in a car. The boy sitting slumped beside her was real, the man in the front seat, hands firm on the steering wheel, was real. She was in the real world.

The real world.

It was unfathomable. Astonishing. Amazing. But all of it meant nothing if she couldn't find a way to get to Tristan. She didn't know how to find him, where to start even. But…

But if she closed her eyes, concentrated with her whole being, she could *feel* him.

He was here. He was close.

And she'd find him.

EIGHTEEN

This was how Tristan must have felt. Dylan sat in a hard, plastic chair in A&E, alone and frightened, and realised that Tristan had been in this position just weeks ago.

It was horrible.

Dylan had been allowed to ride in the ambulance with him, but once they arrived at the hospital the two paramedics had whisked him away. She followed as best she could – *stupid crutch!* – but they wouldn't let her go beyond the expansive waiting room, crowded with people. That hurt, but not in the way she'd come to expect. It hurt because she was scared – she hadn't seen his eyes open since they'd strapped him to the stretcher and wheeled him into the emergency vehicle.

And now... now she didn't feel that tightness of breath, the nausea. The echo of pain in her leg. She couldn't see him, she didn't know where he was, what was happening to him, and she felt nothing – except a sick terror.

It's because he's unconscious, she told herself. *When he comes round, you'll feel like hell – and you'll be grateful for it.*

There was nothing to do but take a seat... and wait. A receptionist came and took Tristan's – very scant – details. A nurse came and asked if Dylan needed to be examined, but even though her leg was throbbing furiously, she refused. She didn't want to be trapped on a bed somewhere when Tristan finally woke up.

A few minutes later, something happened that made her really, really wish she'd gone with the kind-faced nurse: a much less kind-faced nurse burst into the waiting area, eyes raking the crowd for Dylan.

"Are you all right?" Joan barked when she saw her. "Marie said you refused to be seen." Her eyes dropped to Dylan's leg, taking in the stiff, awkward way she held it.

"I'm fine," Dylan said quietly. She tried to draw the limb closer in to herself, moving languidly like it was nothing, but she couldn't quite pull it off. A sharp hiss escaped her clenched teeth. "Do you know how Tristan is?"

"You're not fine, I don't know *what* you two were doing," Joan told her. "You're coming with me to X-ray."

"Do you know how Tristan is?" Dylan repeated her question. "Nobody will tell me anything."

Joan stared straight down at her, lips clamped tightly shut and eyes angry. She knew something; it was obvious. Dylan prepared herself for an almighty fight, but instead, tears filled her eyes. One slipped free and ran down her cheek. "Mum…"

And that was all it took.

"He's fine," Joan sighed. "Well, he's not fine. He lost a lot of blood. They had to put an IV into him," she added, making Dylan gasp audibly, "and he'll need a lot of stitches. But he *will* be fine."

⤺

Joan's words proved true. Pressure on hospital beds, and the fact that he was going home with a nurse, meant that by eight o'clock that night, Joan was bundling Dylan and Tristan into a taxi.

Tristan was pale and moving stiffly, but he was alert and alive, and Dylan was satisfied with that.

Joan was still angry, but her initial blazing fury had cooled into a white-hot blade. She sat in the rear-facing pull down seat in the back of the black cab and glowered at Dylan and Tristan.

"What on *earth* were you two thinking going back to that tunnel?" Her voice was low and cutting.

"Mum—"

"With her barely out of a wheelchair and still limping – I can't *imagine* what you were up to to injure yourself that badly, but it certainly wasn't doing the one thing you're supposed to be doing while you're living under my roof." A hissed intake of breath. "Looking after my daughter!"

If only she knew the truth, thought Dylan. But she had to appease her mother somehow.

"I'm sorry Mum, it's my fault – I begged Tristan to take me to where the train crashed because I thought it might help…"

"Might help? You've set back your recovery, Dylan. And I've had to lie for *him* once again, fudging his details on the forms. Stupid boy, slicing himself up like that. I could lose my job—"

"Tristan was lifting me over the barbed wire and he slipped," Dylan lied. "We both fell down the verge, that's all. Please don't blame Tristan for this, it's my fault."

"I'm sorry Joan," Tristan croaked, shifting uncomfortably. "It won't happen again."

Joan went silent once again, and remained that way until they got home. Still, she hadn't enacted Dylan's biggest fear and kicked Tristan out – *yet*. Perhaps she knew that if she did, Dylan would go too. No matter what Joan said.

Despite the fact that it was barely after nine, Joan announced that Tristan needed to sleep, so they were all going to bed. That suited Dylan. What she really wanted was to speak to Tristan alone and that wasn't going to happen until Joan was safely tucked away in her bedroom. Doing her best not to limp – her leg was throbbing – she did her bathroom routine, threw on her pyjamas and turned off the light. Easing into bed, she shifted right over to the wall and settled down to patiently wait.

⌒

Tristan stood at the living room window, staring out into the darkened street. It was late, but a quiet flow of traffic still ghosted along the road below. There were few illuminated windows in the flats across the street and nobody walked the pavement. It was as peaceful as it ever got this deep in the city.

Nothing. Nothing but the hushed murmur of Joan, on the phone in her bedroom. She'd been talking for a while now, though Tristan couldn't work out who was on the other end of the line. He could guess, though.

He was waiting for her to finish her call, make her nightly trip to the bathroom – then he was going to Dylan.

Tristan needed her. Needed to hold her, feel the gentle rise and fall of her ribs under his hand as she breathed. If Joan didn't hurry up, he was going to sneak in there anyway. He would have done already, if it wasn't for—

He closed his eyes, concentrated. Nothing. Nothing but the road noise and the low tones of Joan's voice and—

There it was again. A tingle, tickling the darkest corner of his mind. A presence, the likes of which he'd not felt since Dylan dragged him into the real world with her.

A ferryman. Here. In this world.

Snapping his eyes open, he scoured the street. He still didn't see anything, but there was an awareness deep inside him. It resonated in a pattern Tristan could not mistake.

Susanna.

The name she claimed. Claimed along with her dark hair and dark eyes. So many nights, he'd sat in the safe house doorway or beside the window and seen Susanna doing the same. What was she doing here? There was no answer from the darkened street.

Sighing, he stepped backwards and turned away from the window. Just that small movement pulled at the would on his shoulder. He froze, feeling pain ripple from the spot, spiking down his arm and trapping the air in his lungs.

"Tristan?" He looked up to see Dylan in the doorway, peering out at him. "What are you doing?"

"Just… looking out the window. I couldn't sleep."

He paused, and the moment to tell Dylan about Susanna hovered in front of him. He let it pass. Susanna was a ferryman – not a wraith. Her presence in the world wasn't a danger to them. If she'd managed to find a way here, had a chance to live a real life, it was no concern of his. Susanna's fate was her own.

"Come to bed," Dylan murmured.

Putting Susanna to the back of his mind for now, Tristan crossed to where Dylan stood waiting for him and put his hand on her hip, guiding her backwards.

"Bed," he agreed. "I need to hold you."

They crossed the hallway as quietly as they could and Dylan motioned for Tristan to lie down first. She settled in beside him, breathing out a deep sigh. "Are you all right? Does it hurt?"

"A bit," Tristan admitted. "Your mum gave me some painkillers."

Dylan snorted. "I'm surprised she didn't leave you to suffer." She paused. "I was scared she was going to throw you out earlier."

"I thought she might," Tristan said. "She still could."

Dylan didn't disagree with him.

"If she does, I'm coming with you."

"You won't have much choice," Tristan said. He sighed. "I'm sorry."

"You know our bond doesn't bother me." Dylan shrugged. It wasn't his fault, he hadn't known what would happen. Besides, she secretly liked the way they were bound together – when it wasn't making her freak out or want to puke or driving needles of pain down her leg.

"That's not what I mean," he said. Dylan furrowed her eyebrows. "When we came through from the wasteland we left a hole, and the wraiths are coming through it. Coming through it and killing people. I should've known—"

"I didn't see a hole, though. Did you?"

"You *felt* the hole," he murmured. "You told me you felt like something was pulling you. That was the wasteland, trying to get you back."

"Oh," Dylan said. "I expected, I don't know – to see a rip or a portal or something."

"Remember the two worlds look identical at that point," he reminded her.

"But you saw it?"

No answer.

"You didn't see it," she said. "The first you knew about it was when I said I was feeling funny. That doesn't mean—"

"Yes, it does, Dylan. I *know* there's a hole there. How else can you explain the wraith appearing like that?"

She didn't have an answer for that.

"Well, you killed it," she said, searching for a bright side.

"I killed that one."

"That one? You think there are more?"

"I don't know," Tristan admitted. "I don't sense them here anywhere near the way I did in the wasteland. I didn't feel that wraith until it was almost on top of me."

"So it's not like we can go and hunt them. And that thing almost killed you."

"It didn't," Tristan shot back, his low voice full of offended male pride.

"You could have bled out, Tristan," Dylan said gently. "You would have, if I hadn't called the ambulance. You can't fight them the same way here."

He grunted, which she took to mean he agreed with her.

"So," she said, "there's nothing we can really do, then?"

She meant it as a statement, but the doubt in her voice – and a growing sense of foreboding – pulled it into a question.

"Yes, there is," Tristan replied. "I can try to shut the hole. Stop any more coming through."

"How?"

Silence. Absolute, blanket silence.

"How, Tristan?"

"By going back through."

"No," she snapped. "No. No way. Not a chance." She was far too loud and she didn't care. "Do you hear me? No."

"Dylan—"

"I said no, Tristan. No. And that's the end of it."

"Shhhh!" Tristan pressed his fingertips to her lips, turning on his good side so that they were face to face in the dark. He kept his hand there, the pressure gentle. "I don't want to fight about it. I just… I just want to be close to you."

The angry words Dylan had been waiting to throw at Tristan died in her throat. He was right. She'd nearly lost him today, had

had to watch the blood soak his t-shirt, run down his skin – and she'd been utterly helpless. Useless.

He was here, he was warm beside her.

That was enough.

Reaching out to grip the bottom of the t-shirt Tristan had worn to bed, Dylan kissed his fingers. Then again. When he took those away and replaced them with his mouth, she kissed that too. Thoughts of his injured shoulder flying from her mind, she pressed herself against him, trying to get closer, taking in his warmth.

She slid her hand up to rest against his chest and she felt his heart beating. It reminded her that the two of them were alive, miraculously, gloriously alive.

That was all that mattered.

As for the rest… they'd fight about it tomorrow.

NINETEEN

"Tristan?" Dylan nudged his good shoulder. It had been two days since he had been stitched up and he could handle a playful shove.

"Mm?" Tristan turned to Dylan, keeping an eye on the streets surrounding them.

"I promise we will sort the wraith problem when you're better – for now can you…"

"Can I…?" Tristan glanced at her through his mop of sandy hair.

"Pretend to be a regular boy with regular-boy problems, just for a little bit?" Dylan grabbed his hand and squeezed.

They'd agreed to meet Dylan's dad at a little Italian restaurant just a few streets from the flat. Joan had insisted that, since she wasn't going to be there this time, they stay in the neighbourhood.

"Right – what should it be? No pocket money, might fail my exams, am I going to be invited to Cheryl's next party?"

"Right!" Dylan took a deep breath, pushed the wraith problem as far down as it would go – which wasn't very far – and turned her head to glance at Tristan. "You nervous about my dad?"

"Why should I be?" He squeezed the hand he still held. "Don't worry about me, Dylan. *You're* nervous."

She was. She was shaking with it.

"I don't know why," she confessed. "I mean, I've met him already."

"You've met him once," Tristan corrected. "He's your dad, and he's still virtually a stranger. This time, you don't have your mum as a buffer, either."

"I have you," Dylan said. "That's better."

That earned her a smile and another squeeze.

"Plus," Dylan chuffed with wry humour, "I can't seem to keep you away from pizza."

That was one of Dylan's favourite things now – introducing Tristan to new experiences and seeing his reactions. Food especially, because his body didn't have to eat in the wasteland. So far, ice cream and apples topped the list – after pizza.

Inside the restaurant there was no sign of Dylan's dad, but he had made a reservation so the waiter led them through to a cosy little table at the back.

Dylan watched the door, unable to contemplate the menu when butterflies were filling up her stomach. Soon, her dad came rushing in the door, his head whipping about as he checked the seats. Somewhat awkwardly, Dylan got herself to her feet and starting waving at the same time as he spotted her. The sheer delight in his expression was almost enough to make her tear up, and though she felt silly standing up, she stayed that way until he'd crossed the room.

"Hi, sweetheart." He folded her into a huge hug. "Sorry I'm late."

"That's all right," Dylan said, pulling back from the hug to offer him a shy smile. "We haven't been here all that long."

"Good, that's good. Great to see you out of your chair and plaster." He turned away from Dylan slowly, as if he was reluctant to do so, and she noticed the look he gave Tristan was a lot less friendly. "Tristan – I've heard quite a bit about you."

As they took their seats, Dylan scowled at the idea of her mum bad-mouthing her boyfriend. "You don't want to listen to anything Joan says." She turned to Tristan. "*I've* said nice things."

Tristan smiled at her, all blue eyes and freckles, and Dylan couldn't help but smiling back, something happy and warm rising up inside her. Then her dad cleared his throat – loudly – and the moment passed.

"Your mum told me you hurt your leg again," James said, picking up his menu and flicking through the pages. "How did that happen?"

"I fell," Dylan told him, thinking the less said about that afternoon the better – and wondering when and why Joan had contacted him about it. It seemed odd that she would do that – she hated him, didn't she?

"Where were you?"

"What?"

Dylan's dad looked up with eyes her exact shade of green. "When you fell. Where were you?"

She had the feeling he already knew, but she answered anyway. "We went back to the tunnel. I was having nightmares and I thought it might help." The same teeny, tiny lie she'd told her mum.

"You didn't just go to the tunnel though, did you? You're bypassing the fact that you skipped out on school." He kept his tone carefully neutral, focussing most of his attention on the menu in front of him – but he was angry. "You went down into the tunnel on a bad leg, and violated a crime scene."

"You're mad at me?" Dylan squeaked. A small part of her brain screamed out that he hadn't the right – just who did he think he was – but for the most part she was hurt. Upset. She'd only just met her dad and already he was disapproving of her.

But he shook his head at her accusation, meeting her gaze again.

"No, Dylan. I'm not angry at you." He flicked a page again, glanced down at it, then back up at her. "Although I am wondering if you're being led astray."

By Tristan. He didn't say it, didn't so much as peek in his direction, but that was what he meant. "Your mother told me this was new behaviour for you," he went on. "Bunking off school, sneaking to places you shouldn't be. She and I are both wondering if your new boyfriend – who she hadn't even heard of before the crash – has something to do with it."

"*She and I?*" It was out before Dylan could hold it back. "You're a team now, are you?"

Her dad didn't react, didn't censor her. He just waited.

"I don't know why you think you can pass judgement when you hardly know me – *us*," Dylan told him hotly, not quite sure where this bravery was coming from. She wouldn't let him think Tristan was a bad influence. She *wouldn't*. "Tristan didn't make me duck out of school. He didn't make me go into the tunnel, and he didn't make me bunk off school to visit you either. *I* did. *I'm* responsible for me. So if you're mad, then I'm the one you have to be mad at." Dylan took a deep breath, gave her dad a chance to interrupt, but he didn't. "Tristan has been there for me through some really hard stuff. You've no idea how hard."

The slightest movement of James's mouth made her aware he didn't take her claim all that seriously. If only he knew how true those words were.

"I love him, and he's in my life." She stopped and stared at her dad, giving him time to hear the unspoken thought – that *he* wasn't in her life – not yet.

The moment went on and on. Dylan risked a quick look at Tristan but he was just sitting quietly, not interfering. She went back to her dad and saw that he looked visibly taken aback.

"You're right," he said. "I'm sorry. I haven't earned a place in your life yet, but I'm your dad, and I worry about you." He smiled at her, made sure to include Tristan in the gesture this time. "Let's start again. Tristan, it's nice to meet you. I have heard some nice things about you... from Dylan."

⌒

Watching Dylan smile and laugh with her dad, Tristan felt only momentary relief from his thoughts. How could he smile and chat along, knowing more people could die if another wraith got through? He'd risked everything by coming here with Dylan – his life, such as it was; her immortal soul. For just a little while, a handful of days, he thought he'd gotten away with it.

But actions have consequences. His actions had ripped open a whole between this world and the next... and living nightmares were seeping through, putting other souls in danger.

He couldn't count how many souls he'd lost over the years – save to say it was far fewer than the number of souls he'd successfully ferried across the wasteland. Still, the four men who had been murdered weighed heavily on him, even though he knew, without doubt, that there was life after death.

Because he also knew, without doubt, that not every soul reached that promised land Dylan had told him about.

And on top of that, it hadn't been their time to go. They shouldn't have died that day. His careless actions had interfered with the lives they had still to live.

He needed to do something, but he knew, he just *knew*, that the only way to resolve what had been broken was to go back through to the wasteland. Perhaps if he just went to the line, one of the beings Dylan had described would speak with him, explain what he needed to do? Perhaps his very presence back in that netherworld would restore the balance and the rift would naturally seal itself. Separating him and Dylan. Maybe even killing them.

Perhaps. Maybe. Possibly.

There were no certainties, except for the fact that if he stayed here and did nothing, more people would die.

And he could not take Dylan back into the wasteland. The fact she had crossed it the first time, surviving the wraiths, was a credit to her bravery. That she had returned, alone, to search for him and lived to tell the tale was unfathomable. To take her back and risk it a third time – that would surely be pushing their luck too far.

Tristan sighed, reached up to rub at his neck, where the muscles were suddenly tight with tension. He tried to pull himself back into the conversation between Dylan and her dad. It was important to her that this man like him, and he sensed James Miller wouldn't sit back and be silent if he thought otherwise.

"Dove had no idea Mrs Malcolm was there," Dylan was saying. "He was shouting 'Boobs! They're boobs! He's drawing boobs!' over and over again. The whole time Mrs Malcolm was just watching, then all of a sudden she hollered 'David MacMillan!' and everyone went totally silent. I thought Dove was going to fall off his chair!"

Her dad was laughing, shaking his head.

"I can't believe that woman is still there. I can't believe she's still alive! She was old when I was a pupil, and that wasn't yesterday."

"I think she's retiring this year," Dylan offered. "It's a shame, I quite like her. At least she can get everyone to shut up so we can actually get on with stuff."

"Yeah, it's a difficult school." Her dad made a face, his humour dissipating suddenly. "Do you do all right there? Nobody... upsets you, do they?"

"You mean do I get bullied?" Dylan asked.

"Well, yeah." He waited, tense, and Tristan could see that he was nervous of the answer. It made him like the man a little bit more.

She grinned. "Now that Tristan's there, I don't get any hassle. Everyone's afraid of him."

"Are they now?" An appraising look from Dylan's dad.

"They're just little idiots," Tristan offered. "You stand up to them and they don't know what to do."

"That's right." Dylan's dad nodded in agreement and Tristan thought he might just have scored a point with him. Dylan was beaming in his direction.

Dinner passed without further incident. Her dad paid the bill and they moved outside. It was a brisk, clear night, though there were no stars to be seen, the vast network of streetlights shining too brightly to make out their distant glow. James offered to drive them home, but then admitted that his car was parked haphazardly on a street corner half a mile in the wrong direction.

"It's fine," Dylan said for the third time. "We'll be quicker walking. It's only ten minutes, and I've got Tristan."

James stared at Dylan for a long moment, deliberating. Tristan could feel his protective instincts warring with the caution not to push too hard given their fledgling relationship.

"You'll call me when you get in," he said at last.

"Yes, Dad!" Tristan watched the little thrill of happiness that lit up Dylan's eyes at using that word, claiming James Miller as family. Something he'd never had. He didn't resent her for it, though. Dylan was all he needed.

"Give me a hug," James said, a little gruffly. He was obviously as affected by Dylan's use of the term as she was. "Go on, then," he ordered as he stepped back. He folded his arms and planted his feet. He was going to stand there until they were out of sight, Tristan realised. Watching out for his little girl.

Tristan took Dylan's hand and, making sure she had her crutch in place, walked with her along the little row of shops and cafés. Most of the shops were closed now, just an off licence window spilling out a bubble of bright yellow light as they passed. The streets were quiet, but a weird prickling feeling kept teasing Tristan.

"What is it?" Dylan asked, after he'd craned his head around for the fourth time in as many minutes. "What's wrong?"

"Nothing," he said, giving her hand a reassuring squeeze. And it probably *was* nothing.

"Tristan," Dylan warned. "What is it?"

"Nothing."

A sigh, then she yanked her hand away from his. "Tell me!"

He shrugged. "I just—"

"You just what?" Dylan tried to look over her shoulder as she walked, and almost tripped. Tristan had to reach out and grab her. "Is someone following us?"

"No." He grimaced. "I don't think so. I just… feel something. It's nothing, honestly."

Dylan stopped dead in the middle of the pavement, in a posture very reminiscent of her father's as he'd watched them leave.

"I have a creeped-out feeling someone's watching us, that's all. But there's no one there. I've looked. I'm probably being paranoid because of the wraith." He took her arm. "Come on, let's go, it's cold."

Tristan resolutely refused to look behind him again all the way back to the flat. He didn't want to frighten Dylan. But that ominous feeling, those uncomfortable needles stippling the back of his neck, refused to abate.

This was nothing like the feeling he'd had when he'd sensed Susanna. She was here still, but somewhere distant; a hint of warmth lingering on the fringes of his consciousness.

No, this was something different. Something cold and angry.

TWENTY

"This isn't right."

Susanna stared hard at the pale expanse of skin that was revealed when she peeled the dressing away from Jack's middle.

"What is it?" he asked. "Is it infected? It doesn't feel like it."

"No," Susanna said, "It looks... it looks really good."

Really good was an understatement. The stitches she'd put in herself under Jack's careful, if unnerving, supervision were neat. There wasn't a scab, just a slightly raised line that, while red, didn't look angry or fresh. It was a normal rate of healing for *her*, but she knew from her souls' reactions to her wounds in the wasteland that humans didn't heal so quickly.

Obviously, Jack hadn't come back to the world of the living quite the same.

They were in Jack's mum's flat. An ugly concrete high-rise decorated with rusting metal balconies. It looked a grim place to grow up. It had been a struggle getting him into the building – especially with Susanna's scant knowledge of buzzers. Jack's mum had hastily paid the taxi fare before tending to her son, showering him with attentive questions and slipping away to her room when he rebuffed her. Of course Susanna had seen Jack's mum in his memories. A small, mousy woman, her hair prematurely grey, and deep lines around her mouth and eyes. She had a perpetually startled look, her shoulders always slightly hunched as if to ward off the world. She'd seen Jack's stepdad in his memories too – at least he didn't seem to be around.

Susanna had spent the night on the sofa in their living room, amazed by the heavy-lidded feel of her eyes; the warm, floaty sensation that was lulling her towards oblivion. Sleep. This was what sleep felt like. Closing her eyes, she revelled in it.

Thirteen hours. She'd slept for thirteen hours. When she woke, she'd come straight in to check on Jack – half-expecting to find him dead – and instead he was well on his way to being fully healed. He was still a little out of it, though, and as he drifted towards sleep again, Susanna heard quiet sounds of someone puttering around in the kitchen. Jack's mum, she presumed. Feeling awkward, like an interloper, she got up and walked quietly through the lounge to the open archway that led to the kitchen. Jack's mum was in her dressing gown, fuzzy slippers on her feet, kettle in hand.

"Tea?" the woman asked, a little too brightly.

"I... no. Thank you." Susanna tried to smile but she felt so out of place the best she could manage was a grimace.

"Jack still asleep, is he?" his mum asked.

"Yeah. He's OK, though."

Jack's mum nodded in acknowledgement.

"Well, I've got to go to work in a bit. You just help yourselves to whatever's in the fridge."

And that was it. The woman added a quick dollop of milk to her cup and then waddled quietly out of the room, that too-bright expression back on her face. She closed her bedroom door behind her with a soft snick, leaving Susanna alone in the living area, stunned.

Where was the inquisition? The questions about who she was and what she was doing there? It didn't seem right; didn't fit with any of the ideas Susanna had constructed in her head about what a 'mum' should be like. Although it did match quite accurately the woman she'd caught glimpses of in Jack's memory. Feeling an uncomfortable rush of sympathy for the woman, Susanna tip-toed past her room and slipped into Jack's bedroom again.

He slept. All day, waking periodically for Susanna to tip water down his throat and feed him bits of toast. When she was sure he was well enough, she would leave, and that would be that.

It gave Susanna a lot of time to think, though really her thoughts were consumed by just one thing. Tristan. Where was he? Somewhere near: she could feel it. What were the chances that in all the world, their souls had led them near to each other? It must be a sign. Now, how could she get to him? She had to sit down, close her eyes and throw her senses as wide as she could. Then, and only then, could she feel a glimmer of him, right of the periphery of her mind.

It was both reassuring and terrifying.

She was fairly sure that the closer she got, the easier he'd be to pinpoint – that was always how it had worked in the wasteland. But she had no money or transport, and after embarrassing herself by not understanding how to work something as simple as the building intercom, she realised there were a million little things she might not know. Things that would give her away, mark her as different.

She needed to avoid drawing attention to herself until she could get to Tristan, and for that she needed someone to help her negotiate this strange new place.

For that she needed Jack.

She weighed it up all day. Remembering how difficult he had been in the wasteland. Worrying about how to go it alone. Several times she found herself on her feet, ready to walk out the front door, but each time she paused, gripped by panic and uncertainty.

If she wanted to get to Tristan, she needed Jack.

Just for a little longer.

When Jack finally woke, he was worryingly chipper. He knocked her hand away as she went to check his bandage a second time.

"I'm fine!" He shoved his t-shirt back down his stomach. "God, I can't wait to have a shower."

"You really shouldn't get it wet," Susanna said, scooting out of his way as he rolled out of bed.

Jack gave her a dismissive look on the way to the bathroom.

"Fine," she muttered to the empty air. "Shower. Get it soaked. What do I care?" She clambered to her knees somewhat stiffly. "I hope you get an infection, stupid arse."

She mouthed the last bit because, even though he was too far away to hear, she wasn't stupid. You didn't mouth off to a thug like Jack.

He took a long time in the shower. She was starting to wonder if maybe he might have collapsed when suddenly the water shut off. Jack emerged moments later, wearing nothing but a towel slung round his waist, the new bandage Susanna had applied sopping wet and sticking to his skin. He was all pale skin and stringy muscles, but there was strength there and once again she was gripped by how easily he could hurt her.

In the wasteland, she'd had some of the power – not to mention he needed her to survive. Now that they were in the real world, that balance had changed. She doubted she could control him with commands any more.

"You can use the shower if you want," Jack told her, sauntering past to disappear into his bedroom.

Susanna hadn't dared take such a liberty while Jack had been laid up in bed. It had been almost impossible to resist – hot water! Just the idea made her weak.

"Thank you," she called softly to Jack's departing back. Then she all but ran to the bathroom.

It was just as good as she had imagined it would be. The shower stall was tight, almost claustrophobic, but the delight of having a cascade of water raining down on her, as hot as she could stand it, made up for the coffin-like feel of the enclosure.

She had to force herself to get out. Wrapping herself in a large towel, she contemplated her clothes. In the wasteland she could alter her ensemble with a thought, but here she'd been in the same jeans and jumper for over a day and to say they were grubby was an understatement. She couldn't bear the thought of putting her soiled clothes back on her scrubbed clean skin.

But as soon as she appeared in the doorway of his bedroom Jack barked out "Here" and flung a bundle her way. Catching it, Susanna saw it was women's clothes.

"Some of Sammy's stuff," he explained. "Should fit you. You're about the same size. But then," his eyes narrowed, "you already know that."

"Right." The least said about that the better, Susanna thought, hurrying back to the steam-filled bathroom to change.

He'd given her a pair of tight-fitting jeans and a blouse-like shirt that wrapped across her front and left a deep, deep v at her cleavage. Oh well, she'd see about using the washing machine and get back in her own outfit as soon as possible.

Susanna lingered in the bathroom, drawing out little tasks like combing out her hair, adjusting her revealing clothes, because now that Jack was up and about it was time to broach a sticky subject. She wasn't sure how Jack would feel about her attempting to renegotiate the terms of their agreement – especially when he'd already gotten his part of the deal. She had nothing to barter with, could only appeal to his better nature.

And she wasn't all that sure that he had one.

When she got finally forced herself to approach him, he was pulling on his shoes.

"I need to go out," he told her, picking up a black leather jacket. He snatched his keys from the coffee table and then finally he looked at her properly, eyes raking over the clothes she wore. His expression remained utterly blank, giving no indication of what he thought. "You going to be here when I get back?"

Caught off guard, Susanna hesitated. Now was the time to speak up, to ask Jack to help her. Staring into his hard, emotionless expression, she chickened out.

"I…" she swallowed. "I can leave if you—"

"Stay," he told her curtly. "Get yourself sorted or whatever. I won't be that long. Just… if you hear anyone at the door, shut yourself in my room."

By anyone, she assumed he meant his stepdad.

"All right," she said. "Thank you."

He grunted in acknowledgement, then headed for the door. It slammed behind him and, for the first time in days, the first time in her life, really, Susanna allowed herself to relax. She breathed out a sigh, tilted her head back on her shoulders and listened to the blessed, empty quiet.

Susanna enjoyed the peace and quiet for all of seventeen seconds.

It started with an unexplained anxiety deep in her chest. After that, her skin began to prickle, to sting. She felt dizzy, light-headed. Sure she was going to be sick, Susanna scrambled off the sofa, but when she got to her feet, her legs couldn't hold her.

"What's happening?" There was no one to answer her. A pain suddenly flared deep in her gut, so searing it sent her to her knees. "Jack!" she screamed, though the sound barely travelled past her lips.

Forcing herself to move, drawing on the times she'd been clawed, bitten, savaged by the wraiths, Susanna crawled towards the front door. Stumbling into the landing, she half-fell down the stairs.

She found Jack six flights down. He lay in a crumpled heap across several stairs, his head against the sharp edge of the top tread. One hand was clamped to his stomach, the ugly red of blood staining his white long-sleeved t-shirt.

"Jack! Are you all right?" she asked, edging round the stairs until she stood immediately below him. The intense pain she had felt in her gut was fading as fast as it had come on, but she still felt weak, her body trembling.

"No." Jack lifted his head, stared down at his stomach at the bloody stain. Tugging up his shirt and peeling away his bandage, he touched the wound, which looked just as it had earlier when Susanna had changed the dressing – despite the blood. He blinked rapidly, like he was trying to bring himself around from a heavy sleep. "What the hell happened? Did I fall?" He eyed her suspiciously. "What are you doing here? Did you follow me?"

Susanna reared back a little at the venom in his gaze. Did he think she'd pushed him?

"I was in the flat," she said quickly. "Less than a minute after you left, I started feeling awful. Really disoriented and dizzy, sick to my stomach. Then I got a burning pain here," she rubbed her side, "right where your knife wound was. It seemed too much of a coincidence so I ran after you. And found you like this."

"You think this happened because I left?"

"I… I don't know." Susanna shrugged her shoulders helplessly.

Jack scowled. "Go back up the stairs."

"What?"

"Go back up. We'll find out."

It was on the tip of Susanna's tongue to tell Jack that he could go up the stairs himself if he was so intent on testing it out, but she bit it back. If their theory was right, they needed to know – and she needed to stay on Jack's good side.

One flight up, she felt OK. A glance down showed Jack watching her, eyes dark in the harsh yellow fluorescents. A floor up and she lost sight of him. The dizziness started to set in and she had to grip the bannister, use it to haul herself up. Another floor and saliva flooded her mouth, her stomach somersaulting. She turned at the beginning of the next flight, contemplated the steps.

"That's enough." Jack's call from below made her sigh in relief. By the time she'd made it back to his side he was sitting up, but his skin was waxy, coated in a light sheen of sweat.

"Satisfied?" she asked, feeling resentful that he'd made her go through the ordeal twice in the space of five minutes.

"Help me up."

She held her hand out and braced when he used it to haul himself to his feet. He wobbled a bit but then steadied. Wrapping a hand firmly around her arm, he started back up towards his flat.

"So what does this mean?"

"I don't know," Susanna shrugged. "I guess... I guess we're connected somehow. It must be a consequence of coming back through from the wasteland together."

Silence as Jack considered this.

"You mean we're stuck together forever?" he asked darkly. "We can't go a hundred feet without each other?"

"I don't know. Maybe." She took a deep breath. "I mean, it seems so."

"Did you know this would happen?"

"What?"

"Did you know this would happen?" He advanced on her, all menace. "'I'll get you back in your body', you said. 'Just take me with you." He was right in front of her, just inches separating them, but still he kept moving forward. Susanna had no option but to retreat. "You said I'd never have to see you again. That was our deal." A thump as Susanna hit the wall. Jack pressed forward until she had absolutely nowhere to go. "Were you lying to me?"

"No, I—"

"Did you plan this? Tricking me into helping you across without mentioning that I'd be *stuck with you*?" He yelled the last bit, right into her face. Susanna couldn't hide her flinch.

"No," she repeated, much more quietly. "I didn't lie, Jack. I didn't know what would happen, I thought we'd be able to go our separate ways. I swear to you."

Jack didn't speak. Susanna was desperate to read the thoughts in his face, but she couldn't seem to lift her eyes from where they were currently burning a hole in his chest.

Finally, when the tension became unbearable, she looked up.

He glowered back down at her. "You need to find a way to undo this."

TWENTY-ONE

"Out with it."

Dylan slammed her tray down onto the cafeteria table, causing little corn kernels to jump out of the main segment of the moulded plastic, right into the custard of her sponge pudding.

"Out with what?" Tristan placed his own tray down much more carefully – he'd sweet-talked the dinner lady into letting him buy chips and cake. No vegetables, no main. It was definitely against their health-promoting school policy, but Tristan had smiled at the server, and she had given him what he asked for. She'd then proceeded to give Dylan extra vegetables to make up for it.

"You've been really weird since last night." He'd spent most of this morning's history lesson trying to look out of the window, and he'd been so distracted as they'd walked to the portacabins for science that he'd actually fallen over. Even more annoyingly, nobody had laughed at him, though he'd sprawled flat on his face, books and bag flying everywhere. Mark and Dove had even paused to help pick his stuff up.

Had Dylan made a spectacle of herself like that, she'd never have lived it down.

"There's nothing wrong, Dylan."

"You're lying." There was an angry edge to Dylan's voice, because anger was better than hurt – and if she let herself feel hurt then she might just cry. Which she was *not* going to do in the middle of the heaving cafeteria. So. "Out with it."

Tristan took her measure, must have realised how deadly serious she was, or maybe he caught the sheen in her eyes, no matter how much she tried to convince herself that she was angry. Angry, dammit!

"Don't do this to me, Tristan," she said, tears thick in her voice. "Don't keep things from me again. You promised."

"Not here," he said. "Let's find somewhere more private."

"Trust me, no one's listening," Dylan contradicted him, getting ahold of herself now that he seemed willing to talk. "What is it?"

He pursed his lips. "It's that weird feeling again."

"Like someone's watching us?"

"Yeah, but I can't explain it. I get this prickly, strange feeling at the back of my neck, but then when I look, there's nothing."

"Who d'you think it could be?" she commented.

"I'm starting to think it's not a who – I'm starting to think it's a *what*."

"A what?" Dylan frowned, then she felt her stomach drop through the seat of her chair. "A wraith? You think a wraith is stalking us?"

"No." Tristan shook his head at once. "A wraith wouldn't do this. They don't think like that. Well, they don't think."

"What, then?"

"I don't know." He grimaced. "That's why I'm worried. I was wondering about—" he hesitated.

"Go on," Dylan gently kicked him under the table.

"I was wondering about those beings you said you met, when you crossed the line. Remember?"

Remember? She wasn't exactly ever going to forget. She'd been heartbroken, devastated. Tristan had lied to her, betrayed her, abandoned her at the line – and this… thing had turned up and told her she had to come with it. Caeli, its name popped suddenly into her head. It had looked sort of like a man and sort of like an angel, only without the wings or halo. Bright white light, that was her most enduring memory of it. She'd never been able to quite focus on its face, its features, but she had thought it beautiful.

"What would one of them be doing here?" she wondered. "Do you think it just found the hole and wandered through?"

"No," Tristan shook his head. "They don't venture into the wasteland. Until you told me about it, I didn't know they existed."

"Well, what would it be doing here, then?"

"Looking for us?" Tristan's expression darkened. "Or, more specifically, for me." He saw her confusion and went on. "Because I've absconded my post. Abandoned my duties. Perhaps it's come to drag me back."

"Tough," Dylan snapped. "It can't have you."

She didn't need to see the grim set of Tristan's mouth to know it wasn't that simple. "I might not have a choice, Dylan."

Dylan thought for a moment about Caeli, tried hard to put her vague impressions into words. "The thing is, Tristan, maybe your experience of the wasteland is skewed by the wraiths."

"What do you mean?"

"Well, on the other side of the afterlife, it was amazing… Caeli made me think of an angel. I was safe." She shrugged. That was the best she could do. "It didn't seem like the kind of place that would send someone to punish you for loving someone. Does that help?"

"Yes and no," Tristan said, his face folded over into a deep frown as he considered her words. "This feeling I get, the eyes on me. They don't feel friendly. They feel dark and angry."

"So it might not be one of those things at all."

"Yeah," Tristan agreed. "It might be something else. Something new."

"Well, what do we do?"

"I don't know," he said. His eyes were dark with worry. "But I think… if I can close the hole we made between the worlds, fix the damage we caused, that might help."

"All right. As soon as we're both well enough we can head there again and try to fix it. If we can get away from my mum." Dylan thought of Joan, who had been watching them like a hawk since their last debacle, tracking their every move. "I haven't been able to sleep right, thinking about wraiths out in the world."

"Me neither." Tristan pressed his foot into hers, clearly conscious of onlookers in the canteen. "Your mum's letting us go to the Halloween dance tonight still, maybe she's starting to loosen off."

"Maybe," Dylan said. "I guess in the meantime we just keep an eye out, see if we can catch this thing in the act. And if we do… I don't know. Maybe we should confront it."

Tristan nodded thoughtfully and Dylan knew his worry hadn't abated. Hers hadn't either, not entirely, but getting Tristan to open up about his worries was a big weight off her shoulders. The thought that he'd still been keeping secrets from her had been her greatest fear. He was her soulmate, her everything. She needed him to trust her, to believe in her – like she believed in him.

⌒

"Is this really necessary?"

"Yes. It is." Dylan tore off another strip of Sellotape and glanced up. "Stop fidgeting, these need to be straight or they won't look right."

Attaching the final piece, she straightened up and stepped back to admire her handiwork.

"Well?" Tristan looked like a martyr about to be sent to the gallows. Actually, he looked like a martyr about ten years after the gallows. The long white strips Dylan had taped onto Tristan's body looked great, but for the full effect—

"Hang on." Reaching across to the wall, she flicked off the light. The strips glowed in the dark, and Tristan's black clothes disappeared, giving the impression of a moving skeleton. Well, a motionless skeleton with his arms folded in an irritated fashion. "Perfect!"

He grunted in response, and when Dylan turned the light back on his expression was still just as grumpy.

"I gave you a choice," she reminded him. "You could've been the Grim Reaper and I would've been the skeleton."

"No," Tristan bit back, just as he had when she'd first suggested it. "I don't ever want to see you as a dead body again, not even as a joke."

"Or we could have gone as Bert and Ernie." That had been Dylan's back-up choice. She grinned as she remembered Tristan's face when she'd shown him a picture of them.

"Only for you would I do this." Tristan eyed himself in the mirror, his expression caught between horror and resignation.

"And I love you too." Dylan squeezed his hand and laughed. "It's a Halloween dance. Dressing up is mandatory."

Actually, it wasn't. But most people would be wearing costumes, and this was her first actual dance, so she intended to go all out. Besides, *her* costume – a little black dress with a hooded robe over it – looked fine. And Joan had given her permission not to use her crutch at last, which made her happy. She could always use her scythe.

"Let's get this over with," Tristan sighed, but he winked at her as he tugged her out of her bedroom.

"Picture!" Joan squawked when they tried to head down the hallway. She shuffled them in front of the fireplace in the living room, camera in hand, and for once, when she looked at Tristan, it was with approval. Gratitude. Dylan knew her mum worried about her at school – how she didn't seem to have many friends, wasn't involved in any of the clubs or teams, didn't go to any school events. Taking Dylan to a dance was earning Tristan major brownie points. And, hopefully, a little more freedom. "Smile!"

"Death doesn't smile, Mum," Dylan reminded her.

"This one does!" Joan retorted. Then she wiggled the camera. "I promised to show your dad."

When, exactly, was Joan having all these conversations with her dad? And why? They hated each other's guts. Shrugging it away, Dylan slipped her arm around Tristan's back, cosying in as he hugged her shoulder, and she pasted a smile on her face.

She felt incredibly foolish.

And she also felt deliriously happy.

Tonight, she was going to a dance with a boy and she was going to have fun. Tonight, she was going to forget about wraiths and murders and holes in the veil between this world and the next. Tonight, she was going to be normal.

TWENTY-TWO

It wasn't a cold evening so they walked through the darkened streets towards school for the second time that day. They joined a host of pupils on their way to the dance, decked out in weird and wonderful – no, mostly just weird, costumes. A horde of zombies pranced in a far-too-lively fashion on the other side of the road from them, and just in front, three demons in skin-tight costumes struggled to walk in sky-high heels. Cheryl and her friends.

At the door to the assembly hall, McManus, their history teacher, had clearly been dragged in to supervise and keep out miscreants. He was also clearly unhappy about this turn of events.

"Tickets?" he barked at them.

Tristan produced the two pieces of card from the depths of his trouser pocket.

"Where's your costume, sir?" one of the zombies called out from behind Dylan.

"He's wearing it," another zombie snickered. "He's come as a relic!"

McManus was decked out, as always, in a pair of brown slacks and a tweed jacket. He had a thick moustache and a bow-tie, almost as if he *wanted* students to take the piss. All he needed was a pipe and he could be a school master from the Victorian era. Especially with that dour, unforgiving expression.

He didn't laugh at the zombie's joke. "McCormack! Consider your access revoked!"

Dylan didn't stop to listen to the argument past McCormack's indignant "What!" – she was too busy taking in the assembly hall in all its glory. The lights had been dimmed and multi-coloured spotlights flashed on and off in rhythm with the pounding music, illuminating the ghouls and monsters and gravestones that decorated the walls, all adorned with mock cobwebs.

"What do you think?" she hollered in Tristan's ear.

"I think I love you," he hollered back. "I must!"

She grinned and shoved him playfully. He might complain, but Tristan was thirsty to drink up as many real-world experiences as he could. This might not have been what he had in mind, but it was definitely a better experience than a microwaveable meal in front of the television.

They ditched their coats in the cloakroom, and despite her fantasies of beheading Cheryl with her scythe, Dylan left that there too.

"Let's get some drinks!" yelled Dylan.

The refreshments were Halloween-themed as well. There were cupcakes topped with fondant spiders and candyfloss masquerading as cobwebs. A huge bowl of 'monster's blood' fruit cocktail waited on a table beside a high tower of paper cups.

"There are probably more E numbers in this than you want to know about," Dylan warned Tristan, scooping up a cupful for each of them.

"E numbers?" Tristan asked, but Dylan took a big swig, indicating that he should do the same. It was just as sugary as she'd expected… though that wasn't what had her choking as she tried to swallow.

"God almighty!" she spluttered, holding her cup up high. "It's spiked."

"Poison?" Tristan asked, an alarmed look on his face. He put his hand out to take Dylan's cup away from her, but she curled it into her chest, out of reach.

"Probably vodka," she laughed, glancing around to see if any teachers were within hearing distance. With the music thumping away like it was, they'd have to be standing pretty close. "You really are from another world, aren't you! It won't kill you – it's cheap booze though, so it might taste toxic."

Shrugging, he took a drink, made a face and then downed the whole thing. Waving goodbye to her taste buds, Dylan did the same.

"Dance with me." Tristan grinned, took her cup and placed it down with his.

Dylan didn't dance. To be fair, she'd never had much opportunity, but whenever it had been on the cards she'd strictly been a take-a-seat-and-watch kind of girl. Now, however, she let Tristan lead her out into the middle of the floor and held on as he twirled and spun her around.

"How do you know how to do this?" she hollered when he yanked her in and whirled the two of them around. "Were there dances in the wasteland?"

"I don't," Tristan shouted back. "I just like the excuse—" he flung her out and hauled her back in again, "to hold on to you in public."

Dylan couldn't disagree with that. They'd been careful in school, restricting touches to under-the-table footsie, the occasional platonic hug and surreptitious handholding when they thought no one would see. It had rankled heavily with Dylan, who had to watch the likes of Cheryl and her friends drool all over Tristan. She'd already caught them eyeing him tonight.

Well, they could dance with him over her dead body. Except they couldn't, 'cause he was hers even when she was dead. She smiled at that.

"Another drink?" Tristan asked in the brief interlude between songs.

Dylan could hear her heartbeat in her ears. She nodded eagerly, but when they got back to the refreshment table the spiked punch had been confiscated so they had to make do with juice.

"I'm sweating!" she declared, waving her hand in front of her face. It was sweltering in the hall with so many bodies crushed in, and Tristan had been flinging her about for – she checked her watch – over an hour.

"Fresh air?" Tristan asked, indicating the fire door, which had been propped open to try and cool the place. He grinned wickedly. "I promised you a little private time, didn't I?"

He had.

Dylan didn't even hesitate. Letting Joan decide Tristan could be her 'cousin' was the worst decision she'd ever made.

But almost as soon as they were outside, Tristan tensed. His head whipped to the side, peering into the dark. "You know what," taking Dylan's hand, he took a step back towards the fire exit. "Let's just dance some more."

"Tristan, what is it?" Dylan whispered.

After the incredible noise inside the hall, outside was eerily quiet. Dylan's ears still buzzed from the assault on her hearing, blotting out the usual city buzz. She could tell Tristan had heard something, though.

Or felt something.

"What is it?"

Tristan said nothing, but as he turned back towards the hall, the fire door slammed shut.

"Perfect timing," Dylan commented sourly. "Bet that was Dove or something, messing around."

"Hmmm." Tristan was glancing jerkily about. "What's the quickest way back inside?"

"We can just bang on the door and—"

"No," Tristan interrupted her. "We need to move, now."

"Tristan?" Dylan hurried along beside him, one of her hands firm in his grasp. It was dark and she was limping slightly, all the dancing having tired out her weaker leg, so she kept her head down, trying to see where she was putting her feet. Tristan was going too fast, but she didn't want to ask him to slow down. Something had him really freaked. "Are we being watched again?"

Tristan nodded curtly.

"They're right here." He cursed quietly. "It was stupid, taking you away from everyone else. I can't believe I—"

Then he stopped speaking.

Stopped moving.

Spinning to look at him, Dylan saw he was frozen like a statue. His gaze was fixed dead ahead.

"Tristan?" He didn't respond. "Tristan?" Dylan turned, stared into the direction that had him so fascinated, so horrified.

She could no longer see the street that ran along the back of the school, or even the school itself. She couldn't see anything except the glow that provided a dramatic backdrop to what had appeared just metres in front of them.

No, she could see something – she could see a pair of piercing eyes.

Oh God, if this was what had been following – stalking – Tristan, then it definitely wasn't a being like Caeli. The only thing that the two had in common was the light that made it hard to see their features.

"Tristan?" her voice wobbled.

But before he could answer her, the thing spoke. If that was the right word. Its words echoed in Dylan's brain.

"Ferryman."

If that was a greeting, it wasn't a good one. Shivers shot down Dylan's spine at the authority, the power in its voice.

"You have erred in your duties."

It paused and Tristan took that moment to unwrap his fingers from around Dylan's hand. Without looking at her, still fixed on the towering creature before them, he whispered, "Dylan, go. Run."

Run? Abandon him? He couldn't be serious. "I'm not leaving you."

The thing spoke again, cutting them off.

"Ferryman, hear your crimes. You failed to deliver the soul you had been allocated to the realm beyond; and worse, you allowed that soul to return to its body and the real world, possessing knowledge that is forbidden."

The creature's disapproval was like needles on Dylan's skin. She was the holder of such forbidden knowledge – the knowledge of what happened after you died.

"Just go!" Tristan growled out of the corner of his mouth. "Get back inside."

"I told you, not without you!" Dylan snagged his flapping hand out of the air. Tugged. "Come with me." It seemed a foolish hope, but perhaps if they bolted around the buildings, back towards the school reception, they'd run into people and the being wouldn't be able to reveal itself. "Come on, Tristan! Come with me!"

"I can't!" Tristan repeated. "I can't move. Please," he ripped his fingers from hers. "Run!"

"You have left the wasteland," the creature continued listing

Tristan's crimes, "abandoning your post and your sacred duty. You have tried to present yourself as human, an entitlement you have not been granted. You have allowed evil to seep into this world, bringing about the deaths of souls before their time. You have—"

"What *are* you?" Dylan blurted out. She didn't want to let it reach its final judgement.

It stopped. Dylan could feel its gaze turn on her like a spotlight, illuminating everything, right down to her bones. Right down to her soul.

"I am an Inquisitor."

She hadn't expected it to answer her. What the hell was an Inquisitor? She tried to ask another question but Tristan shushed her.

"Soul, this is no concern of yours. You should not even be witness to this judgement." Its voice rumbled inside Dylan, sounding frighteningly like a snarl. "You should not be able to see me."

And she probably wouldn't be able to, Dylan realised, if she hadn't journeyed to the wasteland and returned, having somehow mortally attached herself to a ferryman. She wasn't the same person she had been.

The Inquisitor turned back to Tristan. Dylan struggled not to sag with relief as she was released from its stare.

"Ferryman," it thundered. "You have heard your crimes."

Tristan remained frozen to the spot, as he had for the entire time. He still had some freedom of movement in his neck as well as his arms, though. Hearing the Inquisitor's words, he dropped his head. In the eerie glow that eminated from behind the Inquisitor, Dylan could just make out the shadow of Tristan's tightly clenched jaw.

"You are guilty," the Inquisitor went on. "For your transgressions, you forfeit your right to be a guide to those newly delivered to the wasteland."

Though his head was bowed low, Tristan managed a small nod of acknowledgement.

"You forfeit the life you have stolen in this world."

A small hesitation this time, but Tristan nodded again, his eyes scrunched shut. Dylan gasped. Forfeited the life he had stolen? *This* life? No.

"Wait!" she yelped, but the Inquisitor ignored her.

"You will be returned to the wasteland, where you will join the ranks of those forsaken creatures—"

"Wraiths? No!" Dylan choked, stepping towards the Inquisitor. "Wait!"

Tristan snapped his hand out and wrapped it around her upper arm in an iron grip, stopping her in her tracks.

"I accept your judgement," he said. "But please, I beg you not to punish Dylan." He lifted his chin defiantly while she struggled in his grip. "She is innocent in this. It was my fault."

What? Dylan ripped Tristan's hand away, elbowing and wriggling to try to break his grip on her. "No, it wasn't. It was *my* idea – if you're going to punish him then—"

Tristan got his hand over her mouth before she could finish the sentence.

"I have no interest in the soul," the Inquisitor said, eyeing Dylan with disdain. "So long as she does not speak of what she knows, no harm will come to her."

"You can separate us?" Tristan asked, stifling Dylan's scream. "Each time we have tried to move apart, we feel pain. The further we go, the worse it is. As if the injuries that killed her in the train crash are happening all over again – to both of us."

The Inquisitor shifted in a subtle movement.

"Then she suffers. The soul is not my concern. I have come to take you to your fate."

"She'll die!" Tristan said. "If you take me away from her, she'll die!"

"Then she dies."

The Inquisitor could have been discussing the weather for all the emotion in its voice. Given that it was talking about her and Tristan's imminent demise, that annoyed Dylan. Increasing her struggles until Tristan released her, she stepped away from both him and the Inquisitor, giving herself a safer distance from the blazing light.

"You can't do that!" she burst out.

"You should have died already," the Inquisitor pointed out. "I shall simply set things back to the way they should be."

"I don't care about me!" Well, she did, but she cared more about Tristan at this moment. And so did the Inquisitor. "You can't just take Tristan away. We just fell in love! And it was *my* fault he came back with me. I talked him into it."

"Dylan!" Tristan growled at her, but she was out of reach.

Dylan ignored him. "You can't do this."

"I can. I must. You may say goodbye."

"Dylan," Tristan said. The expression on his face was utterly haunted. "I love you."

The words cut Dylan right to the core. Split her open and made her bleed. Instantly, Dylan felt the anxiety, the nausea, the agony that came whenever Tristan moved from her side. Her heart thumped frantically in her chest and she knew she was a beat away from dying. Again. She wanted to say those words back to him, desperately, but if these were their final few seconds she couldn't afford to waste them on that. She had a last opportunity to reason with the thing – she had to take it.

"He can't just disappear. He's made friends, he's registered in the school. If you take him away, there will be lots of questions."

The Inquisitor seemed unconcerned. "They may ask questions, they will not find the answers."

It turned back to Tristan, and Dylan knew this was it. It was going to take Tristan away. In one fell swoop it'd kill her and hand Tristan over to—

"What about the wraiths?" It came out as a yelp, but the Inquisitor paused. "They're finding their way through, and unless we close the hole it will keep happening. But we could get them. We've done it already, at the tunnel."

"You lie," the Inquisitor accused. "Wraiths cannot be killed."

"I'm not lying, I swear!" Dylan stared at the Inquisitor beseechingly. Desperately. "Tristan was hurt during it. Show him your wound!"

The Inquisitor didn't wait for Tristan to reveal it, but moved instantly closer and grabbed his skeleton costume where Dylan pointed, tearing the material and the dressing beneath. The Inquisitor saw the furrow in Tristan's flesh, healing almost human-slow.

"They can be killed here," Tristan said. "They are more solid in this world." He touched his wound. "Like me."

The glow that enveloped the Inquisitor seemed to dim momentarily. "I cannot control the wraiths," the creature admitted. "Nor can I close the tear that you have made between worlds." It fixed its eyes on Tristan, "You see how your actions have grave consequences?"

Tristan said nothing. Dylan opened her mouth to speak but the look on Tristan's face stopped her. It was… hopeful.

What was happening?

Suddenly, the Inquisitor let go of Tristan. "I offer you a chance, though you do not deserve it."

A chance? Dylan's heart soared, the relief overwhelming her so thoroughly she almost didn't hear the rest of the Inquisitor's words. "You will find a way to close this… gateway. And you will destroy any remaining wraiths that have found their way into this world."

"If I do this?" Tristan asked.

"If you do this, I will allow you to remain. To guard this realm, preventing others from coming through, and killing any wraiths you find. Do you accept?"

"Yes!" Dylan gulped. "Yes, we'll do it!"

The Inquisitor completely ignored her, its eyes on Tristan.

"I accept," Tristan said.

"You have three days," the Inquisitor said. "Three days, no more. I will not have mercy a second time."

And it was gone.

TWENTY-THREE

"I need time to think," Tristan said, when Dylan woke to find him halfway into his school uniform. He had laid hers out on his – already-made – side of the bed. "We don't want to go off half-cocked and—"

"Half-cocked?"

"Half-cocked. It means unprepared, to just barge in when you're not—"

"I know what it means!" Dylan snapped, exasperated. "Just… don't say *that word* in front of anyone at Kaithshall, all right?"

"What… half?" Tristan shot her a quizzical look.

"No! The other—" she broke off, staring suspiciously at Tristan. He tried to hold on to his wide-eyed, innocent expression, but his lips were twitching.

"Idiot." Dylan snorted, shoving at his arm, before getting them back on track. "We need to come up with a plan. We've only got three days – we need to *do* something, not go to bloody school!"

"Yes, we need a plan," Tristan agreed. "And for that, I need to think. Until I've worked out the best thing to do, we should follow a normal routine. If you truant now," he said, raising his voice because Dylan had opened her mouth to argue, "then Joan will clamp down on us just when she's beginning to trust us again. We won't be able to do anything."

So they went to school, although Dylan lectured Tristan about how stupid it was all through computing class, and planned to continue doing so until he listened to her.

Dylan couldn't stop thinking about what seemed an impossible task – finding any other wraiths that may have escaped.

"There haven't been any more killings," she said.

"No," Tristan agreed. "I suspect the one in the tunnel was not the one that killed those four men. It's still out there. But perhaps it hasn't killed again because it glutted itself. Eating a real live person is more of a feast than eating a soul. And it went through four."

Dylan made a face against the image that raised in her mind.

"It could get hungry again any time then," she reminded Tristan. "So we need to go there, make sure we're in the right place." No response. "Tristan?"

"Damn…"

His low-muttered curse made her look over at his screen. Rather than the lines of code they were supposed to be working on, his monitor was filled with angry red lettering:

BLOCKED

"What did you search for?" Dylan asked. Dove had been hauled out of class in second year for trying to look at dirty videos, but there were other things that triggered it.

"How to create home explosives," Tristan admitted, looking ⸢ittle sheepish.

⸢hat!" Dylan's yell made every head in the class turn her
⸜ Mrs James looked up from what she was doing. Dylan
and waited until her classmates' attention drifted
·lowering at Tristan. "You can't google that!"

"I can see that," Tristan mumbled.

"Not just 'cause it's blocked – it causes an alert to the government or something. They'll think you're a terrorist!"

"Well, give me your smartphone. I'll search on that."

"That's even worse!" Dylan squeaked. Sometimes she forgot how little Tristan knew about the inner workings of the world. "If you really need to, we'll have to go to an internet café."

"You know what," Tristan said, his gaze suddenly fixed over her head, "I've got a better idea."

"What?" Dylan spun round, tried to see what Tristan was so interested in. All she could see was Dove and his cronies messing around with the wires at the back of their computers. "Tristan, what?"

"I'll tell you in a minute," he murmured, and without another word he got up and went over to join the small crowd of boys, sitting down beside them and drawing Dove – *David MacMillan* of all people! – into conversation.

⌒

"Are you going to tell me what you're up to?" she asked as they left computing. She figured she'd been patient long enough, sitting watching Tristan talk and joke with Dove's gang of morons as if they were all best buddies.

"Explosives," Tristan murmured, opening the door for Dylan.

"What on Earth does that have to do with Dove?"

He looked at her, surprised, and she knew he'd assumed she understood what he was thinking. "I'm going to blow up the tunnel. Well," he shrugged. "*Try* to."

Dylan still wasn't getting it. "But why did you need to talk to Dove about it?"

"Remember the other day in the science lab? He nearly blew

the whole place up. I asked him what chemicals he was messing about with."

"I doubt he remembered."

"He did," Tristan told her. "He knew exactly." Tristan paused to glare at a little trio of first-year boys who'd come too close. As one, they scarpered. "He told me he's tried it at home, just using household stuff. Cleaning supplies, mostly. Nearly took the roof off his mum's place."

No, he couldn't possibly. "You can't do that! Tristan, we'd get into so much trouble! If the police found out, we'd get arrested! And you don't have any ID or anything. Tristan, you *can't*!"

"More trouble than having to tell the Inquisitor we've failed?" He let that sink in. "Dylan, it'll take me back to the wasteland and let the wraiths have me. I'll *become* one of those slathering, mindless vermin, and you – you'll die, Dylan."

"Yes, but—" she shook her head. "Even if you did blow it up, it's one of the main train lines to Aberdeen! They'd just open it back up and uncover the hole again. Think about this, Tristan!"

"I have thought about it," he told her, deadly serious. "I've done nothing but think since we heard the news about those four men who died. And I've got the answer: I'm not blowing up the tunnel here, I'm going to do it in the wasteland."

Dylan just stared at him, absolutely aghast.

⤿

It was disturbingly easy to buy the ingredients for a bomb. They went to Homebase, and Tristan loaded up a trolley with chemicals and duct tape, a small reel of copper wire and some other miscellaneous bits and bobs. He also bought a jerrycan. It all looked very suspicious, but the middle-aged woman at the counter didn't even blink as she stuffed it into a carrier bag. Dylan winced when the bill rang up.

All the way around Homebase and on the long walk home, Dylan barely said a word. They ate dinner with Joan – pork chop and mashed potato – and then sat through a cookery show that she usually really enjoyed. She went through the routine of getting ready for bed like a robot and then, while she waited for Joan to go to sleep, she stared up at the ceiling.

Blank. Expressionless.

It was the only emotion she could manage, because if she let herself feel anything, she might scream.

Finally, Tristan curled in beside her. He didn't even have time to get comfortable before Dylan rounded on him, her words thick with accusation. "You're leaving me."

"What?" Tristan snaked his arms around her, squeezing her closer. "I'm right here."

"You're going to leave me," she repeated. "This plan of yours, going to the wasteland. You know... you know if you leave you won't come back."

Silence. Dylan stayed subdued for the first five seconds of it then tried to wriggle out of Tristan's arms. He wouldn't let her.

"Stop," he pleaded. "Listen."

"Listen to what? You justify yourself? You did this before when you made me go through to the other side alone!" Dylan choked her words off, unable to control her volume. "Please, Tristan. You can't just wander back and forth."

"I'm not leaving, Dylan," he promised, "I've got an idea." She waited. "If I tether myself to the real world, I should be able to go through and find my way back before the bomb explodes."

"Tether yourself?"

"Like a safety line. The sort of thing climbers use."

"So you're going to tie a rope around your waist and hope that you can pull yourself back, that's your plan?" Her tone dripped with derision.

"We have three days," Tristan reminded her. "Two now. Do you have a better plan?"

No. But going back to the tunnel, letting Tristan disappear into the darkness, leaving her all alone there…

"I'll go with you," she blurted. "We'll set the explosion together."

Tristan's grip became steel bars around her. She felt the sudden tension in every line of his body. "No."

"Tristan!"

"No." A hard squeeze to emphasise his point.

Dylan scowled in the darkness. So it was all right for him to go and not her? Did he not think she could manage? She'd survived on her own there… *twice.*

"Why not?" she asked, her voice hard.

"I need you on the other side," Tristan said. "You're what I'm tethering myself to."

Oh.

Well. That did make sort of sense. But she still wasn't happy about him going through on his own, and she'd argue it to death if, as Tristan had pointed out, she had a better idea. Which she didn't.

"If you don't come back," she told him, "I'm coming to get you."

Another squeeze, this one much gentler.

"Good," he said in her ear.

He followed his words with a kiss to her earlobe. Then to her jaw, her neck. Finally her mouth. Residual anger and tension from their conversation kept her rigid and unyeilding for a heartbeat, but when he kissed her more deeply, she melted.

She'd crossed the wasteland for him before, she'd do it again.

TWENTY-FOUR

"Jack?" Susanna slipped into Jack's bedroom. He was standing with his back to her, gazing out onto the urban sprawl below. Tension held every line of his body rigidly still. "Jack, I think I've got an idea."

"What?" he whirled to pin her with his gaze.

"About breaking the connection between us."

"Go on then."

"I think I know someone who can help."

Silence. Only the noise of Jack's mum hoovering the living room carpet – which she'd already gone over twice since this morning – broke the quiet.

"I thought you didn't know anyone else here," Jack said at last.

It was impossible to miss the aggression in Jack's voice.

"He's not from here. Not originally, anyway. He's another person like me. Another ferryman."

"Huh."

Jack didn't say anything further and Susanna forced herself to wait. Jack *had* to agree to this. She couldn't think of any other way to get to Tristan – because nobody moved Jack when he didn't want to.

Please, she thought. *Come on.*

To her surprise, instead of spearing her with his gaze and

interrogating her with a series of rapid-fire questions, he fixed his eyes over her shoulder, down the hallway.

"That's right. Got to make sure everything's perfect before *he* comes home." His lip was curled up into a sneer.

"What?" Susanna blinked, totally thrown. The noise of the hoover increased again as Jack's mum continued to clean. Oh. "Your stepdad's coming back?"

"Yeah, can't wait." It was easy to hear the sarcasm in Jack's voice, but Susanna also caught a tremor of trepidation.

"Where's he been?" she asked, aware that she was on thin ice. Jack didn't like personal questions, and she knew he *definitely* didn't like his stepdad.

"Working," Jack spat out. "He's a truck driver. Long haul, so he's away for days at a time. Wish he'd just stay away." Jack's gaze cut back to her, several things moving behind the dark of his eyes. "This ferryman," he began.

"Tristan," Susanna said. Adrenaline had her heart beating faster just saying his name aloud.

"*Tristan?*" Jack raised his eyebrows scornfully. He rolled his eyes. "You know where he is?"

Ah. That was the sticking point.

"Kind of," Susanna hedged.

"What does 'kind of' mean?" Jack advanced half-way across the room. "You do or you don't."

"I do!" Susanna reassured him, grimacing internally at the tiny white lie. "I mean, I know the general direction."

"What?"

"South."

"South?" Jack repeated, then paused. Susanna nodded. "Just south? That's it?"

"Well... south-west."

"Are you serious?" Another step forward put Jack within arm's reach. It wasn't a big room. "How the hell are we meant to find him if all you know is that he's anywhere south of us, in the whole world?"

"I can sense him," Susanna promised. "He's close. In the same country as us. We can feel each other. And it's stronger the closer we are. If you just take me in his general direction, I'll be able to find him. I promise, Jack."

Susanna was almost positive that was a promise she could keep. And even if she couldn't, she was willing to take the risk. She *had* to get to Tristan. She hadn't gotten as far as she had, chanced as much as she had, to give up now and be stuck with Jack for the rest of her mortal life.

Jack opened his mouth to respond at the same time as the hoover cut off. The sudden quiet was distinctly uncomfortable. As was the way Jack suddenly changed his mind. Reaching to the side of Susanna, he grabbed his jacket off its hook and chucked her one of his mum's thick cardigans.

"Right then, let's go." Jack started purposefully towards the door, an agitated prowl, as if he'd storm right through her.

Susanna did the only sensible thing: got out of his way. Relief made her giddy and her legs felt wobbly as she hurried after him. They were going to find Tristan. She almost couldn't believe it.

"Come on," Jack prodded, and Susanna did her best to move faster, even though she didn't understand the sudden rush.

That became clear just as they reached the front door.

The startlingly loud sound of a key in the lock stopped Jack in his tracks. His mum rushed to the sofa and started frantically plumping the cushions again.

Susanna watched the door as it opened, half-expecting the devil to walk in, even though she'd already seen the man in

Jack's memories. He was very ordinary looking – a wiry build, average height. His brown hair was thinning above a narrow face with sharp features. He wasn't related to Jack by blood, but somehow he seemed to have the same cold, cold eyes. They swept the room as he walked in, only pausing on Susanna for a millisecond before moving on. They ran the length of Jack, who was stood taut and tense, fists clenched, then took in the spotless room before finally resting on Jack's mum. She offered him a timid smile.

"You're home," she greeted.

"I am," he said.

Taking three more steps into the room he dumped his bags and jacket down on the sofa before enfolding Jack's mum in a hug. Did Susanna imagine her slight flinch at his touch? She wasn't sure. She definitely didn't imagine the way Jack braced for battle when his stepdad pulled back and turned his attention to him.

"Jack," he rumbled. His eyes darted to Susanna again, and she felt the chill all the way across the room. "Who's this?"

"Jack's friend. She's been staying for a couple of days." Jack's mum offered the information with a hopeful smile.

"I see." Jack's stepdad licked his lips. "Running a B&B, are we?" There was a razor sharp edge to the words.

"We're just off," Jack blurted to his mum before she had to answer her husband's question, positioning his body between them.

"That's a good idea," his stepdad said, saccharine sweet.

Jack looked like he wanted to say something back – or do something with the right fist that he was clenching and unclenching, but the possibility of escape was too tempting to pass up. Without another word, he stalked out. Susanna followed hot on his heels.

"Jack," she called, chasing down the stairs after him. The fire door burst open as he shoved at it with both hands. "Jack, wait."

He didn't respond, going so fast that Susanna felt the pull between them, a sharp twinge in her side, and had to run, gasping and holding onto the site of the phantom stab wound.

Jack didn't slow until he'd erupted out of the building into the open air of the forecourt. Then he stood, breathing hard, like an enraged bull. With a strangled yell, he turned to the side and threw a fist into the already dented side of a white van.

"Are you OK?" she asked.

"Fine," Jack grunted, the angry glitter in his eyes giving Susanna a different answer.

"Your dad seems—"

"He's not my dad."

"Your stepdad, then, he seems—"

Jack slashed a hand violently across the air, cutting her off again. "I don't want to talk about him. Let's go."

Jack stalked through the streets until the residences thinned into shops and then, finally, businesses and industrial units. It was much quieter here, even though the work day had started. A lot of the buildings had FOR SALE or TO LET signs hanging above them. Even the places that were still open looked in need of some repair. Susanna shivered. It wasn't exactly cold, but there was little warmth about the place.

This far away from the flat, Jack's temper seemed to have cooled and she felt it was safe to try and talk again. Not that that was ever all that safe with Jack.

"What are we doing here?"

"You want to go find your ferryman, right?"

Susanna nodded dumbly.

"Well, we need a way to get there."

OK. She looked around again, still confused. There wasn't a bus stop or a train station in sight. No taxis either. The only vehicle moving was an old transit van chugging out towards the town centre.

Jack read the bewilderment on her face.

"We need to pick up a ride."

"A ride?" Susanna repeated blankly. "But you don't have a car." Or a licence, she was fairly certain.

"I can fix that," Jack crowed, suddenly looking a lot more cheerful. "I'm a master at hot wiring."

Susanna wasn't entirely sure what hot wiring was, but that didn't help her sense of foreboding as she trudged along behind Jack, who had already started scouting for 'something decent'.

That turned out to be a neat little blue hatchback. Parked in a discreet patch of shadow between two looming buildings, it looked clean and well cared for, its age only told by the little spots of rust that were starting to creep up from the wheel arcs.

Jack stepped closer, a sliver of something glinting in his hand. Susanna watched silently as, in one smooth movement, he slid it down between the door and the glass of the driver's side window. There was a quiet click and the next second Jack was tugging the door open. "Ladies first," he said, smirking at Susanna as he held the door open for her to slide over to the passenger side.

Susanna hesitated. Perhaps it was denial, but she hadn't quite realised that they were planning to steal a car until this point. Stealing a car. That wasn't petty shoplifting or graffiti, the kinds of things Jack did on a regular basis. It was a real crime. If they were caught…

But she knew she didn't have much choice. If she tried to balk, it'd be an ugly scene, and she'd still end up riding in a stolen vehicle. Besides, a car was the best mode of transport for her hazy sense of Tristan's location. Grimacing, she ducked down and crawled inside. It would be worth it. Worth it to get to Tristan.

"Now what?" she said. She might not know much about how things worked in this world, but she did know that generally cars needed keys to start them.

"Just wait," Jack said, eyes slicing to hers, crinkled with humour. He held them as his fingers fumbled with something just underneath the steering wheel. Suddenly a tiny light flashed in the darkened well, then the car coughed to life. "Yessss!"

This was him in his element. He forced the car into gear and then, with a screech of tyres, they took off.

Though Jack couldn't have a licence – he wasn't old enough, Susanna was sure – the way he handled the car told her that this was not the first time he'd driven one. With spins of the steering wheel and quick, smooth changes of gear, he whisked them round the tight corners of the industrial estate and then, when he hit a dual carriageway, he hammered down on the accelerator, powering forward so hard that Susanna was thrust back into her seat.

"So," he said, fiddling with the buttons on the radio until a heavy bass started thumping through the speakers, almost drowning out the sound of his voice as he yelled. "South-west?"

TWENTY-FIVE

They took the same route to the tunnel as before, bomb-making kit crammed heavily into their school bags. There wasn't enough space in the luggage compartment for their bags, but Tristan didn't want to let them out of his sight, anyway. He arranged them carefully between their feet on each bus, with a warning to Dylan not to jostle too much.

"They could explode?" she asked in a furious whisper.

"No," Tristan said, though he didn't look convinced. "But there are chemicals in there that really shouldn't mix. At least, not till we're ready."

The walk to the train tracks was much easier this time because Dylan's legs had healed enough to manage the rough terrain. Despite that, she walked slowly, trailing behind Tristan who was burdened with the two rucksacks. Her dillydallying didn't seem to make the walk to the tunnel any longer; all too soon it loomed before them.

Dylan had worried there might be workers on site, the train company feeling the pressure to get the line up and running again as soon as possible. Tristan disagreed, though. He'd read that work would have to halt until the police enquiry into the four men's murders was completed... and given that they'd been killed by a wraith from the afterlife, he doubted they'd have made much progress. As they approached, Dylan saw that Tristan had been right – and wrong.

There were no works vans or signs of construction. No digging, sawing or hammering. But someone had clearly been here since their last adventure, because a wooden barrier had now been erected at the tunnel entrance.

KEEP OUT was spray-painted across the plywood, and police tape criss-crossed over it for good measure.

Dylan paused, but Tristan kept going until he stood right in front of the makeshift blockade. He sighed. "We'll just have to bash it down as best we can." He gave it a frustrated kick and the whole thing quivered. "It doesn't seem very substantial."

It wasn't. Tristan was able to pull the entire barrier away from the opening in one piece.

"Wait!" Dylan said a heartbeat too late as Tristan shoved the ungainly sheets of thin wood to the side. "What about wraiths?"

"It's daytime," Tristan reminded her. He glanced up at the sky, heavy with rainclouds. "This is still too bright for them out here." He made a face. "Just about."

Hunkering down just inside the shelter of the tunnel, he unzipped one bag and pulled out two heavy-duty torches.

"Here," he said, handing one to Dylan. "This might help keep them at bay better than your phone light. You stay here and I'll go and check to see if there are any lurking further down."

He shone his torch briefly down the depths of the tunnel, where its beam was soon swallowed by the dark.

"Tristan—"

"I'll be careful."

He didn't give her any more time to argue. Shrugging one of the rucksacks onto his back, he started walking into the tunnel, the beam dancing and weaving round every curve of the arched ceiling, every dark corner near the ground. Dylan watched too, her eyes hunting for the darting, whirling mass of a wraith, but as Tristan walked further away from her, all the torch did was create more shadows. It was impossible to see.

Wrapping her arms around herself, she turned and stared out across the bleak landscape. The railway tracks cut a straight line across the heather to the horizon, and on either side low hills rose and fell away from her. Unlike in the wasteland, here she could make out the odd farm house or country cottage and further on, the blurred glow of a small town. It was an uninviting setting, but not an empty one.

It started to rain, droplets saturating her hair. Her jacket – new, but still inexpensive – wasn't as waterproof as the label had claimed and she felt the damp chill on her shoulders. She could step back into the shelter of the tunnel, but she found it preferable just to get wet. She didn't intend to spend longer than necessary in there when the time came.

She blew out a breath. She felt sick, agitated – and it wasn't just because Tristan was steadily increasing the distance between them. No, it was just *this place*. God, it gave her the creeps. If Tristan's plan to collapse the tunnel in the wasteland worked, she was never coming here ever again.

Ever.

"Dylan!" A yell, but he didn't sound alarmed or worried.

She spun around, directed the torch beam down the length of the tunnel.

"Yeah?"

"It's safe. Can you bring the other bag?"

Right. For some reason she thought he would've come back to collect her, but that was stupid. And unnecessary. He'd checked the tunnel, for goodness sake. There were no wraiths; there was no danger.

"Get a grip," Dylan muttered to herself.

Hiking the other bag up onto her shoulder, she started down the tunnel.

It didn't take long, just ten or so steps, before its claustrophobic tightness wiped out all sound from outside. The gentle whisper of the wind, the occasional caw of a bird. The distant thrum of traffic driving along the road. It was all deadened in here. There was only the sound of her breath, quick and nervous, the rustle of her jacket and the crunch of stones shifting under her feet. The scuttling and scratching of things – rats, mice, *bats* – shying away from her presence.

It took far too long and no time at all to reach Tristan's side. He was down on his haunches, torch propped up on a sleeper, rummaging in his bag.

"Here?" Dylan asked, confused.

This wasn't the crash site. That was at least a hundred feet away.

"This is as close as I want you to get," Tristan said. "Last time, you told me you felt a pull. Like something was trying to haul you back to the wasteland. Do you feel it now?"

Dylan thought about it, concentrating on her chest, her heart. It was beating faster than normal, and she felt a strange compulsion to keep moving, but not that terrifying yanking sensation.

"No," she said. "I'm OK here."

"Good." He stood up, a curl of rope in his hand. "I'm going to tie one end to the line here. If it goes really taut, or I start yanking on it, pull. As hard as you can. But *don't*," he stepped forward, ducking down to stare into her eyes, "go past this point. Got it?"

Dylan nodded obediently. Of course, if it came down to it,

she would follow the rope through the portal until she found Tristan at the end of it, but there was no need to tell him that.

Tristan finished tying the rope around his waist, then bent and double-knotted the other end to a metal coupling, yanking to make sure it was firmly attached. As soon as he let go and stood up, Dylan went to hold on to the rope where it met the metal.

"You don't need to do that," Tristan told her. "Wait until you see me yanking on it."

"I want to hold it," Dylan confessed. "I'll be able to feel you moving, it'll make me feel better."

"All right." Tristan hiked both bags up over one shoulder, leaving his other hand free to hold the heavy torch. He began to walk away, but turned back suddenly, stepping close and pressing a quick but firm kiss against her lips. "I'll be back before you know it."

TWENTY-SIX

It will be fine, Tristan thought. It *will* be fine.

Still, walking away from Dylan took a monumental effort. He didn't want to take her into the wasteland with him – nothing in this life or the next could make him do that – but he didn't like her out of his sight when he knew there were wraiths around.

He had no idea what was going to happen to them and the weird connection they shared when he slipped into the wasteland, but he'd committed to this plan now, and he needed to see it through. There was nothing else to be done, not if he wanted to appease the Inquisitor and save both their lives.

He was angry with himself – incredibly angry. If he'd just done the decent thing and delivered Dylan across the wasteland and to the line with cold detachment like he was supposed to, like he always did, then she'd be safe there now. Dead, but safe. He'd never have known her smiles, her gentle touch and the kisses that made him feel like he was drowning and flying all at once, but that wasn't important. He loved her, and so he should have made her safe, not tried to take more than he was ever meant to have. A life, a soul to love.

But there was no turning back the clock. All he could do was try to fix the mess he'd made, and hope he and Dylan came out the other side alive.

Despite his determination, he still paused on the threshold of the wasteland. What if, once he went through, he was torn apart from Dylan, linked to a new soul, thrown to another edge of the wasteland, never to find the tunnel again? What would happen to Dylan then?

What if, when he stepped through, he simply severed the link between them and killed them both?

There was no way to know. Taking a deep breath, he reached for the darker, colder atmosphere of the wasteland – and stepped into it.

Nothing happened.

That quick realisation had breath rushing from Tristan's lungs. He knew he was alive, still in Dylan's wasteland, and, as far as he could tell, that meant Dylan was fine too. Putting a hand down, he felt at the rope around his middle. It was an irrational thought, but he had the strangest feeling that the tether he'd created – the physical connection it made between him and Dylan – was preventing the debilitating effects of separation. He gave himself a moment to bask in relief before he got to work.

Moving just a couple of feet from the gateway, he dropped to his knees, threw the torch on the ground, and unzipped both bags. With cautious haste, he arranged the various bottles and wires around him within the torch's glow. He had only a rudimentary knowledge of what he was attempting, but hopefully Dove's instructions would be enough. The key was in initiating the chemical reaction, similar to dropping a Mentos in a bottle of Coke.

With agile but slightly shaking hands, he balanced the little tub of crystals above the container of liquid. He then set up a device similar to a mouse trap – once the timer counted down, it would spring open and tip the crystals in. And... kaboom.

When he had everything ready, he backed up very, very carefully and then grabbed the jerrycan of petrol. Taking great pains not to get any on himself, he doused the area around his little science experiment – the walls and the sleepers and everything in between – with gasoline. Then he sent up a prayer... and pressed the timer.

Thirty seconds. Twenty-nine. Twenty-eight.

Satisfied that the clock was working, Tristan turned and began hurrying towards the portal. He grinned, unable to believe how easy it had been... and a bare second later he felt the talons gripping his shoulders, shredding his jacket and piercing his skin.

A wraith.

Tristan's first thought wasn't a thought at all, more a paralysing eruption of panic. It shot through him like lightning, flooding him with adrenaline.

It was too late to stop the bomb – this wasn't a fancy professional job, it was held together with duct tape, and once he'd set the timer, there was no going back. He had to get the wraith off him *now*.

He whirled, trying to get the creature in front of him, but its claws were embedded in his clothes, his flesh, and it turned with him, trying to tip him off balance. Snarling with frustration and anger, Tristan reached up to grab at its talons, planning to yank it down so that he could get to its vulnerable eyes, its neck. But he couldn't get any grip at all. His hands passed right through the wraith's savaging claws as if – as if he was human. A soul in the wasteland, rather than a ferryman.

The panic surged back, stronger than ever. He knew that an ordinary soul had no way to fight off a wraith. Without their ferryman, it was inevitable that they would be dragged down beneath the ground, their essence consumed until they became another one of these loathsome, mindless creatures. The only remote possibility of survival was escape.

Logically, his brain knew that. But unadulterated fear had made his body take over, and it wasn't listening. He thrashed and twisted, writhed and wrestled, trying desperately to keep his feet so that the thing couldn't drag him under. How many seconds were left? Twenty? Fifteen?

Ten?

He couldn't dislodge the wraith. He couldn't even *touch* it. He'd still be struggling here when the world – the tunnel – exploded. If that didn't kill him, the fire would.

An almighty yank around his middle sent him to his knees. He sprawled across the gravel, his elbow connecting with a sleeper in a shock of pain. Above him the wraith gave a gleeful cackle of joy and swooped, punching straight through his stomach. The sensation made him contract every muscle, forcing the breath from his lungs. Hauling in more air, he tried to get his hands and feet under him, the sharp stones cutting into his palms, but the wraith had a hold of him again and was pulling, pulling, pulling. The ground beneath him seemed to be melting, like thick treacle. It was all Tristan could do to lift a hand, shift a knee forward...

He was sinking.

He was going to die.

The yank came again, dragging him forwards, hauling him up. It freed him for a blissful moment, but the wraith worked its teeth into him, pulling him back. Under.

Another yank. Then another. Tristan felt like he was being broken in half. Blasting forward in a jolt, he felt the air change as he passed through the hole they'd torn in the veil.

He lay there for the briefest instant, stunned, before his brain registered the furious, frenzied shrieking of the wraith behind him. It had piggy-backed across with him, talons sunk into Tristan's side. He was no longer in the wasteland – he could touch it now. He got his arms beneath him, lifted up... and a burst of sound slammed him flat again.

The bomb.

There was a blaze of light as flame licked through the portal, singeing the hair on Tristan's head, then there was utter darkness. Utter silence. Tristan held still, hardly daring to move.

"Tristan!" His name echoed around the tunnel. "Oh my God, Tristan, are you all right?"

Jerking his head up he stared, speechless, at the outline of the girl standing in front of him, the tunnel mouth in the background turning her into nothing more than a silhouette.

Still, there was no mistaking who it was.

"Susanna," he croaked. "You're here."

TWENTY-SEVEN

Dylan stood motionless in the dark of the train tunnel. Beside her, a boy who looked about the same age as Tristan shifted and fidgeted, but she ignored him. Her gaze was fixed dead ahead, where Tristan, *her* Tristan, was staring, mouth agape, at a pretty, dark-haired girl.

The rope that tethered them hung loosely in her hands, but Dylan hadn't been the one to haul Tristan back to safety. She'd tried – God, she'd tried – but it had been ripping through her grip, skinning the palms of her hands. She'd been about to lose control of it when she was roughly shouldered aside and the girl – Susanna – took a much firmer, stronger hold and yanked Tristan back through. Just in time.

They were lucky. A second later, and Dylan would have lost him. A second later, and Tristan would have been caught in the blast. But watching the way the two of them were gazing at each other now, Dylan didn't feel very lucky.

"Tristan?" she called hesitantly.

She wanted an explanation. She wanted to get between him and the girl.

"Stop!" Tristan shouted. "There's a wraith!"

Dylan planted her feet, flicking her torch all over the tunnel. "Where?"

She hadn't seen anything fly past her but then… she'd been distracted.

"It's here." The cause of her distraction took a step to the left and kicked at something on the dirt and gravel floor. Her voice was low and accentless, but strangely compelling. "It's dead."

Tristan sighed and leant against the wall of the tunnel. "It must have got caught by the blast. Here," he gestured to a thick length of metal by Dylan's feet. "Pass me that."

She handed it to him wordlessly and, after climbing stiffly to his feet, Tristan lifted the hunk of steel above his head and smashed down with all his strength. There was no blood, but wisps started to appear above the two lifeless hunks. The four of them stepped back while the wraith disintegrated into a cloud of back poison.

There were a million questions running through Dylan's head as she watched Tristan and the girl standing over the wraith, but first she had to check… "Did it work, Tristan?"

"I don't know." Tristan turned, facing the space where the tear was. Dylan noticed he was avoiding Susanna's gaze. "One way to find out."

Lifting both hands up, he felt for a change in the air, the subtle difference that denoted a move into the wasteland. For two, three cautious steps, he met with nothing. Nothing at all.

The portal to the wasteland had closed.

"I think we've done it!" Tristan said, continuing to poke and prod at the impenetrable doorway.

"Really?" Dylan stepped forward eagerly, but Tristan held out a hand to keep her back. "It's OK – I don't feel it like I did before. There's no pull." She came forward until she stood shoulder to shoulder with him, feeling for the veil herself. When she was done, she dropped her hand and very deliberately intertwined her fingers with his.

She took a moment to glance back and take in Susanna's reaction. The tunnel was too dark to really see, but was that a hint of consternation on her face? Of jealousy?

Jack's face, at least, was utterly blank. Uninterested. He stood beside Susanna, but somehow also apart. Dylan turned back to Tristan.

"We did it," she whispered.

Tristan let go of her hand and went to his waist, where he began to work at the tight knot of rope around his middle. Dylan saw his fingers tremble slightly as he worked at the tangled mass. It had saved his life. If it hadn't been tied around him...

The same thought seemed to occur to Tristan. He gave up untying himself and dragged her into a tight embrace.

"Tristan?" Dylan spoke tentatively, one of her hands stroking through the hair at the nape of his neck. "Who is—"

"You saved me," he mumbled, his face buried in her neck. "If you hadn't pulled on the rope, the wraith would have had me. I couldn't fight it."

"You would have." Dylan tried to reassure him, but a hard lump set in her throat. He didn't know. He didn't know that she wasn't the one who managed to yank him to safety. She could feel Susanna's eyes on her – along with the inexplicable silence between this new girl and Tristan, even though they clearly knew each other.

"No," Tristan denied. "I couldn't get a hold of the wraith. And there were only seconds left on the bomb. If you hadn't pulled me through, Dylan, if you—"

"It wasn't me." The truth came blurting out even though she tried to hold it in. "I didn't save you."

Tristan stiffened for a moment in her arms before drawing back. "What?"

"I didn't save you," Dylan repeated. "It was her." The words tasted like ash in her mouth. "Susanna was the one to pull you back through."

Detangling himself from Dylan, Tristan turned to Susanna. His real saviour. Then he repeated exactly what he'd said before, his voice holding the same stunned shock.

"Susanna. You're here."

Shock, Dylan thought, and something more.

"Let's get out of the tunnel," Tristan said. "Then we'll talk."

TWENTY-EIGHT

The human girl stayed close to Tristan as he led them out of the tunnel. Susanna watched them, noticing the tight grip she had on his hand, the quick, discreet glances she kept shooting back at her. Behind her, Jack tripped along. It wasn't like him to be so quiet, to let someone else take charge. It probably wouldn't last very long.

The lashing rain had stopped. Now the sky hung low and angry. Susanna glanced up at it as they stepped out from beneath the arched opening to the tunnel – and promptly walked straight into the broad strength of Tristan's back.

"Oof! Sorry," she mumbled, bouncing back unsteadily into the path of Jack, who shifted to avoid her rather than catch her. Instead, it was Tristan who shot out an arm to prevent her falling. His grip was strong, the heat of his hand soaking through the damp woollen fabric of the cardigan she wore.

It was the first time he'd ever touched her.

Though they'd known each other for centuries, he'd never, ever touched her.

If the same thought occurred to Tristan, she couldn't read it in his eyes. Or his face. Whatever he was thinking or feeling about discovering her here, in the real world, with him, was completely hidden.

When he was sure she had her balance, he let her go.

"Are you all right?" he asked.

Mutely, she nodded. Opened her mouth, then closed it again. What to say? Every moment, every late-night encounter they'd shared, gazing out at the wasteland, or up at the stars, watching the wraiths gather, had been shared in silence. There had been no need for words.

She needed words now. "Yes, thank you."

"Tristan." The girl standing beside Tristan was still clinging to him like a limpet. Something passed between them and Tristan turned back to Susanna.

"This is Dylan," he told Susanna. "She is—"

"The soul you used to cross over," Susanna finished for him. "I know, I saw."

"I didn't *use* her," Tristan scowled. "We did it together."

"So you're a ferryman too – like him?" Dylan chipped in.

"Dylan," Tristan said. "This is Susanna. Yes, she's another ferryman." Tristan's eyes flicked over to Jack and then back to Susanna, one eyebrow raised in a silent question.

"This is Jack," Susanna offered.

"Hi." Dylan offered him a tentative smile and Jack gave her a brief chin jerk in response. His eyes were watchful, wary, and mostly focussed on Tristan.

Tristan dismissed Jack with the tiniest shrug of one shoulder and then turned back to Susanna, piercing her. "What are you doing here?"

Susanna startled, shocked by the question, though she supposed she should have expected it.

I came to be with you.

The words were on the tip of her tongue, but they wouldn't come out. This wasn't going at all like she planned. In her mind, Tristan was thrilled to see her, hugging her and smiling.

He wanted to take her under his wing, show her this new world where they could actually live; where they could actually have a life.

Instead, she could feel the disapproval – disappointment? – rolling off Tristan in waves. And the frostiness from his soul was palpable. Susanna chewed on her lip.

It was Jack who answered.

"We're stuck together," he said, speaking fast. "Since we came back through, we can't go more than ten metres from each other. Susanna said you'd know how to fix it." He stared hard at Tristan. "Do you?"

"No." Tristan shook his head. "The same thing happened to us. Every time we separate, it's like Dylan's dying all over again. Only this time, I feel it too."

"You haven't figured out how to cut it?" Jack's temper was rising.

"No," Tristan repeated, eyes narrowing on Jack, "I haven't."

Susanna's nerves skittered to life at the power, the menace, in Tristan's tone. But in typical Jack style, he either didn't notice it, or blithely ignored it. He rounded on Susanna.

"You told me!" he snapped. "You told me he'd be able to help! But that was just another lie. You don't have a clue, do you?" Jack was getting into full rant mode, but this time, Susanna didn't feel scared. Out of the corner of her eye, she saw Tristan take his hand from Dylan's and shift his body weight. Still, Jack went on. "Well, you know what? You're the one who doesn't belong here! If I just get rid of you—"

Whatever threat Jack had been about to deliver was silenced as Tristan grabbed him by the collar of his jacket and propelled him backwards until his shoulders smacked off the stone edge of the cliff beside the tunnel mouth.

"Stop," he snarled. "Not another word."

"Get off me!" Jack tried to fight, to rip Tristan's grip from his jacket, but he couldn't. "Get your bloody hands off me!"

"You should be dead," Tristan hissed. "Do you get that? You should be dead. And if you were really lucky you'd be across the wasteland by now. If not, you'd be one of the wraiths. Did you see them in the wasteland? Do you know what they are? They're souls who were too stupid to keep their traps shut and do what they were told." Pulling back, Tristan let go of Jack's jacket.

To Susanna's astonishment, Jack stayed exactly where he was. Even more shockingly, he stayed silent.

"You'd be a wraith, I reckon," Tristan went on. "You've got that look about you. You think you know best, but guess what? In the wasteland, we know best. You're not dead, are you?" He waited until Jack gave a tiny shake of his head. "Be grateful, then. Got it?"

Without waiting for an answer, Tristan turned his back on Jack. When Jack didn't react, didn't move a muscle, Susanna released the breath she'd been holding. She watched as Tristan went straight back to his soul and enfolded her in his arms.

"We don't know how to break the soul bond, Susanna," he said, "but the Inquisitor might."

"The Inquisitor?" she managed to ask. "Who the hell is that?"

"It's the reason we're here," Tristan replied. "It's from the wasteland. Two days ago it cornered us, told me it was going to pass judgement on me. It's got powers, strong ones. It had me frozen in place. I couldn't move, couldn't even speak unless it let me." At that, Susanna felt icy dread grip her own gut. Anything that frightened Tristan was something to be terrified of. "It made a deal with us, told me that if we want to stay we need to undo the damage we caused crossing over. Close the hole, kill the wraith that came through." Tristan paused. "That's how you came through, right? You saw me go – and followed me?"

No. That was the truthful answer. No, Susanna had found a soul and convinced him to fall back into his dead body and – according to Tristan – ripped her own hole in the veil between the wasteland and the real world.

Which meant an Inquisitor thing might be hunting for her now, too.

She needed to tell Tristan. Tell him and ask for his help. He'd closed theirs; he could close hers too, or at least tell her how it was done. Susanna opened her mouth to confess, but she couldn't do it. It just wouldn't come out.

She didn't want to be a burden to Tristan. She didn't want to admit to the deceit, the manipulation she'd had to do to convince a soul to take her back. If Tristan believed she'd merely followed him through, taken the soul she had with her at the time...

That didn't seem so bad.

That didn't seem so devious.

Glancing back, she saw Jack was ignoring them, staring off across the countryside, fuming. Seething over his damaged pride. She turned back, gave Tristan her most winning smile, the one she reserved for the trickiest of souls.

"Yes," she lied. "I saw you go and followed." She took a deep breath. "I wanted a chance at life too – and so did Jack of course. He was too young to go."

Tristan nodded – his face hard to read again.

"You said you had to kill a wraith," Susanna continued. "That wraith?" She pointed back into the tunnel.

"No," Dylan spoke up this time. "We think there might be more, because the gap has been open a while. One of them murdered four men in the train tunnel days ago. We saw it on the news."

"But," Susanna shook her head. "They could be anywhere by now. How on earth are you meant to find them?"

"We will," Tristan said, squeezing Dylan, who had paled considerably. "We will because we have to. I can sense them if we get close, so we just have to figure out where to look."

"Why?" Jack asked, daring to step back into the circle, although he deliberately kept his distance from Tristan. "What happens if you don't?"

Dylan's words were soft, haunted. "The Inquisitor will kill us both."

Dylan's words hit Susanna as a punch to the stomach. What had she done? Followed Tristan to the same awful fate, and doomed Jack's life too, in the process. She couldn't tell them the truth now – but she could learn from Tristan. And save his life in the process.

"We'll help you," she stuttered. "Come with us – we've got a car. We'll find your wraiths and kill them together."

TWENTY-NINE

As Susanna and Jack led them to the car, Dylan pulled at Tristan's arm to slow him down. She could tell he didn't want to talk, but she had to know.

"Tristan—"

"Yeah?" he mumbled, his voice rough with worry.

"Who is she?" Dylan asked.

"You know who she is," Tristan said, lifting his shoulders in a small shrug. "A ferryman."

"You know what I mean, Tristan. Who is she – to you?"

"We worked together," he offered, but Dylan shook her head.

"You work alone," she said. "That's what you told me. Only ever meeting souls, and transporting them through the wasteland." She swallowed past the glass that had lodged in her throat. "So how do you know her? Is she – are you and her—"

"Me and her?" Tristan leaned closer, frowning. "There's no me and her. Past tense or present. Each ferryman works alone, but we have set routes, and hers was alongside mine. When our souls' journeys overlapped, we'd see each other and we'd know we weren't quite so alone. That's all." He gave Dylan a sympathetic smile and reached out to hold her hand.

"Don't." Dylan shifted back out of easy reach, putting her hands up to ward him off. "Don't make me out to be some jealous

215

girlfriend." OK, she was. But that wasn't all there was to this. She kept her voice low. "Why didn't you tell me about her?"

Tristan sighed. "I know," he said. "I'm sorry."

Which part are you sorry about? Dylan waited but Tristan didn't say anything more. "You knew she was here, didn't you? You didn't seem surprised she'd crossed over."

She'd intended to stay calm and rational about things. But then, she'd never been calm or rational where Tristan was concerned, not even in the beginning – when his surly attitude had driven her nuts – and she just couldn't keep the accusation out of her voice.

Dylan watched Tristan's reaction carefully. She could see his face working. Whatever expression he was going for – nonchalance? innocence? – it wasn't working. He just looked guilty.

"I knew," he admitted. "I sensed her as soon as she came through. A few days ago."

"A few *days* ago?"

"Dylan, that's the thing. I knew it was a ferryman – it felt different to when the Inquisitor was watching us. It wasn't malevolent, so I didn't want to worry you. It was more like a resonance. A harmony."

Dylan didn't like the sound of that. Not one bit. "Could you tell it was Susanna? Before you saw her, I mean."

"Yes," Tristan said. "I recognised her straight away. I didn't know why she was here, but I knew it was her."

It all came back to that, for Dylan. He'd lied to her – an omission was as bad as a lie. It felt like a betrayal. Like he didn't trust her. That hurt.

"And you chose not to tell me?" That, that was the real problem. If Susanna was nothing to him, why not tell her? Another ferryman had crossed over! Of course she should have known about it!

"I don't know." Tristan fixed his eyes forward to where Susanna and Jack were reaching the car.

"You don't know," Dylan echoed. She stared at him, hard, waiting for more than that non-answer.

"I just…" he gave another shrug, one that made Dylan want to strangle him. "What with everything that had happened. Your injury, the murders, the wraith at the tunnel, your dad… I just, I just figured you had enough to worry about."

It was a good answer, sensible. Rational. But—

"You should have told me," Dylan said quietly. "After you lied about the wraiths, and then wouldn't talk about it when you were feeling watched… I can't *believe* you would do this to me again!" Her voice raised with every accusation, so much so that Susanna turned to look at them as she and Jack waited.

Tristan blew out a breath through his nose, then acceded the point with a sharp jerk of his chin. "I'm sorry," he whispered. "I know I've said it before. I know I promised I wouldn't keep things from you." He closed his eyes and shook his head, a tiny gesture. "It was stupid." Another tiny gesture, this time a grin, there and gone in a flash. "I'm used to operating on my own. Making decisions alone. I'm not used to opening up to someone else. This is new to me – I'm not very good at it yet, but I want to be, Dylan."

Dylan believed it; his sincerity, the regret in his eyes, was impossible to doubt. But the hurt of another betrayal was too raw, and they were about to get in a car with the girl he had lied about – the girl he had shared his whole life with, who knew what it was like to be…

The only other ferryman in the whole world.

THIRTY

It didn't take long for Dylan to realise Jack's car wasn't exactly Jack's car. She watched him fiddling about under the dash, hot-wiring it.

But getting in a stolen car was the least of her worries. She was finding it hard to breathe past the cold, hard lump in her chest. Every time Susanna spoke to Tristan, every warm look she sent his way, made that lump throb in a painful spasm.

It felt like her heart was breaking, but with the Inquisitor's deadline hanging over their heads, and the wraiths still out there, getting hungrier with every moment that passed, she had to swallow it back. She had to.

She could fall apart later. Right now, they had wraiths to kill.

They set off, Dylan in the passenger seat while Jack drove. Tristan and Susanna sat in the back, their eyes closed, concentrating. Apart from a slight frown furrowing Susanna's forehead, their faces were expressionless, which was good – because they were *holding hands*.

Tristan and Susanna could just barely feel the presence of the wraith, the presence of evil, and they'd discovered that their sense of it was amplified if they were touching. The discussion about how to find the wraiths had been awkward for everyone, but Dylan had a sense that Susanna had enjoyed that particular discovery. Especially now they were squashed together in the back seat, fingers entwined, while Dylan and Jack tried to navigate with directions as vague and unhelpful as "north", "that way" and "over there". Dylan tried to keep her gaze ahead, but she couldn't resist turning every ten seconds – checking to see if they'd shifted any closer, checking for signs that they were enjoying the closeness – because Dylan certainly wasn't.

Eventually, Jack drove them into a village called Bridge of Allan, and Tristan snapped his eyes open. Gaze snagging with Dylan's, the first thing he did was take his hand from Susanna's. Good. Dylan watched him as he looked around them, taking in the location.

"This is it," he said. "I can feel the wraith is close by even on my own."

"Me too," Susanna agreed.

Teacher's pet.

Jack parked in front of a café, the outside seating area deserted, tables filled with puddles of rainwater. Through the steamed-up windows, Dylan could see clusters of what looked like University of Stirling students staring at their laptops, oblivious to this carload and their deadly task.

"Do you know exactly where it is?" Dylan asked Tristan, sitting forward in her seat so that she could pull off her jacket.

"No," Tristan shook his head. "We'll keep searching. It can't come out during the day of course, so it will have found somewhere safe to hide. Like a cave or a drain or something like that."

"Somewhere dark and creepy, you mean?"

"Exactly that. The closer we get to it, the easier it should be to find." Tristan turned to Susanna. "Like when you were searching for me."

"Brilliant." This time Dylan didn't bother to disguise her caustic tone. "Where do you suggest we start?"

"Those woods." Tristan nodded to a patch of evergreens, rising moodily up the hill that hid the University of Stirling campus from their view. "I can sense darkness coming from there."

"Pain and death," Susanna agreed. "And hunger. We need to move fast."

"Yes, we know." Dylan took a deep breath. "Lead on, Macduff."

Tristan sent her a confused look, but he started walking, and Dylan and Susanna plodded along in the rain behind him. Jack took up the rear.

It took less than ten minutes to reach the wooded area. Tristan and Susanna climbed over the waist-high wire fence at once, but Dylan paused. She really, really didn't want to go in there. Into the dark, where shadows stretched out like reaching fingers and roots rose up out of the ground to trip her, bring her to her knees. Oh yes, and where a wraith was probably hiding, hungry to feast on human prey.

If it wasn't for the sight of Tristan and Susanna walking away from her, shoulder to shoulder, looking like a pair, a couple, she might have stayed there. But as she watched, Susanna turned to say something to Tristan, and he crooked his head and smiled.

"Right," Dylan mumbled under her breath, and scrambled over. Jack followed. Rushing a little, she strode ahead of him until she was just a step behind Susanna and Tristan.

"Remember how I told you in the wasteland that I hated hiking?" Dylan huffed, out of breath after just a minute or so of following the two ferrymen uphill. "And hills?"

Tristan grunted. Turned to flash her a quick, sympathetic look.

"Well, it's still true. Know what else I hate?" She swiped at a low-hanging hank of Douglas fir. "Trees! And mud. And rain. Nature," she finished, her trainer squelching into the boggy ground.

"I'm sorry," Tristan replied, turning to walk backwards, his feet annoyingly confident and secure on the rough terrain. "If I could, I'd leave you down in the town. Nice and warm in a café, with cake."

That sounded unbelievably good at that moment. It didn't matter that Dylan was literally tied to Tristan's side, though. She wouldn't have let him leave her behind anyway – not with Susanna.

"After," she told him. "You can buy me cake after. A big slice."

Of course, Tristan didn't actually have any money of his own, so it would be Dylan paying with her rapidly decreasing funds, but it's the thought that counts.

"Promise," Tristan told her. "Now… shush! This wraith will be a lot easier to deal with if we can take it by surprise."

Dylan did as she was told, though it smarted to be told off in front of Susanna. For ten, then fifteen minutes, they traipsed about the woods in silence.

Between the heavy cloud cover and the thick overhang of the trees, the light was dimming fast. That wasn't good – if wraiths were here, they would wake soon…

"Tristan," she whimpered. "It's getting dark. Maybe we should just come back tomorrow."

Never mind that they were going to be in almighty trouble for skipping school and likely grounded for eternity. The Inquisitor could fight it out with Joan over who had the right to damn their immortal souls.

Dylan's money was on Joan.

"Tristan." She stumbled over a thick tree root.

"Shhhh!" He stopped dead, held out a hand for silence. Hurrying the last few paces, Dylan stopped just behind him, next to Susanna, and peered over his shoulder.

A leaf-covered mound, the front face oddly made of brick

with an entrance built into it, no more than a metre high. The door was broken, the rotten wood hanging at a drunken angle. It looked like a bird hide, or maybe an old bomb shelter.

"You think it's in there?" Dylan breathed.

"Yes," Susanna whispered. "It's practically pulsing." She gave a tiny, delicate shudder.

"What do we do?"

"You go and stand over there. With Jack." Tristan nodded with his head towards an oak tree just to the left of the bunker. "I'll go in and see if the wraith's there. Susanna, you wait here and if it gets past me, grab it!"

"Wait! What?" Dylan stepped in front of Susanna. "I'll do that."

"No," Tristan shook his head and gave Dylan's shoulder a gentle push, urging her back. "Susanna's used to dealing with the wraiths. She can do it."

"Tristan!"

"I'm not arguing, Dylan. Go and stand over with Jack."

"But—"

"Shhh!" Susanna's hiss cut across their argument and Dylan turned to her, ready to tell her to mind her own business, when she heard it. A thin, high-pitched wail. The wraith was awake.

It knew they were there.

"Susanna, are you ready?" Tristan asked.

"I'm ready." The ferryman gave a tight nod, her face set, composed.

"Tristan, let me help, please!" Dylan gave it one last try, grabbing Tristan's arm.

"I can't," Tristan told her. "I won't be able to concentrate if I think you're in danger. Please, Dylan, do this. For me." He lifted her hand from his arm and gave it a squeeze.

This time Dylan shifted over towards the tree. From her

reluctant point of safety, she watched him creep towards the opening and then, without a moment's hesitation, slink inside.

Susanna stood guard. Though Dylan hated to admit it, taking in the girl's crouch, the way her hands were lifted, ready, she looked like she knew what she was doing. Like she could handle anything that came out of the little hut.

Of course she would be brave as well as pretty.

As soon as Tristan was out of sight, Dylan started casting about for a weapon of her own. Bending over, she wrapped her fingers round a thick length of fallen wood about the size of a baseball bat. It felt solid in her grip. Satisfied with her makeshift weapon, Dylan hurried over and took up position… right behind Susanna.

Just in case.

Glancing over her shoulder, she looked at Jack. He stood as far away as possible. Safe, and unconcerned.

Dylan's attention was ripped from Jack when a sudden commotion erupted from inside the bunker. The sounds of banging and scraping echoed in the quiet of the wood. Dylan gritted her teeth and resisted the impulse to call out – the last thing he needed was for her to distract him. Instead, she tightened her grip on the branch and shifted her stance a little, balancing on the balls of her feet.

A snarl escaped the half-open door, like an angry cat. Only bigger, scarier. A thump followed, and a clatter, like something falling over. Dylan wished she could see what was happening inside, but she didn't dare release her hold on her club to yank the door wide.

A second later, she was very glad she hadn't. The door shoved open of its own accord. Or, more accurately, to free the screaming wraith who zig-zagged wildly out of the opening. Even though she'd been ready, Susanna started, jerked slightly back – and it skirted right past her. She reached out for it, twisting desperately, but it ghosted through her fingers.

Dylan cried out a warning a second too late. Then, realising she was the next obstacle in the wraith's path, she gathered herself… and swung.

Thwack.

Her bat connected solidly and the wraith crashed to the ground several feet away. It didn't stay, though. After a bare instant to gather itself, it launched skyward again, claws extended. Adjusting her grip, Dylan swung again. This time, she missed.

The wraith dived under her arcing arms, talons fixing themselves to the sodden material of her jacket. Dylan felt the fabric tear and rip, but long and wickedly sharp as the wraith's claws were, they couldn't penetrate all of her layers. Still, she felt the pressure of the needle-like tips against the vulnerable flesh of her abdomen.

Letting go of the branch with one hand, she reached down and grabbed at the wraith. It felt… revolting. It had a wispy coat of what appeared to be tattered scraps of black cloth, but beneath that its skin had the texture of raw meat, cold and wet. Dylan tried not to focus on that, tightening her grip, nails digging in. She tried to wrench it away, but its hold was too strong. It bucked and writhed against her, its head whipping this way and that, gaping jaws straining to slash at her with misaligned and jagged teeth.

It would have gotten her, would have snapped its jaws shut around her wrist, if Tristan hadn't appeared at her side. He grabbed it round the neck, hauling it to the ground. He pinned the wraith with one firm hand and shifted his body out of the way.

"Now!" he shouted. "Dylan, smash it!"

Taking the time to draw in one deep breath, Dylan lifted her bat above her head and brought it down with all her strength. One, two, three times. After that, Tristan pulled his hand away, but Dylan continued to pound the thing. She might have gone on hitting it indefinitely, but Tristan caught hold of one of her wrists.

"That's enough," he said softly. "It's dead."

It was. Dead, dead, dead. Dylan stared down at the mulch that was left of it, breathing hard. Before her eyes, it started to melt into vapour. She'd killed it.

Dropping the branch, she wrapped her hands over her mouth, shocked. A sob escaped.

"It's all right," Tristan wrapped her in his arms, guiding her a few feet away from the wraith's smoking body. "It's OK."

"I'm sorry." Susanna's voice came from over Dylan's shoulder. "I reached for it, I should have had it, but—"

"It doesn't matter." Tristan gave Dylan another squeeze. "Dylan got it."

More than anything he could have said, those warm words allowed Dylan to get a handle on herself, to stop crying. She stayed put in Tristan's embrace, though. Letting him hold her, feeling his warmth; letting Susanna see he was hers.

"Although," Tristan murmured moments later, just to her, "You were supposed to be by the oak tree."

"And if I had been?" Dylan threw back, just as quietly.

"Then the wraith would have gotten away and we'd be in serious trouble," Tristan admitted, grinning at her ruefully. "I'm glad you can't listen to instructions."

Dylan held out for another few moments, then she had to smile back at him.

They'd done it. They'd closed the hole and killed the wraith. The Inquisitor no longer had any reason to punish them. To send them back. Stepping away from Tristan, Dylan drew in a deep breath. It felt like the first one she'd taken since… since the night of the dance.

THIRTY-ONE

Susanna watched Tristan and Dylan laughing and smiling as they celebrated their victory over the wraiths. They were free, but Susanna's task had only begun. How long before the Inquisitor appeared and gave her the same judgement? How long before innocent lives were taken by wraiths who found her gap in the veil?

God, she was so stupid. Why had she lied to Tristan? *Why?* She hadn't wanted to admit what she'd done, that she'd deliberately connected herself to a soul like Jack just to get to him. What must he think of her for turning up like this? If she told him the truth about how she'd gotten across, he'd hate her even more.

It had been such a relief, seeing him in the tunnel and then working with him to find the wraith, holding his hand and feeling that sense of oneness, of connection. It had been so much more than they'd ever shared in the wasteland, his body so close she was able to bask in his warmth.

But then he'd let her go – and it had been Dylan who'd helped him destroy the wraith. Who'd wrapped herself around him, held him in victory. The two of them were going to return to the life they were carving out. Susanna had no option but to try and fix her problem alone – well, with Jack. Which was worse than being alone.

This day had not ended the way she'd hoped.

They waded back down the soggy field towards Bridge of Allan, Susanna deep in thought about how to close the hole she and Jack had made in the veil. Until Tristan broke the silence:

"Wait." He stopped dead, causing Dylan to stumble. "Before we celebrate too much, we should check we can't feel any other wraiths around. I don't want to risk it."

Susanna's stomach dropped. She knew she couldn't find them without Tristan's help – they could only detect them together – but that meant…

"Susanna?" Tristan held out his hand, causing Dylan's face to flush red.

Susanna hesitated, her hands wavering by her sides. There was only one thing to do. She knew it, but that didn't make it any easier to accept. She had to come clean. She had to confess to Tristan what she'd done – and that she'd lied to him.

Tristan's hand was still held out for hers, his eyebrows raised in question, and she knew what would happen when they touched. He was never going to look at her the same way again, and Susanna wasn't sure which revelation would disappoint him the most.

Tears burned as she fought a desperate battle within herself, the cowardly, selfish side of her frantically trying to think of some way, any way, to fix this without losing part of Tristan – his respect, his approval, or, dare she hope it existed, his love.

But there wasn't a way.

"Tristan, there's something I need to tell you."

"What is it?" The look he gave her almost made Susanna change her mind, but she knew she couldn't do that. It was time to take responsibility for what she'd done.

"I lied to you." She paused, delaying her confession for just one more moment.

Tristan didn't fill the silence. At his shoulder, Dylan took a step forward, her expression wary.

"We didn't come through the hole you made. We made our own."

Dylan gasped, horror and shock clouding her face. But it was Tristan's reaction Susanna was waiting for – and he kept his expression blank. Unreadable.

"That's why you and Jack are bound together," he said slowly. "Because you used his body to cross over. If you'd just followed us…" He let that thought tail off and Susanna fought the urge to flinch when she realised how simple it could have been.

It was too late now. Far too late.

"Tristan, I'm sorry," Susanna said. "I shouldn't have lied to you," she said. "I just… I panicked. It was stupid, I know it was. And I'm so, so sorry.

"Another tear." Tristan's face was impassive.

"I'm so sorry."

"We'll have to close it, too. We promised the Inquisitor." He paused. "And Susanna, you can't stay in this realm. I don't know where else you can go, but you'll have to find somewhere."

"What?"

"We promised the Inquisitor that we would stop anyone else coming through the veil – not just killing wraiths, but making sure nothing else got through ever."

"I'll explain to the Inquisitor," Susanna swore, almost in tears at Tristan's cold reaction. He was angry at her, disappointed. And he wanted her gone. "I'll tell the Inquisitor that the second hole is my fault, that it wasn't anything to do with you, and we'll get rid of all the wraiths for good."

"I don't think it will matter to the Inquisitor," Tristan told her. "We made the bargain; it'll expect us to uphold it."

"But if I explain, if I take full responsibility—"

"You didn't meet it," Dylan interjected. She looked ashen now. "You don't know what it's like."

"Plus," Tristan added, "it'll know you can't take full responsibility. It's clearly my fault you're here." Underneath his anger, there was questioning in his eyes – or was it pity?

Susanna didn't know what to say. There didn't seem to be any way to fix this, to undo the damage she'd caused.

"Look," Tristan continued, "Let's at least work out what we're dealing with. Where did you come through?"

"The place where I died," Jack answered.

"And where was that?" The scathing edge to Tristan's voice made Susanna wince.

"An alleyway in a small town between here and Glasgow," she cut in, worried Jack would say something smart.

"Denny," Jack muttered.

"Right. Not too far. Let's see if we can sense any wraiths." Again, he held out his hands to her – and again Susanna just stared at them.

It was everything she had wanted – sliding her palms over Tristan's, feeling their fingers interlock – but not like this. Not with Tristan's censure so thick in the air it was hard to breathe.

Susanna shut her eyes and felt the tingles in her nerve endings as her abilities were amplified by Tristan's. Dreading what she'd find, she reached out… and immediately shrank back from the thick, oily chasm of darkness pulsing on the edge of her mind.

She opened her eyes as Tristan ripped his hands from hers, his face bone white.

"What's the matter? What is it?" Dylan took Tristan's elbow and he immediately dipped his head down to look at her.

"Wraiths have definitely made their way through," he said.

"Wraiths?" Dylan squeaked. "Plural?"

"A swarm," Susanna whispered.

"You said an alleyway," Tristan said, and Susanna understood what he was thinking.

"It was right in the middle of the town," she replied. Her hand crept up to cover her mouth. "If a swarm has come through there—" She was going to be sick. Images of the carnage a swarm could cause in a populated area flooded her mind. "What have I done?"

Jack only grunted in response to this news. Did he realise – or care – that these deaths were almost certainly their fault?

"Why did you do it?" Dylan asked, drawing Susanna's attention away from her soul. "Why did you follow us here?"

"I—" Susanna looked at Dylan's hand wrapped around Tristan's arm, his body turned unconsciously towards her. She just couldn't do it, she couldn't give voice to the secret dreams she'd created. Not when they were crashing down around her. "I made a mistake."

"Yeah, but—"

"Dylan." Tristan hushed her with a swipe of his thumb across her cheek. "It doesn't matter – it's done now."

He gave Susanna a sombre, thoughtful look. She wondered whether he'd guessed her reasons, and ducked her head, unable to hold his gaze.

"Tristan, what are we going to do?" Dylan asked quietly. "The Inquisitor's coming tomorrow."

"We need to fix it tonight," Tristan said.

Susanna gave a small nod so that he'd know that she was on board with the plan. Tristan gave her a tiny smile of acknowledgement, but she knew it didn't change things. It didn't absolve her.

"It'll be easier to deal with the hole in the veil while it's dark," he said. "Especially if it's in a public place."

"But the wraiths," Dylan reminded him. "Won't they be more dangerous at night?"

"We'll have to wait until daylight to deal with them," Tristan agreed.

"That's day three, Tristan," Dylan reminded him.

"I know." His expression was troubled, but he held her tighter. "It'll be OK, I promise. I'll take care of it."

Susanna wished it was her face he was holding, her he was comforting.

She needed Tristan to tell her that it was OK. She needed him to tell her he forgave her for how she'd used Jack, for how she'd lied to him.

But she knew she didn't deserve it.

THIRTY-TWO

They stood in a long street of flats and terraced houses. From the state of the scrubby footpaths and the crappy cars lining the road, it wasn't a well-off neighbourhood. Dylan eyed a group of young men lingering outside a newsagent. They reminded her of the idiots who went to her school – only these guys actually looked dangerous.

"I don't like this place," she whispered to Tristan.

"I know." He grabbed her hand comfortingly, though she was more reassured by the fact that he didn't look intimidated by the gang. Turning his back on them, he looked to Susanna. "Take us to where the tear is."

It only took them four minutes to walk there, and they could have found it without Susanna or Jack's guidance. The site of the stabbing was still liberally coated in police tape. The whole section of pavement around the alleyway and a bit of the road itself had been cordoned off.

"This is it," Jack growled, his lip curling up. He took another step closer, rage lighting a fire in his eyes, which quickly turned to alarm.

Susanna gasped as he tripped back several paces, clutching his chest.

"Don't get too close," Tristan murmured to him, although he didn't sound all that concerned.

Dylan knew it would meet the Inquisitor's demands if Jack's soul was dragged back into the wasteland.

"Do you feel anything?" Tristan squeezed Dylan's hand. She knew he was uncomfortable having her this close to any kind of opening to the world of the dead.

Dylan waited a moment, then shook her head. "Nothing."

"Really?" Tristan sounded surprised. "It must be because it isn't your wasteland." He brightened. "That's good." Tugging his backpack off his shoulder – hastily refilled again as the nearest Homebase was closing for the night – he looked up at Susanna. "We'll deal with this. You and Jack can keep a lookout for wraiths, scout the place to see if you can feel any nearby."

"I can help you," Susanna said faintly. She glanced at Jack then turned pleading eyes to Tristan. "I did last time."

"Dylan can help me," Tristan shot back. "She knows what to do."

"But last time—" Susanna began, and Dylan squirmed. Last time Dylan hadn't had the strength to yank Tristan back through the veil.

Last time, if Susanna hadn't turned up, she'd have lost him.

"Maybe Susanna should—"

"No." Tristan turned to her, his expression unyielding. "I only need you." Dylan's breath caught, happiness expanding in her chest, even though she knew Tristan was only talking about closing the tear in the veil. Still, Susanna looked stricken, as if she'd also taken two meanings from the words. Good.

"Come on, Susanna," Jack called, breaking the awkward silence. "Let's keep a lookout for the bloody wraiths."

After throwing a heavy glance at Tristan, Susanna hurried after Jack.

"Wow," Dylan muttered after they had moved further up the road. "They are *not* a good match."

"They're not," Tristan agreed. "He's not the right kind of soul for her, she should never have been given him to guide."

"Why was she?" Dylan wondered.

"Well," Tristan dropped his backpack on the ground and busied himself rummaging inside it. "Probably because the ferryman who should have been his guide wasn't there."

Dylan gasped. "You mean—"

"Yeah," Tristan said. "He'd have been mine, I'm sure of it." He sniffed and yanked out the rope that would act as their tether. "So that's another reason we need to help them."

"All right." Dylan paused, her mind still on Susanna. "I still don't understand… why didn't she tell us sooner? She saw what we were doing, and she came with us to hunt the wraith, for goodness' sake. Why wouldn't she say anything?"

"I don't know." Tristan shook his head, staring at the rope. He gritted his teeth, jaw tight. "I don't know why she'd lie to me. We've known each other for so long, I just assumed… I mean, when she said she saw me and you leaving, I just assumed she'd followed us through." He shook his head angrily. "It never even occurred to me that she'd work out how we did it. *I'm* not even sure how we did it. But I should have checked. Should have asked her more questions. That was stupid. Stupid!"

Dylan watched him tie the rope around his middle and then frowned. Something about his anger at being lied to reassured her, but she still wasn't satisfied with Susanna's motives.

She glanced around. While the street wasn't busy, there were cars flowing past at regular intervals and she could see a handful of people milling about. None of them were close, but if she could see them, they could see her. And Tristan.

Looking a lot like teenagers in an alleyway in the dark, up to no good.

"You're going to do it now?" Dylan asked uncertainly. "Anyone could see!"

"We only have one more night – the Inquisitor is coming tomorrow and we don't know when."

Dylan snapped her mouth closed.

"I know what I'm doing," he promised. "I won't take long."

"Tristan," Dylan said, considering the alley afresh. "Are you sure this is going to work? There's no roof to collapse down this time."

"I know," Tristan said, "But the walls are closer together, I'm hoping they'll topple in."

"And if they don't?"

"I don't know," Tristan said. "Let's just hope it works and save worrying about it until it doesn't."

He snuck under the cordon to attach the other end of the rope around a lamppost and then, nipping back under the tape, shouldered his bag.

"Wait!" Dylan yelped, stopping him short before he'd had the chance to take his first step. She ran forward quickly and hugged him, her arms encircling him awkwardly because of the bulging rucksack.

"It'll be fine, Dylan." Tristan smiled at her. "Remember," he pointed behind him, "the wraiths don't usually come this close to the veil anyway."

Only slightly reassured, given last time, Dylan let Tristan go. He gave her a brief grin, running the back of his knuckles down her left cheek, then he stepped into the alleyway... and disappeared.

Dylan stared at the spot where he vanished, at the rope that seemingly stretched into nothing. If anyone saw that...

She turned her back on the alleyway and eyed the street. This was so dodgy, they could easily be caught. Just feet away, traffic glided past. The group of loiterers at the shop were still in sight. Across the road, a pensioner was peering out a window, staring right at her. Discomfited, she smiled, but that only made the old woman's face sour even more and she dropped her blind with a snap. Dylan chewed on her lip anxiously. She hoped the old lady wouldn't call the police, report her for violating a crime scene.

How on earth would they explain themselves?

"Hurry up, Tristan."

She couldn't expect him to reappear any time soon, though. He'd only just gone through, and it was a pretty complicated operation.

Unsettled, Dylan glanced at her watch. It was just before 10 p.m. She wished she'd checked the time when Tristan went in, but it was too late to fix that now. He'd been gone for five minutes, maybe. Or was it even less than that?

How long did it take him at the tunnel? Dylan had no idea. It had felt like an eternity... and then the tugging and jerking of the rope had started and she hadn't thought about anything else other than getting Tristan back through the portal.

Tristan's rope was still lying relaxed and limp on the ground – so far so good. Blowing out a breath, she returned to monitoring the street. The little gang had broken up and three of them were headed her way.

Terrific.

They moseyed up the pavement, all swagger and confidence. Cheryl would be beside herself with glee in her situation, Dylan thought. These were the sort of idiots she drooled after. The kind of boys Dylan tried to avoid. Especially at life-or-death moments like this.

They had obviously registered her on their radar. A teenage girl, on her own at night; clearly not from around here. Dylan was aware that she probably looked as uncomfortable as she felt.

A prime target, in other words.

She repressed the urge to flee. To lead them away from Tristan. She had to be here, right *here*, in case she had to haul him back through to safety.

Damn it.

"Hurry up, Tristan," she mumbled again under her breath, bouncing lightly on her heels with agitation as she tried to will him to appear again in the alleyway. "Come on."

Still nothing, the rope limp – but a bark of laughter made her rip her head back round. God, they were getting close now. They couldn't continue down the road on this side, the pavement was blocked off. And they knew that, which meant they were heading for her.

For the second time that day, she felt herself looking for a weapon. Unless she planned to garrotte them with police tape, however, there was nothing to hand. She'd just have to talk to them, keep the peace, and then, when Tristan appeared out of thin air…

"Bloody hell," she said under her breath, trying hard to avoid their gazes. Fifteen metres. Ten.

Oh God. Oh God. Oh God.

"Hey gorgeous!" One of them – a skinny pale boy around seventeen or so, with a piercing in his right ear – grinned at her. It wasn't a friendly grin. It was more like the kind a cat gives a mouse – right before it eats it. "You all on your lonesome?"

Dylan opened her mouth to deny it – although right at this moment it was technically true – but nothing came out. Which was just as well, because a hand clamped down on her shoulder.

"You OK, Dyl?"

Dyl? Since when the hell was she Dyl? She didn't question it, though, because the three thugs in front of her were suddenly looking a little less confident, a little wary.

"I'm fine," she said, and tried to sound like she meant it. At her back, she could feel Tristan fumbling with the rope. He was jerking roughly at the tether, trying to get it undone before…

Oh.

An eruption of sound behind her. A wave of heat singeing her ears. Tristan pushed forward *towards* the boys and held her firmly.

The three thugs in front of her each wore identical – hysterical – expressions of shock and astonishment. They tripped backwards.

"Shit! Did you see that?"

"The alley just exploded!"

Recovered from their initial disbelief, they surged past Tristan and Dylan, intent on discovering the source of the explosion.

At the same time, Tristan started shepherding her away from the alley.

"Wait!" she hissed. "The bag."

"There's nothing important in it. Leave it."

"The police could—"

"There's nothing in it to identify us," Tristan said. "Let's just go."

As soon as they were beyond the line of sight of any witnesses on the street, Tristan broke out into a run, hauling Dylan along with him. She kept up for as long as she could before she had to stop.

"Give me a sec," she pleaded. "God, I'm so unfit."

"Come on, Dylan. Walk at least."

Panting, the cold air stabbing knives into her lungs, Dylan pushed herself to a limping half-jog.

"Now what?" she asked Tristan.

"Now," he said, closing his eyes to concentrate, "we find Susanna – and the wraiths."

THIRTY-THREE

"What does it feel like?" Jack asked. It was the first time he had shown an interest in the entire time Susanna had known him. Bizarrely, the thought made her smile, as did the feeling that Tristan was getting closer, which must have meant he and Dylan had succeeded.

"It's like a sticky, oily, grasping feeling. The closer we get, the stronger it is. We're close enough for me to feel them on my own." They'd been walking for less than ten minutes since they'd left Tristan and Dylan.

"They?"

"Yes, it feels like more than one. A lot more."

"And they're just hanging out in Denny?"

"It makes sense," she said, grimacing as she gazed about the street. "The wraiths haven't moved too far. Why would they, when there's so much fresh meat right here?"

Jack made a face and she knew it was because she was referring to people as 'fresh meat'. But that's what the wraiths did; that was what they were, when you came right down to it: cannibalistic souls. Normally Susanna tried to avoid thinking about that. Especially when, in the very near future, she was about to confront one. Or many. They were going to have a hell of a time dealing with them, even with the four of them – and two of them ferrymen – and she'd no idea how they were meant to do it without any witnesses seeing things they shouldn't.

She hoped Tristan had an idea about that, because she didn't.

God, she thought for the umpteenth time, this wasn't going *at all* the way she had planned.

She and Tristan were meant to be exploring this new world. Together. They were meant to be free of their old life, their old obligation. Free to just *be*.

Instead, she was still stuck with Jack, and Tristan was only helping her because he needed to clean up the mess she'd made. Not for her, but so that *Dylan* would be safe. The soul he was happy to be tied to. He'd come through the veil, through to the real world, to be with *her* – so she could live her life and he could live it with her. Susanna was so stupid!

Was there even a place for her here? *Any* sort of place, even just as Tristan's friend? She couldn't go back to the wasteland, go back to ferrying soul after underserving soul. She just couldn't.

"OK then," Jack jolted her out of her pity-party. "What do we do?"

"We're almost there, I'm sure of it – and when Tristan and Dylan get here we'll work out how to attack." Susanna scrubbed her hand across her cheeks and was relieved to find they were dry. "Just… be careful now it's dark. Look out for sheltered, creepy places."

"Like the bunker?"

"Kind of," Susanna nodded, "But a little bigger. And Jack? Be careful – every time you move away from the street lights you're more vulnerable. They don't like the light."

They checked the line of garages that ran along the back of the terrace, then gingerly lifted the lids on all the bins. Susanna even snuck into an abandoned ground-floor flat, disturbing a homeless man and a litter of cats.

Nothing. Without Tristan, Susanna felt disoriented. She could feel the wraiths' presence getting stronger, but she couldn't pinpoint them as easily on her own. She wasn't as sensitive, as strong, as the two of them were together.

She was beginning to feel stirrings of panic, when she heard Jack stifle a yell.

"Susanna!" Another gasp. "Over here!"

Bags of garden waste – the reason he'd come over for a second look – hid whatever it was he had found. Tall slatted fences on either side of the path made the space tighter, darker than the alley Jack had died in.

"What is it?" she asked, coming closer.

A foot. That's what she saw first. In a heavy-duty black boot, jeans overlapping the ankle. Another step revealed more. Blood stained the entire bottom half of the t-shirt he wore under a leather jacket. Horror gripped Susanna by the throat and she should have stepped away, but she had to see his face. Another step, and it came into view.

His features were screwed up, as if he'd been in agony when he died – and all because of her. Susanna's stomach lurched. She was about to throw up.

"Look at this," Jack crouched down, hunkering over the body. "Looks like someone's punched a hole right through his middle. Someone with a big fist."

"That's what wraiths do," Susanna rasped. "In the wasteland, they don't do this kind of damage. Here…"

"Shit," Jack whistled quietly. He glanced up at Susanna and for once she didn't see the surly, cocky teenager looking back at her. He was pale, a sheen of nervous sweat glistening on his upper lip.

"There's probably more," Susanna warned. "This would only be a meal for one wraith."

That made Jack blanch again.

"Come on," Susanna said, feeling, strangely, a little more in control. "There's nothing we can do for him." Backing out onto the main path, she peeked round the fence, into the house next door. She didn't see any faces peering back at her.

But she saw something much more disturbing than that.

Blood spatter. The room wasn't well lit, but she could just make out the splashes and sprays of red across the beige wall. Moving on silent feet, she ghosted up the steps of the house, pushing open the already ajar front door. There was silence inside.

More blood spatter decorated the hallway. That, and a body. Just like the body in the alleyway, this man looked like he had died a horrible, painful death. This time, it was much easier to see the injuries that had killed him.

This must have happened so recently they hadn't even been found yet.

Jack entered the house behind her, his footsteps echoing on the bare floorboards. He passed by where Susanna was frozen in the hallway and headed further into the house.

"There are more," he called. "I reckon three, maybe four bodies?"

Susanna closed her eyes briefly, horrified. All this death, all her fault. Because she'd wanted something that had seemed so simple, so small.

She just wanted a chance to live.

"Susanna, you need to come and see this." Jack's voice came from deep inside the house. It was pitched low, steady, but there was an edge to it.

He'd found something.

She didn't want to go in there. She really didn't. She moved though, one foot in front of the other. Out of the corner of her eye she took in the room that had first drawn her attention, the lamp-lit front room. She purposefully didn't look, didn't turn her head even a fraction of an inch towards it, but she was still aware of the carnage inside.

"Susanna?" His voice was closer now. Susanna followed it until she reached a back room. Jack knelt beside a fallen chair, his hand on the floor tracing a seam in the floorboards.

Her sense of the wraiths set off like fireworks inside her head. It wasn't needed now, though. She looked to Jack, who had his head cocked towards the floor.

"I know where the wraiths are. Listen."

THIRTY-FOUR

"Nest?" Dylan whispered. "What do you mean, nest?"

The wraiths, likely sluggish from their feast, had holed up in the basement. By the time Tristan and Dylan arrived, Susanna and Jack had discovered three entrances to the underground space: the trapdoor in the dining room, a narrow window at the rear of the building, and a door along the side. The trapdoor was bolted, and the window was small and jaggedly broken, a rag stuffed into the hole as a quick fix.

That left the door.

It, too, was locked, but both the wooden door and frame were rotten and bloated with moisture, and Tristan thought he could force it open with little effort.

It wasn't morning, but the sky had lightened just enough for them to see in the shadowy back garden, and Tristan didn't want to wait any longer.

"So what do we do?" Jack looked to Tristan for the answer, Dylan saw, and she decided that Tristan was very likely right: he should have been Jack's ferryman. Would have been, if he had still been in the wasteland.

"Tristan?" Susanna prompted. She, too, was putting all of the responsibility on Tristan's shoulders.

Absentmindedly, Tristan kicked the wooden door. A chorus

of snarls rumbled through the narrow gap between the door and the frame. Though Dylan didn't really have the experience to judge, it sounded like there were a lot of wraiths hiding out in there.

"Fire," Tristan said at last. "We set a fire. Burn them in their nest."

"A fire?" Dylan echoed. She bit her lip. Her eyes rose to the house, the bodies within. Susanna had described the scene inside, and Tristan had gone in to look for himself. His face when he came back out told Dylan she didn't need to see.

Still, it didn't seem quite right to light a funeral pyre beneath them before anyone even knew they were dead – they must have family and friends. If they burned everything to ashes, would anyone even be able to identify the bodies?

"Tristan—"

"I know," he told her quietly. "But they're gone now, flames can't hurt them. Besides, it's not as if the police are ever going to be able to investigate these murders, are they?"

It was hard to argue with that. The police could search and question for the rest of their lives and not even get close to the truth.

"You're sure that'll work?" she asked. "Burning them?"

"In the wasteland, no. But here, they're like me and Susanna. They're more solid. It'll work. They'll be sluggish after their feast, and we can try to keep them in there until the damage has been done. If they escape, hopefully they'll at least have been weakened enough for us to finish them off."

"All right."

"Let's get on with it," Jack added. He, for one, didn't seem bothered by the idea of setting a fire. Looking at him, Dylan figured it probably wouldn't be the first one he'd set in his life.

In the rubbish-strewn street and surrounding gardens, Jack and Tristan found as many things as possible that could burn – including a bottle of lighter fluid. They went back into the house briefly – using the back door so that no one on the street would see them – and poured it down through the trapdoor. By jamming a knife under the edge, they were able to wedge it open just enough for the nozzle of the little can.

"There wasn't much left," Tristan said when the pair came back out, "but I think it should be enough to get the fire going strong."

"That's us?" Dylan asked when he stood. Tristan nodded. "All right."

They returned to the backyard to find anything they could use as a weapon. The garden wasn't much of a garden, but at least it seemed to be a dumping ground for junk.

"Here." Tristan finally selected a spade and a rusting crow bar. He tried to hand Dylan the spade. "I want you to stand by the window. I don't think anything of them will try and come out that way, but if they do, whack them."

Dylan kept her hands by her side. "I'd rather have the crowbar."

"The spade will be easier to hit things with," he pointed out.

"It looks heavy."

Tristan shifted his grip on the spade and bounced it in his hands a couple of times. Then he handed Dylan the crow bar. "Don't miss."

Jack had a jagged piece of wood that he was wielding like a baseball bat, and Susanna held a smashed glass bottle in each hand.

Before Dylan could do more than brace her legs, Tristan had lit a rag. He gave it a few precious seconds to let the flames catch, then yanked back on the edge of the door with all his strength. As he'd suspected, it broke free, the bolt screw tearing out of the damp-softened wood. There was an escalation of hissing and growling from the basement, but nothing emerged.

Flinging the rag into the heart of the basement, Dylan saw

Tristan pause, staring intently through the tiny gap. Probably waiting to ensure the rag set off the petrol, she thought. It must have done, because he slammed the door shut, a satisfied expression on his face.

Dylan concentrated on her window. It was plugged with a cloth, but the glass was broken and the wraiths had to have been getting in and out some way. It certainly wasn't the trapdoor. Nothing happened at first. Then the wraiths started getting louder.

They hissed. Yowled. There was some thumping and banging, wailing. Dylan glanced at the houses overlooking the garden, expecting to see curious faces peering down at her. Nothing yet. She crossed her fingers for an instant, hoping that the people nearby were asleep.

When she turned back to the window, wisps of smoke were curling through the hole in the glass. They twisted then disappeared as they hit the open air, but more followed. In just the space of a minute, the smoke got thicker, darker. The basement was really burning. Hopefully the wraiths were, too.

They started screaming. It sounded inhuman, but it was loud enough to reach beyond the basement, beyond the yard. Loud enough, probably, to wake the neighbours.

"Tristan," Dylan called. This wasn't going to work. People were going to come and investigate before they had the chance to finish. They'd be arrested. God, setting fire to a house was arson, and they couldn't exactly explain themselves… or the dead bodies.

"Tristan!"

But he must have had the same idea. Abandoning the 'burn them alive' plan, Tristan flung the stunted door open. Fresh air would feed the flames, Dylan knew, but it would also give the wraiths an escape route.

They took it.

After just a second or so, one barrelled out of the opening, right at Tristan. Dylan watched as he swung with the spade, a heavy 'thunk' hitting its mark. The wraith spun and landed several feet away. Tristan had already turned, ready to face the next creature that was emerging more cautiously, but as Dylan watched, the wraith on the ground twitched and writhed, flopping about on the dirt and gravel. It wasn't dead.

Before Dylan could yell a warning, Jack was there. With one vicious, downward chop, he split the wraith in half.

"Dylan!" Tristan's yell made Dylan look up, but he wasn't looking at her, his attention was fixed on the window. Dylan looked, too, and saw a wraith squeezing through the ragged gap in the glass. It hissed and thrashed as it struggled through.

"I've got it!"

In three steps she was there. Her first swing missed – the crowbar connected with the brickwork just beneath the window frame, sending shockwaves up Dylan's arms – but her second attempt hit true. She put all her weight behind the strike, but the wraith still didn't die. She had to hit it again, and again. On the final swipe, she caught the edge of the window as well as the wraith. It was enough to finish the evil creature off, but it also shattered the remaining glass. The fabric fell free and black smoke billowed out.

So did a wraith. Two. Three.

Hidden within the acrid curls in the pre-dawn sky, they soared out at Dylan. When she whirled to face the first, the thing was close enough for her to see the razor-sharp claws, the black pits of its eyes. She would have screamed, but there wasn't time. Instead she brought the crowbar up as fast as she could. She almost took out her own eye, but she managed to bat the wraith far enough away that she could arc the metal tool back around. She hit it as hard as she could, and she knew it was dead even before it hit the ground.

A shattering sound of glass right beside her left ear made her duck and cry out.

"It's all right," Susanna gasped, using the jagged remains of one of her glass bottles to shred another wraith down the middle. "I've got it."

"Where's the other one?" Dylan asked.

"Tristan killed it," Susanna told her.

Breathless, her heart pounding in a heady mix of adrenaline and fear, Dylan wiped the sweat off her brow and looked around. The fire was obvious now. Smoke curled out of ground floor windows as well as the little basement casement in front of her. Flames licked out of the door where Tristan stood. They were out of time; if they lingered here any longer, they'd be discovered.

Tristan seemed to reach that conclusion at the same instant. Chucking down his spade, he turned to look at the rest of them. "That's them all." He looked to Susanna, who nodded her confirmation. "We need to get out of here."

The wraiths they'd despatched were dissolving into vapour that swept up and joined the thicker, acrid smoke tunnelling out of every crack in the building. Tristan closed the basement door over as best he could and moved with quick, purposeful steps to Dylan's side.

"Let's go."

Instead of taking the path around the building, Tristan had them hop the neighbour's fence and then slip across their garden so that the four of them emerged onto the street a house away from the fire, and two houses away from the dead body in the narrow pathway. Tristan started walking in the opposite direction immediately, head down and steps rapid, Jack just a pace behind, but Dylan couldn't resist a quick look. Susanna, too, stopped beside her.

A crowd had gathered on the road. Some of them, still in pyjamas, loitered nearer the house, pointing at the escaping smoke. As she stared, one of the throng turned to look at them. Dylan whipped her head away at once – she didn't want this person to remember her face.

"Should we run?" Dylan asked, jogging a few steps until she came level with Tristan and Jack. They were still far too close to the scene of a crime – *crimes* now that they'd committed arson – for her liking.

"No," Tristan said, grabbing her hand so she couldn't give in to temptation.

"It just makes you look guilty," Jack agreed.

He would know, Dylan figured.

Please, thought Dylan, as they hurried away, *please let that be it*. She was so done with souls and extra ferrymen and wraiths and Inquisitors and holes into other worlds.

No more excitement, no more calamity. She just wanted a nice, normal life with the being from another world that she'd convinced to come back with her after dying in a train crash. Really, was that too much to ask?

THIRTY-FIVE

Fourteen steps. Twenty-seven seconds.

That's how long Susanna had to hope that things would all be all right.

Jack and Dylan seemed not to realise that anything was wrong, but beside her Tristan froze. At first she thought he'd just felt it too, the strange sense of danger, of menace. The sense of being watched by unhappy eyes. But then a moment later she realised she was frozen to the spot, unable to shift her feet. Moving her arms was like trying to wade through cement, but she managed. Reaching out, she gripped Tristan's arm.

"What's happening?" she gasped.

"He's here."

"Who?" Then understanding dawned. "The Inquisitor?"

Tristan managed a nod.

The distant glow from the fire was suddenly overwhelmed by a cold white light.

Dylan was instantly by Tristan's side, her whole body pressed against his. She was searching the street for the Inquisitor and, taking in her braced stance, the determined set of her jaw, Susanna realised she was preparing to defend Tristan.

Rather than hiding behind him, seeking protection, she was trying to protect her ferryman.

Astonished, Susanna looked for Jack. He was glancing around, fists clenched defensively. Step by small cautious step, he was taking himself away from the three of them. Susanna had the horrible realisation that he'd leave them if he could.

As soon as she had that thought she felt a piercing, stabbing pain in her gut. And she saw Jack cover his lower stomach with both hands. Drops of blood seeped from between his fingers.

"Jack," she hissed through the pain. "Come closer."

He didn't want to, she could see he didn't want to, but he was obviously hurting as much as she was. Every step he drew towards her lessened the agony and soon he was hurrying. Susanna didn't fully breathe until he stood beside her.

"What the hell's happening?" he bit out.

She didn't get time to answer, however, because suddenly the Inquisitor stood before them. Between one blink and the next, it filled Susanna's vision.

"Ferryman." The being spoke, pinning her with its eyes. There was no question who it was addressing. "Do you know who I am?"

Terrified out of her mind, Susanna managed a jerky nod. Tristan had told her the Inquisitor had powers, could freeze her muscles, steal her will – but knowing it was nothing like feeling it.

The being briefly turned to spear Tristan with a look. Susanna had only a heartbeat's reprieve before she was back under the spotlight.

"Ferryman, you have erred in your duties."

Susanna opened her mouth, but no sound came out.

"You have not fulfilled your primary responsibility, to deliver your soul to the realm beyond, and worse, you brought that soul back to its body and the real world."

The words came without feeling, without passion. As if the

Inquisitor was reading from a script, rhyming off regulations from a rule book.

"You have left the wasteland, abandoning your post and your sacred duty. You have tried to present yourself as human, an entitlement you have not been granted. You have allowed evil to seep into this world, bringing about the deaths of souls before their time." Here the Inquisitor paused, and Susanna felt the heat of its stare burn painfully hot. "You have caused the murder of innocents. The blood that has been spilt stains your hands."

Though she knew the Inquisitor was speaking metaphorically, Susanna looked down, expecting to see the thick, viscous substance smeared across her palms.

She saw only her own pale, unblemished skin until Jack's fingers, rough skin and blunted nails wrapped around the slender bones of her wrist and tugged. Hauled against her.

"I don't know what the hell's going on," he hissed in her ear, "but let's go!"

For the first time, Susanna found herself in complete and utter agreement with him. The problem was, she simply couldn't. Her feet were glued to the ground, her muscles unresponsive. A cry tore from her lips as her shoulder joint strained and threatened to pop under the pressure from Jack's tugging.

"I'll leave you!" he threatened. "I mean it! I'll leave you."

Susanna looked back at the Inquisitor, who watched impassively. Unconcerned.

"You can't," she told Jack as she swivelled back to him. "You'll die. We both will."

That took some of the fight out of him. Detaching her wrist from his grip, Susanna turned to the Inquisitor.

"Ferryman," it intoned, continuing on as if Jack's threats to leave were of no consequence. "You have heard your crimes.

Have you anything to say before your judgement is passed?"

Judgement? Susanna scoured her mind, searching for a feasible defence. Nothing came. The only thing she had left to offer was the truth.

"I only wanted to live," she told the Inquisitor. "I'm sorry, I…" she swallowed, glanced over at Tristan. It wasn't fair to drag him into her decision. Not when he might have a chance, him and his soul. "I just wanted to live."

The Inquisitor watched her with those glowing eyes that never seemed to blink. Time stretched painfully, the sound from the world around her thinning until she barely heard Jack hissing "Susanna!" repeatedly in her ear.

"You are guilty."

Susanna felt a brief instant of relief as the tension burst, quickly followed by a rippling wave of horror as she waited for what came next.

"You forfeit the life you have stolen in this world. The living world cannot be subject to the whims of those who are not mortal. You will be returned to the wasteland, where you will be punished."

"Punished?"

"To hell with this." Jack spun away. "I'm leaving."

"Jack! No! You know we can't." Susanna watched with wide eyes as Jack stormed away. He made it ten feet, then twenty. At twenty-five, he stumbled. Clutched his side. At the same time, Susanna felt the echo of the knife that had been thrust into Jack's flesh. "Jack, stop!"

Dimly, she was aware of Dylan yelling, too. Telling Jack to stop. To come back. He ignored her as he had Susanna. Tristan, the only person he might have listened to, was silent. Tears in her eyes, from panic and pain, Susanna turned beseechingly back to the Inquisitor.

"Please!" she gasped. "Make it stop!"

"You chose your soul poorly," it admonished her. "I can see the bond between you. It is black, made of greed and selfishness. You have caused innocents to die so that you could fulfil your own self-centred desires. You are not deserving of my pity, or my mercy."

"Please," Susanna repeated. She fell to her knees.

"No," the Inquisitor shook its head. "You will return to the wasteland. You will return to your post. And you will be grateful that I grant you this, instead of turning you into a mindless savage."

"What about Jack, my soul?"

The Inquisitor turned its passionless gaze to Jack, who was still trying to crawl away, a blood trail slick on the ground behind him.

"Your soul chose death," the Inquisitor said. "I need do nothing."

No sooner had the Inquisitor uttered these words than Jack collapsed. He made one more valiant attempt to rise, then dropped. His chest rose once, twice, three times. Then was still.

The Inquisitor swept back to Susanna and raised its hand.

"Wait!" Tristan jerked like he'd tried to step forward, but of course he was just as trapped as Susanna. "Give her another chance! She's helped us, tried to fix—"

"I have yet to deal with you," the Inquisitor intoned. "You would be wise to save your pleas for yourself."

Tristan opened his mouth as if he'd like to argue more, but a quick glance at Dylan, who was watching the whole exchange, wide-eyed and mouth agape, and he fell silent. He shot Susanna an apologetic look. She understood. She had known Tristan for a long, long time, but he had never looked at her the way he did Dylan. She was his friend, maybe. Dylan was his soulmate.

Tears glistening on her cheeks, Susanna whispered, "I'm ready."

THIRTY-SIX

Dylan watched Susanna flicker out of existence.

She blinked, but it wasn't an illusion. One moment, the dark-eyed, dark-haired ferryman stood before her, frozen to the spot as the Inquisitor passed judgement, the next she was gone. In the background, Jack lay motionless on the pavement where he'd dropped. He was gone, too. All that was left was an empty shell.

Pity welled up inside her, but she was too afraid for herself and Tristan to let it fully take hold.

"Now, ferryman," the Inquisitor turned its attention to Tristan. Dylan felt her heart stutter.

"I did what you asked," Tristan said, pre-empting whatever the Inquisitor had been going to say. "The wraiths are dead and I've closed the tears into the wasteland, both of them." The Inquisitor didn't reply. "That was the deal."

Dylan searched the Inquisitor's face. There was nothing there to read. Nothing.

"You think you are in a position to speak to me thus?"

Warily, Tristan lowered his gaze. It seemed that was the right thing to do because the Inquisitor gave an almost indiscernible nod.

"Consider yourself fortunate," the Inquisitor told him, radiating disapproval. "I could – and I should – sentence you to the same fate." It paused, looked from Tristan to Dylan and back again.

"The bond between them, it was an evil thing, born of greed. What is between the two of you is bright and shining. It glows, and I will not be the one to extinguish it." It took a threatening step forward. "But should this happen again, should any other wraiths appear in this plane, I will expect you to deal with them."

Dylan whimpered quietly beside him, horrified by the thought, but Tristan nodded without hesitation. That had been what they'd agreed, after all.

"You and your soul may never tell others of the knowledge you possess. If you do, your lives will be forfeit, and the lives of any you have told."

Again, Tristan nodded. Dylan did too.

The Inquisitor's threats didn't matter; neither of them would say anything about this to another living soul. Ever.

The Inquisitor bowed its head. "Then we are finished."

Relief made Dylan sag against Tristan. She watched the Inquisitor turn, hardly able to believe it was over. Then it disappeared, and the dawn light seemed dark.

Tristan shifted suddenly and Dylan knew he had regained control of his body. The very first thing he did was grab her with both hands and haul her into a bone-cracking hug. Dylan couldn't breathe, but rather than pulling back she wound her own arms around him and squeezed tighter.

"We're free, Dylan."

"Please," she whispered, face pressed into the thick fabric of his jumper, the scent of smoke rising from him. "Please, can we go home now?"

"Yes." Tristan said, his voice hoarse with emotion. "I think we can."

THIRTY-SEVEN

It seemed a long time later that they finally stood outside Dylan's building. Their building, Tristan supposed. He lived here now.

He had a home.

Hopefully, he still would tomorrow.

It had taken them hours to return to Glasgow, silent, stricken and without Jack's car for transport. And Tristan had the feeling that it wasn't over yet. A glance at his watch told him it was almost midday, well over twenty-four hours since they had left the day before. Dylan's parents were going to be frantic. Frantic and very, very angry.

"Come on," Dylan mumbled beside him. She was so knackered, she was swaying on her feet. "Let's get this over with."

It took her two attempts to slot her key in the lock and she couldn't quite get her hands to work together. After two aborted attempts, Tristan gently ushered her out of the way and turned it for her. He practically had to carry her up the steps.

"Well, this is going to add credence to our story," Dylan told him sleepily as they reached the front door of the flat. "I feel drunk."

They had tried to come up with a plan for why they'd been gone an entire night. A party? An accident? A roadtrip? They knew whatever their story was, Joan wasn't going to let them get away with it.

After everything they'd been through, everything they'd done since the appearance of the Inquisitor. Something as trivial as an alibi for Dylan's mother seemed nonsensical to Tristan, but Dylan was right to be concerned. It was Joan's flat, not Dylan's. And, no matter how mature she seemed to Tristan, Dylan was a minor. If Joan threw him out, Dylan's mother and the authorities could, and would, stop her going with him.

That would be a death sentence.

They stepped into the hallway.

"No, wait just a moment, officer," he heard Joan's voice saying. "That's somebody now."

Dylan's dad, James, stuck his head into the corridor.

"It's them," he said to Joan. Then he advanced on them.

He was a big guy. Taller than Tristan, fit for an older man. As he came prowling down the hallway Tristan wondered if it might make a better impression to back away, as if intimidated – and he was, slightly – but there was nowhere to go.

"You have some nerve!" James growled "Where the hell have you been?"

"Just out," Dylan mumbled, blinking owlishly. She didn't seem to realise that her dad wasn't talking to her.

"Dylan?" Joan's voice was tight and tense, though it didn't hold the threat of violence embedded in James's. She rushed down the corridor. "Are you all right?"

James gently but firmly took Dylan by the arm and led her into the living room. Tristan followed, and sat down next to her when her father had deposited her on the sofa.

"Where have you been?" Joan this time. Arms folded and eyes narrowed.

"We went on a trip." Dylan uttered.

"A *trip*?" Joan's eyebrows rose up until they almost disappeared into her hair. "You have been gone *all night*. What sort of fifteen year old goes on an all-night trip without telling anyone?"

"Well, I don't know," Dylan said, sounding perfectly like a sulking teenager. Tristan couldn't tell if it was an act or real, it was so convincing. "It was sort of spontaneous. Sorry."

"Sorry?" Joan echoed. "Sorry!" She waved one arm dramatically in the air. "You've been gone almost *two days* with no contact. You made me think you were dead – *again*. I have to stay home from *work* so I've lost the money from today's shift, we've been worried out of our *minds* and all you can say is *sorry*? Where did you go? What on earth were you doing that was so important?" Dylan opened her mouth, but she didn't get the chance to say anything. "I don't know what's gotten into you lately, young lady. In fact, I do."

A change of focus. Now it was Tristan pinned under the spotlight.

"You." Joan pointed at him, finger piercing the air. "You. That's what's changed."

James moved to stand at Joan's shoulder, a menacing presence. "I don't know much about you, but it seems this change in Dylan has happened since you came on the scene." There was a hard edge to his words. "You're clearly older than her, and I don't know your background, but it seems to me you're leading my daughter astray."

"It isn't Tristan's fault!" Dylan butted in. "It was my idea, and it was me who wanted to go on the trip."

"Right, OK," James stepped between the two of them. Neither Joan nor Dylan looked remotely impressed by his intervention. Undaunted, he turned to Tristan. "I notice you're keeping quiet. What have you to say for yourself?"

Tristan stared at him. As Joan's anger had escalated, his had calmed.

"I'm sorry," he began softly.

Joan scoffed.

"James, Joan… I love your daughter," Tristan continued, "I really do. She's everything to me." A quick glance at Joan. She looked stiff and unyielding.

"Out." James's voice was quiet, but firm.

"No! You don't understand!" Dylan made to reach for Tristan, but her father sliced his hand through the air.

"We've given him enough chances, Dylan. Something weird is going on and it's putting you in danger. You've been helpful, Tristan, but you've caused too much disruption. We don't need you under Joan's roof any more – not now Dylan has almost fully recovered."

"Please—" Tristan began, but James had already strode out of the living room and opened the front door for him.

"Out."

"You don't understand, I can't—"

"Don't make me call the police, son. Just go." James moved back towards him, grasped him by the shoulder and started manoeuvring him forcefully back down the hallway and through the flat door. Tristan fought the urge to wrestle with him – redoubling his efforts when he heard Dylan screaming at her mother.

The tightness in his chest hit on the landing outside the flat. Shards of pain raked his legs at the top of the stairs. He tried to brace, reluctant to go further, knowing Dylan would be feeling the same pain – or worse.

"Tristan, don't fight me," James warned, softly forcing Tristan down another step. "Leave. Now."

"Please, listen," Tristan gasped. "You don't understand what you're doing to Dylan. You're hurting her."

"She'll get over it." James gently pushed him one more step away.

No, Tristan thought. *She won't.* But the words wouldn't come out, he was in too much pain.

They'd been further away from each other before, but never like this, knowing they were about to be truly separated.

"Dad!" Dylan burst out of the flat door and stumbled towards her father. "Stop! You can't do this."

She didn't get as far as the top of the stairs. Her legs gave out on the landing. Tears were streaking down her face and she clutched at her back.

"Dylan!" Tristan croaked.

"Look what you're doing to her." James's voice was rough in Tristan's ear as he shook his shoulder. "Just go, so she can pick herself back up." Without warning, he charged forwards and Tristan had to move with him to stop himself from toppling down the full flight.

Three more steps and they were on the floor below. Dylan's scream of agony ripped through the air.

"You're killing her," Tristan ground out through gritted teeth.

"She'll be all right."

"No, she won't."

Unable to take the pain any more, Tristan dropped where he stood, sprawling across the first-floor landing. Aggravated, James clambered roughly over him and went to haul him up by the arm.

"Tristan!" Tilting his head, Tristan could see that Dylan had pulled herself to the top of the stairs. The hand that she stretched out towards him was covered in blood.

"James," Tristan begged, "*look* at your daughter."

James hesitated for a moment, looked up and gasped. "Dylan! Stay there, sweetheart. You've hurt yourself!"

"No," Tristan mumbled, disoriented by pain. "*You've* hurt her."

James looked down at him, at his slumped body, and all the

colour leeched from his face. Tristan knew that the blood he could feel saturating the back of his shirt must be smeared across the floor.

"What the hell...?" James whispered.

"I told you," Tristan said. "We can't explain. But you can't keep us apart. You just *can't.*"

For several long seconds, James simply stared. Tristan could hear Dylan's soft sniffles above. Her father must have, too, because he looked towards her and something changed in his expression.

"All right," he said gruffly. "All right, let's get you back up the stairs first."

It took some doing, because Tristan's legs didn't feel like they could support him, but James managed to hoist him up to the second-floor landing and drop him down beside Dylan. Ignoring James, who was hovering protectively over his daughter, Tristan drew Dylan against his chest. She was wracked with shivers, pale as a ghost.

"I don't..." James shook his head. "What's happening?"

"It was the train crash, Dad," Dylan admitted quietly. "I'm not the same as I was. And I *need* Tristan."

"But—"

"We can't say any more," Tristan said firmly. The Inquisitor had been clear. The little they'd given away might already have been too much.

James sighed, reached up to run his fingers through his hair. "Let's just get you back inside, deal with your injuries. Joan can—"

"No!" Dylan shook her head. "You can't tell her. It's important."

"Dylan, you're bleeding."

"She's not any more," Tristan promised. Then, to Dylan, "Show him."

Somewhat awkwardly, because Tristan couldn't bear to let her go just yet, Dylan swivelled and lifted her shirt at the back. Tristan knew what James would see beneath the blood-soaked material: the smooth skin of her back, marred only by faint white scar lines.

"That's impossible," James murmured.

"You see, Dad?" Dylan said. "We have to be together. I know it seems crazy, but it's real."

"What's going on here?" Joan's sudden appearance in the flat doorway made the three of them jump. "Why is he still here?"

"Mum—"

"It's all right, Dylan," James cut in. "I'll deal with this."

"Deal with what?"

"We've had a discussion, the three of us," James said. "Tristan and I have had words – man to man – and I think we've sorted a few things."

"Man to man?" Joan's voice carried a hint of scathing, but more than anything she sounded weary. Worn thin with worry. Tristan felt a pang of guilt for everything the woman had been through.

James cleared his throat. "I think we understand each other now. There will be no more skipping school, no more keeping Dylan out late."

Tristan dipped his chin in a meek nod. "Yes, sir." He lifted his head to see James staring at Dylan's mum, something soft in his face.

"A second chace, Joan?" James breathed.

THIRTY-EIGHT

"I can't see what they're doing!" Dylan complained.

She looked back at Tristan. He was reclined across her bed, reading her Kindle, the glow from the screen illuminating his face, since she'd made him turn all the lights off.

"I'm going to have to open the window."

He didn't say anything, so she unhooked the lock and, as quietly as possible, opened up the sash. Tilting out as far as she could, she craned her neck until the front of the building came into view. What she saw there made her jerk back inside and leap onto the bed.

"Ew!"

"What is it?" Tristan didn't look up from his book.

"They were *kissing*!"

He kept on reading, but a slight smile hitched his lips. "Well, what did you expect? They were on a date."

"But they're kissing!"

Giving up, Tristan put the Kindle down and gazed at her, his eyes laughing. He pulled her to him. Then, as he had every day for the past four months, he whispered into her ear, "I love you."

And as they had every day for the past four months, the words made Dylan glow, inside and out.

"I love you too," she told him. "Before you came, I was so

unhappy. I didn't have anyone – I just wanted to hide away. Now, I can't wait to go out and explore the world with you. I want to see everything, do everything – with you."

"We will," Tristan promised. "We have time now – time to live. Although," a twinkle glittered in his eye, "I really hope you don't want to experience any more of those school dances, because one was enough."

"Oh, but you haven't been to a Christmas dance yet!" Dylan told him. "You can't miss that! You haven't tried the Gay Gordon! Strip the Willow! You'd make a great Dashing White Sergeant!"

Tristan groaned and Dylan laughed, delighted in her teasing, in her boyfriend – in her life. Staring into his cobalt blue eyes, she dipped her head down and kissed him. His arms wrapped around her, pressing her even closer. They were wonderfully, heart-poundingly alive.

EPILOGUE

The wind was howling. Or was that the wraiths? Susanna wasn't sure. She felt dizzy, disoriented.

This wasn't how it usually happened. Where was the world? Where were the tower blocks and rusting cars? Where was the blood stain on the pavement from Jack trying to haul himself away from danger – and towards death.

"What is this?" Jack hollered. It was hard to hear him over the whooshing, whirling and screaming.

"The wasteland," Susanna shouted back.

"Why doesn't it look like it did before?"

Because it was real now. The bloody red core that lay beneath every soul's projection. This was the underbelly where the wraiths didn't have to follow the rules of sun and shadow, because the burning ball in the sky shone deep red, keeping the landscape in a permanent state of semi-darkness.

Susanna stared at Jack, dread bubbling in her stomach. This is how the Inquisitor had punished them. Crossing the wasteland like this – following the thin sliver of inky-black pavement that wound through the blood-soaked sands – was almost impossible.

It was a death sentence.

"Jack," Susanna said, turning to the soul she'd led too far from his path, "I'm sorry. I'm so, so sorry."

Acknowledgements

Thank you very much to the following people:

To Ben Illis at The BIA. The train just goes on and on and on. Here's to the little book that could.

To my family, thank you for letting me disappear inside my head. For all the hours I spent saying 'hang on', 'just a minute' and 'nearly done'. I hope you agree they were worth it.

To Floris Books, thank you for welcoming me into the family. I look forward to continuing this exciting adventure with you.

And to you, if you read *Ferryman* and came back to see how Tristan and Dylan fared in the real world. Thank you readers. (A special nǐ hǎo to readers in China. Wǒ hěn gāoxìng nǐ yě ài Tristan hé Dylan. I hope that makes sense – I tried!)

Claire McFall

TRISTAN AND DYLAN HAVE A LOVE LIKE NO OTHER

DISCOVER WHERE THEIR STORY BEGAN

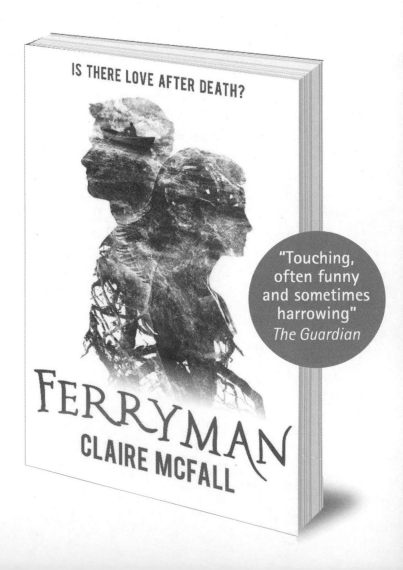

IS THERE LOVE AFTER DEATH?

"Touching, often funny and sometimes harrowing"
The Guardian

FERRYMAN

CLAIRE MCFALL

Follow KelpiesEdge or search "Ferryman soundtrack" on ⬤ Spotify to listen to our specially selected soundtrack for the FERRYMAN novels.

Together The xx

I Will Follow You Into The Dark Death Cab for Cutie

Skinny Love Bon Iver

Burning House Cam

In Dreams Ben Howard

The Killing Moon Echo & the Bunnymen

The River PJ Harvey

First Day Of My Life Bright Eyes

A Thousand Years Christina Perri

Riverside Agnes Obel

We Found Each Other In The Dark City and Colour

I Will Wait Mumford & Sons

Lucky Bif Naked

All the Little Lights Passenger

Say Something A Great Big World

KELPIESEDGE

SCOTTISH BOOKS WITH ATTITUDE

GET INSIDE **KELPIES**EDGE

EXCLUSIVE CONTENT, COMPETITIONS
AND SNEAK PREVIEWS

WWW.KELPIESEDGE.CO.UK

FOLLOW US FOR

BOOK NEWS AND AUTHOR CHAT
🐦 @KELPIESEDGE

THE FIRST LOOK AT NEW BOOKS
📷 @KELPIESEDGE

BOOK-INSPIRED PLAYLISTS
🎧 KELPIESEDGE

TRAILERS AND INTERVIEWS
▶ KELPIESEDGE